W9-CMZ-475

Please Come Back To Me

FLANNERY
O'CONNOR
AWARD
FOR
SHORT
FICTION

Nancy Zafris,
Series Editor

Please Come Back To Me

STORIES BY JESSICA TREADWAY

The University of Georgia Press *Athens & London*

Published by the University of Georgia Press
Athens, Georgia 30602
www.ugapress.org

Designed by Walton Harris
Set in 11/15 Garamond Premier Pro
Printed and bound by Thomson-Shore
The paper in this book meets the guidelines for
permanence and durability of the Committee on
Production Guidelines for Book Longevity of the
Council on Library Resources.

Printed in the United States of America

14 13 12 11 10 C 5 4 3 2 1

Library of Congress Cataloging-in-Publication Data

Treadway, Jessica, 1961–.
Please come back to me : stories / by Jessica Treadway.
p. cm. — (The Flannery O'Connor Award for short fiction)
Contents: The nurse and the black lagoon — Dear Nicole —
Oregon — Deprivation — Shirley wants her nickel back —
Revelation — Testimony — Please come back to me.
ISBN-13: 978-0-8203-3584-1 (hardcover : alk. paper)
ISBN-10: 0-8203-3584-3 (hardcover : alk. paper)
I. Title.
PS3620.R43 P55 2010
813'.6—dc22 2010005958

British Library Cataloging-in-Publication Data available

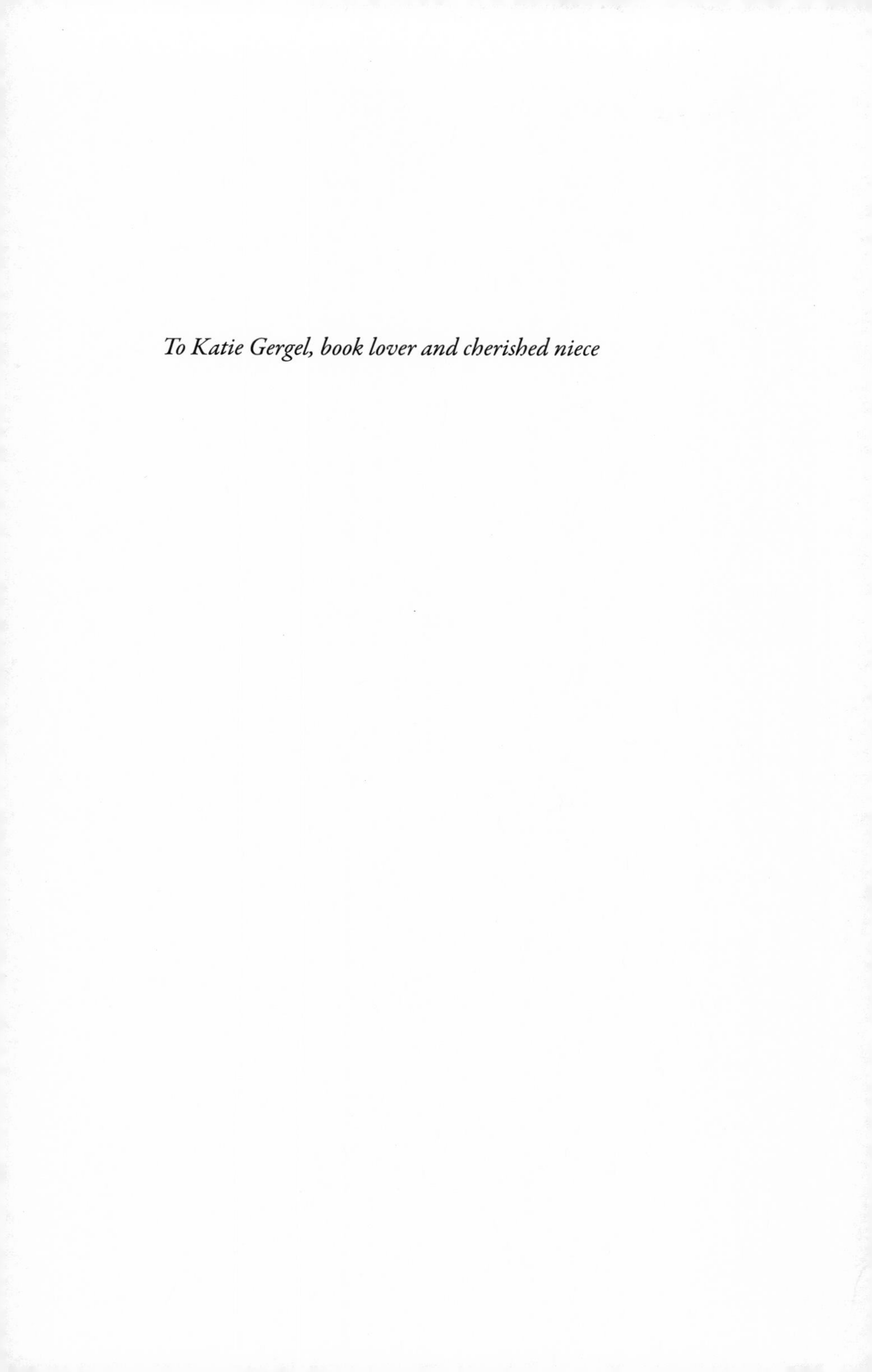

To Katie Gergel, book lover and cherished niece

Contents

Acknowledgments

My deep gratitude to Nancy Zafris, series editor for the Flannery O'Connor Award for Short Fiction, for her faith and abiding nurturance, and to Dorine Jennette for her astute and elegant editorial assistance. My thanks as well to the editors of the publications in which the following stories have, in slightly different form, appeared: "The Nurse and the Black Lagoon" in *Five Points*; "Dear Nicole" and "Shirley Wants Her Nickel Back" in *Ploughshares*; "Oregon" in the *Boston Book Review*; "Deprivation" in *Eclipse*; "Revelation" in *Shenandoah: The Washington and Lee University Review*; and "Testimony" in *Glimmer Train*.

Please Come Back To Me

The Nurse and the Black Lagoon

WHEN THE PHONE RANG, Irene let it go because it came in the middle of a reality show she would not have wanted her children to waste their time on, it was so stupid; but since nobody else was home, she'd decided to indulge herself. She didn't listen to the phone message until the commercial. A man's voice, deep toned but without inflection, rumbled through the wire: "Lieutenant John Scully of the Morton Police here, I'm looking for Joseph or Irene Ludwig. We have your son Brian in custody at the station. You probably know where it is on Elm Avenue, the old Hardy school. Please call us or come down as soon as you get this message. Your son is safe, but something of a serious nature has occurred." He disconnected without saying good-bye, as if he knew that to do so would compromise the urgency he felt obliged to convey.

Irene stood frozen over the phone with the remote control still in her hand. Her show had come back on and she meant to mute it, but her finger wouldn't work. When she managed to move again, breathing sounds of anxiety out of her nose, she started to dial the number printed on the neon orange Town Information sticker that had puckered and faded from sitting in the family room's direct sunlight over the years. *Police, Fire, Poison Control.*

But before she could complete the call, she hung up and, instead, pressed the necessary buttons on the remote control to record the remainder of the reality show. Joe was appalled at this later, and she was surprised herself when she realized what she had done. "I think it was my way of not letting it sink in, the phone call," she told her husband. "I didn't want to know what it was." By the time they had this conversation, she had bailed Brian out and he had sequestered himself in his bedroom. Joe and Irene were trying to decide what to do next. Katy was ignoring the phone messages from her friends, watching and rewatching the stupid program her mother had recorded.

When Irene had arrived at the police station Sunday night, she'd let herself entertain, although only for a few seconds, the idea that the "something of a serious nature" had happened *to* Brian, even though the officer had assured her that her son was safe. But then, she reasoned, the police would have come to the house if he'd been in an accident. Wouldn't they? That's how they notified parents on TV. So she allowed her mind's eye to wander in the other direction on the spectrum of possibilities, imagining that Brian might have been caught with other kids in the woods by the high school, drinking beer.

It made her sad to realize that this was wishful thinking. The drinking-beer-in-the-woods behavior would belong to Katy when she got a little older, not to Brian, whose few friends were more apt to spend their time alone in their rooms like him, playing computer and video games.

When she saw him in the room where the police were holding him, she felt a rise of the fresh, uncomplicated joy she hadn't remembered since before her children were teenagers. *There he is.* And he didn't appear to be injured.

Yet clearly, something was wrong; he wouldn't look at her. "Is your husband with you, Mrs. Ludwig?" the lieutenant asked. "It would be best if you both could be here."

"He's in Chicago," she told him, "for work. I'll call him. But I wanted to find out what was going on, first."

"Mom," Brian said. It was the voice of her six-year-old son from ten years earlier, confessing to her on Christmas afternoon. She'd found him crying next to the Christmas tree, next to the 215-piece airport-and-helipad set she and Joe had spent hours assembling in front of the kids' stockings the night before. "I heard you guys," Brian had cried into her sweater, where he pitched himself after she asked him what was wrong. "I sat on the stairs and watched you and Daddy put it together." They'd had the Santa Claus talk then and there, much earlier than Irene had planned or wanted, and without Joe, who had taken a noon flight to Florida on Christmas — "Christmas Day, damn it!" she'd snapped at him on the phone that night — for a convention he had to set up.

"He'll get over it," Joe'd told her. "For God's sake, Irene, it's *Santa Claus*. Tell him children are starving in Africa."

"He's six," she'd said. "Don't be ridiculous."

"He's old enough to understand starving," Joe shot back, before some client called and he had to get off the phone.

"I'm sorry," Brian said to her, now as he had then, and she felt herself preparing to tell him he hadn't done anything wrong.

"It's okay, honey," she said, realizing that though it was silly she still wished he would throw himself at her, as he had then, in the belief that there might be some comfort for him in her arms.

But her son was backing up against the white wall. "What, honey?" she said. The sight and feel of him retreating made her skull go cold.

"Have a seat, Mrs. Ludwig," the lieutenant told her, and she sensed in him the sympathy of one who has the delicate duty of changing somebody's life for the worse.

What Brian had done, the police told Irene, was burn down the playground at Eastbrooke Elementary School. A neighbor whose yard bordered the playground called 911 at 6:16 p.m., during halftime of the Giants game, to report the fire. By the time the trucks got there, the whole thing was gutted, the entire wood-based structure in which every piece of equipment — the round drum of the crawl tunnel, the monkey bars, the spiral stairs climbing to yellow slides — was connected to another. The only parts left remotely recognizable were the chains connecting rubber tires through the obstacle course, and the steering wheel that encouraged kids to pretend they were captaining a ship full of playmates through a cedar-chip sea.

Of course, Lieutenant Scully didn't go into these details. Irene knew them because of the pictures she saw on the news that night. All the officer said was that Brian was being held on suspicion of "malicious destruction of property" at the school. He had been seen watching the firemen from the hill to one side of the playground, overlooking the kickball field. He didn't try to run when the police approached him, but he had no account of why he was there. He didn't respond when they asked if he'd set the fire.

"This is impossible," Irene said, but she didn't go into why — the memory of the day the playground had been built, a Saturday in May at the end of Brian's second-grade year. One of the Eastbrooke fathers, an architect, had presented a plan to replace the metal jungle gym and swing set that had been collecting dents and rust since the '70s. Irene joined the committee of parents charged with applying for permits, renting equipment, and organizing a schedule. The new playground could be put up in one long day of work by volunteers under a construction supervisor, the architect said, so a date was designated and more than a hundred people showed up, with many entire families, including Irene's. A group of mothers babysat while other parents took up pieces of the prefab "circuits" constituting the new playground. It was the first stunning spring day of the year, the sun high over a faint warm breeze. Irene had never been so exhausted as at the finish, when everyone gathered on the hill to eat pizza and admire what they had accomplished, the gleaming and colorful structures the kids swarmed as soon as the safety inspector deemed it okay. Irene remembered imagining that this was what it must feel like to the Amish during a barn raising: the sense of pride and fulfillment in belonging to a group whose members worked so hard for the common good.

Thinking of that day as she listened to what Lieutenant Scully told her, Irene tried to recall if there had been anything negative about the experience. She remembered a brief but palpable panic when Laura and Stew Bender's daughter Ellie went missing; she was found moments after the search began, having chased a cat into the woods. Afterward, Laura Bender was part of the pizza cleanup crew with Irene. "I *knew* she had to be somewhere," Irene remembered Laura saying several times, giddy with relief. "There's that line, you know? Between thinking they're okay and thinking they might actually be *gone* somehow? I never crossed that line this time, but one more minute — well, I was getting close." The other mothers, including Irene, nodded; they all knew which line she meant.

Now that Irene thought about it, she remembered that Brian, who was in Ellie Bender's class, had gone blank when it first seemed she was missing. *Gone blank* was a phrase Irene used to herself, to describe what she saw in her son's face sometimes (and what she felt sometimes in her own): an expression that might have looked mild or innocuous to a bystander, but that in fact actively concealed a measure of emotion he did not want to risk showing, because he was afraid it could not be contained.

Unlike her brother, Katy hadn't inherited this trait of Irene's. Their daughter took after Joe, who had little talent for hiding anything. It meant that Joe and Irene didn't have to worry about her using drugs or having sex they wouldn't know about, and this was a relief; but it also meant that when she was angry at one or both of them — which, lately, was often — she didn't stomp out of the room to sulk in private, but remained to let them feel the full force of her fury. Even after unleashing a torrent of words she would not leave their presence, as if she wanted to be sure their focus would not shift from whatever complaint or passion of hers had inflamed the fight.

Facing Brian in the police station, Irene found herself wishing that her son could be more like his sister. She felt she would give anything to be able to read his now-more-than-ever-*gone-blank* face. Was it outrage at having been accused of something he would never imagine doing? Was it fear? Or — this possibility was one she had to avert her eyes to consider — could it be guilt?

"This is impossible," she'd said, and she meant all of it: the trip to the police station, the information about the playground being burned down, the fact of Brian being held in connection with the crime. "This is impossible," she'd said, but the truth (she saw, when she could finally look up) was that it wasn't.

Joe took the first plane he could book after the meeting on Monday he couldn't get out of.

"You'd get out of it if he were dead," Irene accused him over the phone. "If he was in the hospital."

"But he's not." Joe made the clicking sound with his tongue that drove her crazier than any other habit of any person she'd ever known. He said he couldn't help it — that it was a reflex — but she believed he could stop if he tried, so it was a steady source of conflict between them, especially because it became more pronounced when he was tense or afraid. "He's neither of those things. He's fine. We'll figure it out, Irene."

The flight put him at the airport at six o'clock, rush hour, and Irene, who hated driving on the highway, asked him to take a cab home. "I don't want to do that," he told her. "We need to talk without the kids around."

"Couldn't we just go out somewhere when you get home?" she

said, but she knew he was right, and she also knew that if she were to be honest with herself, she was trying to put this off — talking with Joe — because until then she might be able to pretend that it wasn't such a big deal, even if it *were* true that Brian had burned down the playground. Maybe it had been an accident. Maybe he'd been experimenting with cigarettes, or — what else? What else could it have been? There had to be something that made sense. When they'd come home from the police station, she tried to talk to Brian. She went to his room carrying a plate of cut-up apples with the skins peeled off, the snack she always fed him when he was three and four and five years old, watching *Thomas the Tank Engine* videos before bedtime.

He'd come to the door when she knocked, and opened it halfway and timidly. When he saw the plate of apples in her hand he just stared at it, even as she held it out to him. Then he said, "You've got to be kidding, Mom," in a voice that, despite the words, wasn't mean — in fact, it was so gentle she almost didn't hear it. Then he closed the door, also gently, and she could tell he remained just on the other side of it, listening, as long as she did. She wanted to ask, "Brian, can't we talk?" but if she were being honest, she had to admit that she had no idea what to say to him, how to talk about this, or how to act. She had to admit the relief she felt when he left the door closed and she could feel him waiting for her to walk away.

Joe wanted her to drive home from the airport because of the Ativan he'd taken during the flight. She liked it when he took Ativan because it made the clicking sound go away. She asked for one and he declined and she said, "Why not, you asshole? One little *pill*," and he turned toward her and said, "You just called me an asshole?" and she said "You heard me," and he flicked the dashboard with two ineffectual fingers, and Irene laughed.

"What the hell is wrong with you?" Joe said. "Have you gone crazy, too?" He put his hands in the *Let me explain things to you* position that had annoyed Irene since their first date. "I go away on Wednesday and everything is fine. Monday I come home because my kid burned down a playground, and now my wife is calling me an asshole because I won't give her a medication that was prescribed for *me*." He pressed his palms together in a martyred prayer. "Do I have that right?"

"Stop being so sanctimonious," she told him. She pulled over to the shoulder, where she collapsed her face over the steering wheel and began to heave.

"Ah, Reenie." He hadn't called her that in years — more than thirty pounds ago, she realized. "Ah, God." Joe was patting her knee and at the same time craning in his seat to look at the traffic whizzing past them in a blare of horns. "We really should keep going here — this isn't safe. *Honey*." She knew he was right but she didn't seem to be able to stop crying. Crying was what it felt like, anyway — there were no tears. "Reenie, let's switch. Come on. I'll drive us." Another round of beeps and blasts as they opened their doors and each walked to the other side of the car, Irene still holding her face. It was another five minutes before they found an opening to ease back into traffic. They spent the time silent as the car filled with their dread.

At home they sat in the driveway instead of going straight in. They watched as Katy, in her bedroom, pulled her curtain aside, looked out at them, then walked away from the window without giving them any sign. "What's *he* doing?" Joe asked, giving a nod toward the other window.

Irene shrugged but only halfway, leaving her shoulders raised. "I don't know. Neither of them went to school today. He wouldn't come out." Slowly she allowed her posture to deflate. "What should we do?"

Joe pinched his nose with his thumb and forefinger, a gesture she had come to associate over the years with stalling as he tried to figure out what to say. "Maybe this isn't as bad as it seems," he began, but Irene interrupted him.

"I already tried that. It doesn't work." She opened her door and he looked at her; she felt like reaching across the seat and smacking the fear out of his face. "Come on." His reluctance to follow her out of the car reminded her of the days when Brian and Katy were children, dawdling over some toy they'd been playing with during a ride. "Just a minute, Mom," they told her, slow to exit their booster seats at two and four and six years old, eyes focused on the handheld pinball game as they practiced being teenagers, affronted by her power.

The house was quiet, an eerie sign. Usually, if the kids weren't watching television, there was at least the beat of a stereo thumping from one or both of their rooms. Irene resisted the impulse to turn on the TV for benign company, a laugh track or talk show or even the smarmy sounds of paid programming. "Hungry?" she asked Joe, and he looked up surprised and hopeful at the solicitude in her tone. Then she saw understanding cross his face, the realization that now *she* was stalling, and that her question had nothing to do with how he felt — with his hunger or nervousness or guilt about why he'd been called home early, his boy suspected of a crime. So he would not give Irene what she wanted, the time she would have welcomed to make a sandwich or pour him a beer. "No," he said, "Let's go get him," and they were both aware that he sounded like a man about to hunt the one who was stalking his family, instead of his own tall sweet son.

Irene climbed the stairs first, feeling Joe's step behind her, heavy on her heels. In the hall they ran into Katy on her way to the bathroom. Her face looked swollen, not from tears but with an influx of knowledge too big for the space it occupied. "Be nice to him," she told her parents. "He feels bad."

"Well I would *hope* so," Joe said, and mother and daughter sent him silent rays of contempt.

Irene asked, "Are you going to Chelsea's?" but Katy gave her a look that implied she was crazy.

"I can't go anywhere," she accused them. "We're going to have to move, you know. To a whole new town somewhere. In a whole new state."

Irene said, "Don't be ridiculous."

"Oh, don't *you*." Their daughter shut the bathroom door with as close to a slam as she dared.

They knocked on Brian's door and when there was no answer, they went in. He was sitting at his desk looking at the computer, where an avatar game filled the screen. "Turn that off," Joe said, and without swiveling to face them, Brian complied; the sound of the computer going dead was a grievous sigh.

"Brian," Irene said, "what happened?" She sat on the bed, but Joe remained standing. Brian stood up from the computer and leaned against the desk as he had leaned against the wall at the police station, backing away from Irene. He was so tall he had to bend so his head wouldn't hit the bookshelf above him. When he was younger, the shelf had been squeezed tight — with *National Geographic* volumes about the solar system, Encyclopedia Brown mysteries, King Tut pop-ups, all the Narnia books. (One weekend, inspired by Narnia, he had created his own universe on a piece of poster board; Irene remembered some of the planet and continent names, even now: *Spartica*, *Willing*, *Playhow*.) Now the bookshelf contained the boxes from computer games, discarded pieces of Lego sets, and bottles of the aspirin he downed more often than Irene suspected was healthy, for the headaches neither he nor the doctors could explain. He reached for one of the bottles now, but it was empty. He slammed it into the wastebasket, which wobbled from the force.

Joe said, "Did you do this thing, Brian?" Irene could hear in her husband's voice the desperate plea for a denial.

Brian shrugged, but she could see it wasn't meant to be elusive or insolent — just a preliminary gesture to answering. "Yeah."

Joe let out a breath she sensed he had been holding since she'd called him from the police station the night before. She waited for him to say "Why?" but when he didn't, she understood; it left a space for her to ask the question, but she couldn't bring herself to do it, either.

"Because he's a freaking wack job." They hadn't heard the bedroom door opening, or Katy coming in. She stood with her long arms crossed in front of her. The small wings of her black hair stood up beside her temples, as if she had been able to shape them with her anger, instead of her usual gel.

"Kate," Brian said. He made a barely perceptible movement toward his sister, but stopped himself as if realizing she would not welcome it. Irene felt the crack in her heart widen. "I'm sorry."

"*Sorry*? How about *crazy*?" When Katy spoke lately, she tended to raise her eyebrows so high in her forehead they disappeared into her bangs. This time the brows came back down almost immediately in a melting motion, and Irene saw that it wasn't anger her daughter felt now — it was fear. And this Irene understood, because she felt it, too. In fact, as she stood between the walls of her son's room, which seemed too small to contain the whole family, she recognized that fear was what they all felt, including Brian.

"Could I be alone now, please?" Brian gestured with his head toward the door.

Katy told him, "Whatever you say, freako," flouncing into the hall, down the stairs, and out the front door. Irene — who would be ashamed of this for the rest of her life — took the easy way and followed Katy out of the room, even though she sensed (and knew she was right in sensing) that her son, despite what he said, did not want his family to leave.

Joe stayed. "I'm not moving till I get some answers," Irene heard him say as she shut the door behind her, closing the truth inside.

She went to the basement. She was sure of what she was looking for, and yet she could not find it. It was the oddest thing, so odd that she convinced herself for a few moments that someone — Katy, or — no — *Brian*, it would have to have been — had taken the boxes and hidden them, specifically so she would not be able to locate them at a time like this. But why? It took her several minutes of searching and puzzling to remember, slowly, that the boxes were gone, and that she knew this; they had not survived the flood that soaked the basement two or three Aprils ago, and though she had tried to air everything out and to fool herself into believing it would dry, all of it was lost. After that they put down pallets but it didn't really matter, because they would never have anything again as valuable as what the storm had already ruined.

The boxes had contained the children's artwork and other projects from nursery through middle school — all the poignant artifacts of childhood seeped through and puckered, warped or dismembered beyond value even to the mother of their creators. "What do you need this stuff for, anyway?" Katy had demanded, as Irene surveyed the sodden boxes and couldn't hold back her tears. The crying made Katy madder, and Brian had gone blank and turned away. Joe had to be the one to cart the boxes to the curb.

Irene had forgotten all of this until now, as she stood in the basement with her hands twitching, knowing what they wanted but finding nothing to light on to take the twitch away.

When the kids were little she used to bring them to the crafts store every couple of weeks. They always came home with a new project, which the three of them put together at the dinner table when the dishes had been cleared. *I am a good mother*, Irene could hear in her head as she dropped the items on the counter in front of the cashier. Actually, what she heard was *She is a good mother*, projected back toward herself in the cashier's unheard voice.

Brian's favorite things to buy at the craft store were bound pasteboard books with blank pages, in which he wrote and illustrated his own stories. Irene's favorite was titled *The Nurse and the Black Lagoon*. When he showed her the cover, Irene said, "Do you know what a *lagoon* is?" and Brian said, "No" as if it couldn't have mattered less.

Menny pursons hav bin to the nurse, went the first page. The "inventive spelling" system favored by the school district drove Joe nuts. "How are they supposed to learn what's right?" he said to Irene, when the letter came home from the teacher explaining the protocol, and adding that parents should not correct their children when they made mistakes reading aloud. "Why don't they have inventive math, then, too? What's the difference between letting them spell *cat* with a *k* and saying two plus two equals seven?" Irene didn't have an answer. Joe brought it up with Brian's teacher when they had their conference, and the teacher explained the rationale. It made sense back then, but Irene couldn't remember it now.

Menny pursons hav bin to the nurse. Brian started having his headaches that year, in the first grade. They had his eyes examined and eventually the doctor even ordered a brain scan, but the physical tests revealed nothing. "It's probably just nerves," the doctor told Joe and Irene. "Some kids get stomachaches, his probably just shows up in his head."

"But what can we do about it?" they asked the doctor. The pain was as real as if there had been a tumor. They could see it pounding behind his soft gray eyes.

The doctor shrugged. She had no children, Irene felt sure — she was too young yet, wore no ring, and didn't seem to *need* to relieve their boy's suffering, the way a parent would. "Try to help him relax," she suggested. "Does he have some favorite music? Maybe a washcloth on his forehead, before he goes to bed."

Irene recalled how angry this had made Joe. "*Maybe a washcloth on his forehead*," he muttered on the way home, low enough that Brian couldn't hear. "Brilliant. A washcloth on his forehead — Jesus Christ."

So a couple of days each week, Irene had picked Brian up at the school nurse's office, and brought him home. In the book he wrote and illustrated, he drew the office in detail, with its cot in the corner, the nurse's desk and its bowl of candy corn (all year round), the blinds she pulled against the sun in the hope of soothing what he called "the hard hurt" at the sides of his head. The nurse's name was Mrs. Rising and Brian loved her, so Irene came to love her, too. Mrs. Rising never intimated that there was anything wrong with Brian psychologically, and she treated his symptoms as real. "I wish I could do more," she whispered to Irene once, as Brian pulled on his shoes. "I'm sure it's because he's sensitive, which is a *good* thing. He'll outgrow the headaches. But he'll always be sensitive. As soon as he learns how to modulate it, he'll be all right."

Irene knew it was true — that she had a sensitive son. She remembered, from his kindergarten year, his face in the school bus window as he waved at her madly in the mornings, trying not to cry. Katy never had separation problems; even on the first day of nursery school, Irene had to ask for a kiss before leaving her daughter to start bossing the room around.

Menny pursons hav bin to the nurse, Brian wrote. *But not menny pursons hav bin to the black lagoon*. Turning the page past the illustration of the nurse's office, Irene had felt crazily curious, wondering how Brian would draw a picture of something he could not describe or define.

But it was just a black page: he had taken a crayon and colored the whole page black, with not a single jot of white space left uncovered. Holding it up toward the ceiling to see if any light could get through (it couldn't), Irene realized that without knowing what a *black lagoon* was, he had rendered it perfectly, through instinct — a metaphor for nothingness, the dark, invisible depths.

It was the only reference in the whole book to the black lagoon, and it was here that the story ended. Usually, Brian felt compelled to fill all the blank pages of the book, but not this time; it was a two-sentence story (*Menny pursons hav bin to the nurse. But not menny pursons hav bin to the black lagoon*), and now that she thought about it Irene could remember Joe shaking his head when he saw it and asking her, "Why can't he write about cowboys, or astronauts? Something more normal? I mean, how many kids his age go around writing about the school *nurse*?"

"He likes her," Irene said. She was folding socks into balls.

"Well, he shouldn't. He shouldn't even *know* her." Joe picked up the second book on the bed, the one Katy had written with Irene's help. *Cats Know How to Build Sandcastles*. "Now that's more like it," he said.

She left the basement quickly, once she realized that there was nothing for her there. She could feel in the house that Joe and Brian were still in Brian's bedroom. It was too early to go to bed yet. She turned on the TV, sat down with a magazine, and waited to see what would come on.

After a half hour Joe came downstairs and told her, "He wants to talk to you."

"What is it?" she asked, but he was shaking his head.

"I couldn't really get it. The cop's probably right, he needs therapy. Jesus. I'd better go look up what we have." He headed for the desk where they kept the insurance papers. "Where's Katy?" he asked over his shoulder.

"Not home yet."

"Well, let's find her. We've had enough surprises for one week."

"Call Chelsea's," she told him, knowing that he would have no idea how to do this, but also knowing that Katy was okay. "I'm going up."

Brian was waiting for her in his doorway. He showed her in like a host. "What's going to happen to me?" he asked. She saw how scared he was, and she also knew that he wasn't referring only or even primarily to the courts. Yet she decided to address this part first, because it was easier. Even though she didn't have a precise answer, she could find something to say.

"Well, that policeman seemed to think we had a good shot at probation, since you don't have any record." She decided not to tell Brian that Lieutenant Scully had said teenage boys often set fires to send up a "cry for help."

"It depends on whether the judge sees it as an act of arson or what they call *malicious mischief*," the officer had told her, after taking her into a side room of the police station. The room felt familiar to Irene, despite the fact that she had not been inside this building since two of the town's four elementary schools had been combined, and the Hardy school transformed into public safety headquarters. With a start that made her feel, absurdly, like laughing, she realized that where she stood now with Lieutenant Scully was the old nurse's office — Mrs. Rising's room, where she had picked Brian up on so many deadened afternoons. She had the idea to mention this coincidence to the officer, until she realized that it would likely be treated as more than just a coincidence — perhaps Scully would use it, even if only anecdotally over beers with other guys on the squad, as early evidence of Brian's being disturbed.

"Probably, since he's been clean up to now, he'll get away with probation and a fine, maybe five hundred dollars," the lieutenant said. He noticed Irene's wince when she heard *get away with*, and he waved at his own words as if to clean his spoken slate. "Or there's a program over in Ravena for teenage fire setters. When they get enough kids from the surrounding towns, they send them through the program together. One afternoon a week plus Saturday mornings."

"What for?" Irene knew she sounded stupid, but she really wanted to know.

Scully shrugged. "To help them find out why they do it."

"Well, in Brian's case, it must be some kind of mistake." She knew how she sounded — every mother in the world would say the same thing, right? — but she also believed herself. "He must have lit a match for some reason, and it got out of hand."

"He smoke?" the officer asked. Irene shook her head.

Scully shrugged again. "Maybe you're right," he told her. She thought she might hug him — he was somebody's son, she realized, perhaps somebody's brother.

But the impulse passed; he was also the person who had arrested Brian.

Now, stretched across his bed, Brian was waiting for her to tell him what neither of them could possibly know. "Dad and I were thinking you might want to see somebody," Irene said. "Besides whatever the courts do. Like a therapist?"

Brian looked at her without registering any expression. She thought he was going to say something, but he didn't.

"Do you want to tell me what happened?" She held most of her breath as she pressed the words out.

"I want to," Brian said, and she coughed on a mixture of relief and fear as they met in her throat. The look he gave her was almost like pity. "But I can't."

And just what was it she thought he might say? That there was a girl involved, maybe — some tough and unloved sophomore who had sucked Brian into the problems of her own life, turned him into a rescuer and confidant, so that he lost his own sense of values in trying to salvage hers? Irene couldn't quite bring herself to see how this would translate into Brian's having set fire to the playground, but she was desperate to make it be true.

But when she asked Katy about it she found out that no, there was no girl. There had never been any girl, not since Ellie Bender in first grade. "Doesn't that strike you as odd, Mom?" Katy said. They were having this conversation in the kitchen and Katy was dipping pretzels in the peanut butter jar, washing the bites down with grape juice from a can. Irene had made dinner, a goulash, but she ate it alone; Joe was still at work and Brian never ate with the family anymore, just stole out of his room to take things from the kitchen, which he ate in front of his computer or in bed. He had stopped going to school and had lost a week already. Irene didn't know what to do.

"I don't know about *odd*," she answered Katy, though now that she thought about it, there had been times when she'd wondered why Brian hadn't wanted to go to dances or, in junior high, the Friday Night Flings, when once a month all the grades got together at the school to play games in the gym, eat pizza, and watch movies like *Night of the Living Dead* in the auditorium.

She'd never asked him about it, though. When he was younger, he used to like spending Friday nights with Irene and Joe, and Katy too if she didn't have a sleepover at somebody's house. They'd either order in pizzas from Sam's and rent a movie, or have dinner at Sam's and see a new release (*Shrek*, *The Lord of the Rings*, *Spy Kids*) in the cineplex at the mall.

"You're not trying to tell me he's gay, are you?" Irene asked.

"Not gay. Just weird. *Off.* Like he still lives on this planet, only he's tilted somehow. Gay would be better, really," Katy opined. "At least then you'd know what it was."

"He always liked Ellie Bender, I remember that."

"You can't even *count* Ellie Bender." Saying this caused Katy to spray pretzel salt from the corners of her busy mouth. "That was just kid stuff. Not real."

"Of course it was real." Irene put her fork down. "He loved her. I know what you're saying, it wasn't a grown-up kind of love. But it *was* real. You should have seen him that day, when he thought she had been kidnapped."

Katy snorted, barely recovering before the pretzel went down the wrong way. "Kidnapped. Yeah, *right*, Mom. You still don't know what happened that day?" Katy took a long gulp of juice. Irene could feel puzzlement and danger tugging at her brow. "He was the one who found that kitten, and he like *lured* Ellie into the woods with it. Then, once they were in there together, he told her to hide and not come out when the grown-ups called, because they'd both get in trouble." Finally satisfied, Katy replaced the lid on the peanut butter. "I can't believe you don't know this, Mom." Uncharacteristically she hesitated, then decided to go ahead. "Everybody else does."

She had not correctly gauged the nature and level of her mother's response to this statement; it had been a long time since she had miscalculated by so much. In the moment after she spoke, Katy flinched, as if to do so could mitigate her mother's pain. She rarely showed this much attention to what somebody else felt, so the foreignness of the impulse made her need to sit down.

Irene, too, lost a beat, and took a step backward. Regaining her breath and balance, she looked at her daughter with a measure of hatred she could recall feeling, previously, only for people who'd threatened her children in some overt or implicit way. And Katy felt it; she would always remember this as the moment of her own growing up, the separation of herself from the illusion of a mother who would love her no matter what.

"I don't know how you could say something like that," Irene said, barely getting the words out between her teeth. "Of course that's not what happened. Did he tell you that? He's just trying to get you on his side." Even as the words emerged, she knew they made no sense. Get Katy on his side in what? How would telling a story that made him the villain contribute toward that end?

And when and how did it happen, that they weren't all on the *same* side?

Katy saw that it would be better if she didn't advise her mother not to go postal, which was her instinct. Instead, she continued the story. "Brian caught the kitten and showed it to Ellie and made her go with him into the woods." She paused and pursed her lips to indicate that Irene might not want to hear what was to follow.

"Are you going to tell me they played doctor or something?" Irene felt her stomach girding, muscles clenching to fend off an attack. "Every kid does that. *You* did it with Jeff Meade. Remember?"

"It wasn't doctor," Katy said.

"Yes, it was. Jeff's mother called me."

"I mean with Brian." Irene had never seen her daughter's eyes flashing so dark. "It was the kitten. He dug a hole and he put the cat in it with Ellie watching, feet first. The cat of course was trying to get out and it scratched his arm up — don't you remember how he came out of the woods all bleeding and stuff?"

Something crackled in Irene's brain — the physical equivalent of all the lights in the house dimming and surging again at the same time. Then the power stayed on and she forgot the flicker.

"But he wouldn't let it. He filled in that hole with only the cat's head sticking out, and he made Ellie promise not to tell." Katy paused to take an especially deep breath, as if relating all of this to her mother exhausted her. "She did, though. Not right away. But eventually, everybody found out."

"This is ridiculous," Irene said. And yet. And yet. With a jolt of clarity she saw her son's arm dotted with *Flintstones* Band-aids, which was all she could find, in the glove compartment, the day the playground was built. Brian was embarrassed and tried to refuse, but Irene prevailed, and it was she who covered all the scratches, which Brian said he'd gotten from thorns while looking for Ellie when she disappeared in the woods. Now that Irene thought about it, she remembered that the scratches and the Band-aids came *before* Stew and Laura Bender raised their alarm. It hadn't made sense to Irene at the time, and she had forgotten about it instantly upon realizing that it didn't make sense.

That moment — the one just before forgetting — was the one she found herself in now. Even Katy could tell how hard it hit her. "Sorry, Mom," she said. "But maybe this was a *good* thing — the fire. Maybe now he can get some help."

The therapist's name was Nathan Winkle, though he told them they could call him Nat. Driving Brian to his first appointment, Irene tried to make a joke of it. "Nat Winkle to the rescue!" she crowed, in as bright a tone as she could muster. "Nat Winkle, PhD. *Who you gonna call?* Nat Winkle!" Gamely, pained, Brian tried to return her smile.

Irene didn't like Nat, because he was always on Brian's side. Again with the *sides*, she thought, driving home one day, but it really did seem that way. She and Joe were the bad guys. Somehow, the reason for their son's arson lay with them. Nat liked Brian and Katy, and Irene found herself hoping that he would give her some credit for that. Did he think it was easy to raise likable teenagers? She doubted that he had any kids of his own, though there was no evidence either way. He was overweight and unkempt, qualities Irene knew Joe would hold against him.

In the family sessions, Irene kept encouraging Nat to surmise how it might be possible for physiology to be responsible for the fire. "The headaches," she kept saying, and though she knew it was silly, she couldn't help pointing at Brian's head as he sat in the chair next to hers. "He just wasn't in his right mind, because the pain is so bad."

But Nat Winkle thought it was the other way around. He believed Brian's headaches were the result of internal stress.

"What kind of internal stress does a six-year-old have?" Joe demanded. "That's how old he was when they started." Irene knew her husband didn't like Nat, either — aside from his lumpy body and uncombed hair — though neither of them had admitted this to the other. She could tell by the way Joe kept pressing his glasses up on his nose, jamming them against his forehead. What he really wanted to be pushing was the therapist, Irene saw.

Nat said, "You'd be amazed at how early kids can catch on to things. Especially if they're sensitive, like Brian." *Sensitive* — that word again.

"What's there to catch on to?" After he spoke, Joe's breath came out of his nose in a rush, fuming. "What are you saying? That there was something at home that made him nervous? Because let me tell you, Natty boy, you're shooting blanks up the wrong tree with *that* theory."

He reached for a Kleenex and blew his nose fiercely as Irene laughed. "You think my blowing my nose is funny?" Joe said, and Irene said, "No. But *shooting blanks up the wrong tree* is. You're mixing your metaphors."

Joe looked as if he might want to put her in a sack and toss her off the nearest bridge. "Well, excuse me for not going to college and learning something useful, like metaphors."

"There were things. *Are* things," Katy said. She hardly ever spoke at these meetings, and she looked almost surprised that she had said something now. She didn't look at either of her parents, or at Brian, as she continued. "There's always the question of whether Dad's going to be home for dinner or not. How many places to set at the table. If we put down four plates and he doesn't come home, Mom gets mad, because the extra plate reminds her he isn't there. If we put down three and he *does* come home, *he* gets mad that nobody set a place for him. Stuff like that happens all the time.

"See, we have these jobs," Katy went on to explain to the therapist. "You know, chores, which is fine. Believe me, I have friends who don't have to do anything for their allowance, and they're total princesses.

"Now it's more like mow the lawn and take the recycling out, stuff like that. But when we were little, setting the table was one of Bri's and my jobs, and you just wouldn't *believe* the tension that went into it every night.

"When it was my turn to set," she continued, looking at her lap as if it contained a screen showing her the memory, "I'd start worrying about it at, like, two o'clock, in the line for the bus going home."

Irene interrupted her, because she didn't want to hear any more. "I just wish he would call, that's all," she told the therapist. "If he doesn't call, it's like he doesn't remember that I exist." She didn't seem up to addressing her husband directly.

"Do you people have any idea what's going on in the world?" Joe's voice actually contained disdain for his children, which Irene had not heard before. "Ever hear of Iraq and a thing called the war? Not to mention global warming and the economy. And you're going to sit there and tell me you get nervous about *plates*?"

"Yes," Katy said. She sat up straighter in her chair and leaned toward her father. "Yes, that's what I'm telling you." She let her heel kick rhythmically at the bottom of her chair.

"Why is it that sometimes you're not home for dinner, Joe?" Nat asked. He kept his own voice neutral, matching his beige flannel shirt.

"Because I have to work late. I realize that selling cash registers probably doesn't impress you very much, Nat, because it's all about machines, instead of getting in touch with our feelings. But you know what? I make a pretty damn good living." Joe paused to let this linger for all of them, not only Nat. "You think there's no stress involved in what I do? But you don't see me setting fires at playgrounds because of it."

They all looked at Brian. He just shrugged and raised his eyebrows, as if to concede that his father had a point.

"Brian," Nat said, and Irene felt her stomach relax a fraction, because the focus was deflected from her. "What happened just before you set the fire? What were you thinking about?"

Irene was sure Brian would not answer the question, so she was surprised when her son spoke as if he had given the subject some thought. "It's like I get these pictures in my head of things that could happen. Things I could actually *do*, but that I shouldn't. That *no one* should, because they're so bad. The headaches are worse, then."

See, Irene wanted to say to the therapist, but Nat sent her a warning look.

Katy asked, "Is that what happened with the kitten?"

Irene was afraid Brian would take offense at this because it had never come up in a family session, but when he just sat there and reflected upon Katy's question, she realized that Nat Winkle already knew about the day Ellie Bender went into the woods.

"It is kind of the same," Brian acknowledged. "The pictures-in-my-head part. And then I do the things, in the pictures, to show myself that it isn't as bad as what I imagined. But it *is*. It *is* that bad. It's not like I get any relief from it, or anything." He leaned over in his seat, clapping the heels of his hands against his eyes. "So why do I *do* it? Why don't I know better by now?"

"Because you keep hoping it will be different next time." Nat had leaned forward, too, so that he and Brian were almost touching, while the rest of the family sat in an excluded circle around them. "Do you know anything about Alcoholics Anonymous? Their definition of insanity is repeating the same behavior, over and over, each time expecting a different result."

"My son is not insane," Joe said, standing, and after a second Irene realized that she should stand, too. Their children remained seated, still not looking at their parents. "But I think maybe *you* are, Nat. You're insane if you think I'm going to listen to any more of this horseshit from some guy who wears flannel to the office, charges two hundred bucks an hour, and can't find the time to comb his hair before a client walks in. Couldn't you go out and buy a decent suit?"

Irene's breath had stopped in her chest, but in the next moment she let it out. "I could," Nat Winkle said, tilting his head up calmly, "but I prefer not to."

Brian laughed, and they all looked at him. "'I prefer not to,'" he said, by way of explanation, and when that didn't help any of them, he said, "It's from 'Bartleby, the Scrivener.' Herman Melville. We did it in English this year."

"You see that?" Irene asked Nat. "He's in AP English *and* AP History. That means Advanced Placement, and he can get credit for college when he's only in high school."

"I know what AP means," Nat said quietly.

"This guy Bartleby just keeps saying he prefers not to do anything. I mean, everything they ask him to do, he says he doesn't want to. It's hilarious." Brian was cracking himself up, and he and Nat seemed to be the only ones not alarmed by this.

"It doesn't sound hilarious," Joe said. "It sounds stupider than hell to me."

Nat said, "I think we're getting off track here."

"That's the most brilliant observation you've made today." Joe picked up his coat from the sofa arm; he had declined to leave it on the waiting room tree rack, with the rest of theirs, because he didn't trust that some lunatic wouldn't run off with it.

"Why don't you sit down, Mr. Ludwig." Nat spoke so softly that Joe had to lean in to hear him, and Irene saw that this was what the therapist had intended. "There are only a few minutes left, anyway." He turned to Brian, and behind him, Joe set the coat back down. Katy and Irene still sat in their chairs, each looking at some spot on the table in front of them. There was one of those gravity-ball knockers on the table — the kind where two silver balls take turns hitting each other in the opposite direction — and for a moment Irene was tempted to start it going, but she couldn't remember if the point of it was that it would, once activated, never cease. Then she thought that maybe — did she remember this from a lecture at the museum, when she was chaperoning a field trip? — the friction between the balls would eventually cause them to stop. But she couldn't remember, and she wondered why Nat had this toy on his table. Or was she wrong and it *wasn't* a toy?

"Are there any feelings attached, when you've done these things, Brian?" Nat Winkle asked him. He dropped his voice further. "Any anger?"

Brian shook his head. "No," he added, for emphasis.

"Not any anger at all? That's unusual."

Brian shrugged. "So I'm unusual. So what?"

"Are you angry at me, right now?"

"No."

"Who are you angry at?"

"Nobody." He barely whispered the word, and in it they could all hear what Nat Winkle had been hunting for. They could all hear it, except Brian. "Can I go now?" he asked, and Nat nodded. Brian stood up and slunk toward the door, which even Irene wished he would slam behind him, because it was so painful to witness such unexpressed rage.

The rest of them got up to leave, too. "I'll get back to you with my recommendation," Nat told them. "I think he can be helped, but it'll be tough on all of you, not just Brian."

"Great," Katy said, flipping her hair out of her sweatshirt hood. "Just what I was hoping for when I got to high school — a brother who could go postal at any time."

That final appointment (the juvenile court judge had ordered eight sessions before the therapist would make a recommendation to the court about how to proceed with Brian's case) took place on the Thursday before Halloween. For weeks, Irene had been collecting applications for all the colleges Brian had ever mentioned, or for which she thought he might be a suitable match. She laid them out on the dining room table in color-coded folders — red for the long shots, blue for the could-go-either-ways, yellow for safeties. Primary colors. She was proud of herself.

As she was putting the remaining, empty folders into a manila envelope she labeled *Katy/College*, the phone rang. Nat Winkle did not engage her in any customary how-are-you chitchat, and she wondered if he was like this, plunging straight to the point, in his personal calls as well, or whether it was just his manner with clients (a word she preferred, of course, to *patients*). "I'm glad you answered instead of one of the kids," Nat told her. Irene sat down at the kitchen table and began picking at the fringes of one of the placemats. "I'm going to recommend probation for Brian," Nat said, "provided he continue therapy, and I think he needs twice a week. I don't have room in my schedule myself — I think I told you, I do a lot of these evaluations for the courts over the short term, then recommend patients out. But I can give you the name of this great guy over in Ravena. He specializes in this sort of thing."

"What sort of thing?" Irene realized it was probably a stupid question, but then she told herself, *No, he's not being specific, I have a right to ask.*

"Fire setters," Nat said, and the blunt speed of his answer made her cringe. "Juvenile arsonists. It's more common than I'm sure you'd guess. That's the good news — there are programs to address this particular criminal behavior."

"My son isn't a criminal," Irene said, the fringe coming off in her fingers.

Nat Winkle cleared his throat. "He set fire to a playground," he reminded her. "How did he know there wasn't some child asleep in there somewhere? It's happened before. Little kids who live in the neighborhood wander out of their yards, and their parents call the police, who find the kids sleeping up in that little clubhouse above the slides. That *used* to be above the slides." He paused, and for a moment Irene prayed that something had interfered with their connection. Because they went to see the therapist at his office in the next city, it had not occurred to her that he might live in their town, not to mention near the Eastbrooke playground. She was on her way to feeling renewed chagrin when he added, "Then it'd be manslaughter, and you'd be looking at a whole different ball of wax."

"But it isn't manslaughter," Irene said. In her head, the word became *mans laughter*. "It's just a fire set by a teenager who didn't know what he was doing. They must make some allowance for that."

"They do." On the other end of the line, Nat held his hand over the mouthpiece, but Irene could still hear him speak to someone in a tone that indicated he was calling from home instead of his office. She pictured him in a kitchen, wearing the same flannel shirt, microwaving leftover coffee in a mug. "That's why Brian's not in jail, and that's also where I come in. The court listens to me — that's why, as your husband noted, they pay me the big bucks." He made a wry sound resembling laughter. "I'm going to give you a couple of names and numbers, and you can set up some appointments for Brian and figure out which is the best fit. He'll be on probation for six months, at the end of which I talk to the therapist he's been seeing, we all meet, and I make a report to the judge. As long as he stays out of trouble during that time, his record will be clean. Got a pencil?"

Irene said, "But is this really necessary? I understand that he did a wrong thing. I get that. But I don't really see why he needs to go to a therapist. What's he going to talk about, all that time?"

Nat said, "Well, of course I don't know what the details would be. But — and I understand this is hard, Mrs. Ludwig — we already know about the fire and about the kitten incident, all those years ago. It's not really possible that there haven't been other things between then and now. You see that, right? This type of thing is usually a progression, and takes place over time. Got a pencil?"

She took down the names and phone numbers, thanked him, and hung up. In the next room the dryer was humming, and then it buzzed. She sat at the table until it buzzed again, at which time she got up to take the clothes out, and folded them.

When she'd put all the piles in the appropriate bedrooms, she went back to the kitchen and got out the yellow pages, sat down at the table with the phone, and started dialing. By five thirty, she had a pad filled with notes and figures. Katy was the first one home. She'd had soccer practice, and her ponytail hung sweatily down the back of her green jersey. "What're you doing?" she asked her mother, but Irene shook her head and gave a smile she had not brought out since the children were little and could be sent into paroxysms of excitement by the promise of a trip to the Tastee Freez.

"You have to wait until Daddy gets home," she said.

"What about Bri?"

"Go get him, will you? He'll want to hear this."

By the time Brian and Katy came to the kitchen, Joe had arrived.

He asked if he could change into his jeans before hearing whatever it was Irene had to tell them, but she said, "It'll only take a minute, just sit down." They all took their places at the table.

Before she could say anything, Brian asked, "Did Nat call?" The three of them were looking at her, trying hard — all of them, she could see — not to appear as invested as they were in her answer.

"No," she said, "but it's only Thursday, and Halloween's coming."

Katy said, "What the hell does that have to do with anything?"

"Language, missy," Joe said, but Irene could tell he agreed with his daughter's question.

"I just thought maybe he has little kids, and he'd be helping with costumes or something." Irene was doing what she had heard Katy refer to, on the phone with her friends, as pulling an excuse out of her ass. She hated the expression, of course, but it seemed apt; she'd had no idea what she was going to say before she said it. And no idea where it would come from, when it did.

Brian said, "He didn't call? He said he was going to," and Irene summoned her highest, most protective courage to reiterate that no, she had not heard anything from Nat Winkle since the last family session they'd had.

From her vehemence they all knew better then, but none of them said so. "So what's the big announcement?" Katy asked.

"Well — " Irene tried to re-create the smile, but felt it sagging at the corners of her mouth. "You remember how we used to talk about putting in a pool?"

"That was like ten years ago," Katy answered. "When I was in *nursery* school."

"I don't remember that." Brian looked confused, and Irene believed that he was telling the truth. If Katy hadn't just confirmed it, she might have wondered if she recalled correctly herself. But her daughter's certainty spurred her forward.

"Remember, you wanted one of those winding slides?" she said to her son. "You used to talk about celebrating your half-birthday, in the summer, so you could have pool parties. Don't you remember that?"

But Brian had gone blank, and Irene, feeling the blood rush to her stomach, put more expression into her own face and voice to compensate. "We just couldn't afford it before now. But Daddy's doing well, like he was telling us the other day, and I called around and got some estimates, and — well, Katy, remember Hannah Craigie, from your first soccer team? Her brother puts in pools for a living. He's coming over tomorrow to make sure it would all work, with the grading and everything, but he says he's seen our backyard and he thinks it should be fine."

Her family was staring at her. Then Katy started to laugh. Joe said to Irene, "Are you insane?" and Katy, through her hysterical-sounding mirth, said, "*Postal* is more like it. Try *postal*, Dad." Only Brian remained silent, and his eyes when they looked at Irene held neither mockery nor fear.

"A pool'd be nice," he said, and the quietness of his voice calmed the mood at the table.

"But it's about to be winter," Katy told her brother. "Not to mention we're not kids anymore."

"Not to mention," Joe added, "that a pool isn't exactly the most important thing going on in our lives right now."

"I was thinking it would be so nice in the summertime," Irene said. "Can't you just see it? — one of those perfect sunny days with absolutely no wind, and in the backyard we have this beautiful pool with blue water, and the sun bouncing off it in sparkles. It would be like Hawaii, or that time we went to Florida for February vacation. Remember, watching the Weather Channel in the hotel? If we'd stayed here, we would have been freezing and shoveling out our cars, and instead we got to lie by the pool and relax the whole time. By the time we got home, everything had melted."

"Pools are a pain in the ass," Katy said. "They look good on TV, but somebody has to be skimming crap off the top all the time. And I'm telling you right now, I'm not going to be the one."

"I'll skim," Brian said. He was pulling fringe off a placemat identical to the one Irene had mutilated an hour ago. "That could be my job."

Dear Nicole

THEY GREW UP playing hockey on Everett Pond, long after supper, after homework and *Happy Days*, after they said good night and went to their rooms yawning as if headed to sleep. The grown-ups pretended not to know about the rendezvous at the rink, but some of the fathers had, as boys, given birth to the midnight game, a raucous winter lullaby at the far end of the street.

Allie Sprinkle was one of five or six girls who listened for their parents to fall quiet behind their bedroom doors before they padded downstairs in their nighties, tucked hems into leggings, pulled on boots and big jackets and mittens but left their hats behind — because of what hats did to hair — and went out to the cold where their friends were waiting. They gathered at the top of King's Hill and locked arms for the slippery descent to the edge of the pond, where there was an extra wooden crate, like the one the boys used as a goal box, turned over for them to sit on.

When they saw them coming, the boys halted their game so the girls could settle. They paused to lean on their sticks, glad for the excuse to catch up on their breathing, then resumed darting and slapping with a louder, sharper energy because they were being watched. The game was dottily lighted by the moon and stars, and by four bulbs strung on a parade of extension cords around the rink. The girls clapped their mittens together and gave soft shouts of "Way to go, Burkie," and "Guard that goal!" When someone scored, a cheer rose from the players and their crowd, and Allie turned her face straight up to the black sky, closing her eyes, tasting a love and safety she knew would never be duplicated, that certainty a sweet stab in her heart.

The winter most of them were twelve, the season came to an end without warning on a crinkly December night. Nicole Rueger was sitting on the crate next to Allie, coughing into her gloves, when Gerald Burke hit the puck with such force that Allie Sprinkle swallowed the ball of Beech-Nut gum wedged in her cheek. There was a moment during which they all lost time — they knew the puck was flying somewhere, but they couldn't see it — and then Allie felt the cold whish of it by her face. She turned her head to follow the puck and watched Nicole fall from the crate beside her, headfirst into the hard bank, making a cracking sound as she landed. The boys skated over and stood in a bigger circle behind the one the girls formed around Nicole.

"Get her up," Gerald Burke said. He was wobbling on his blades.

Allie bent over to touch Nicole. There was no blood, but they all knew she was knocked out.

"Don't move her," said Mike Usiak, whose father drove an ambulance for Memorial.

"Well, what are we supposed to do?"

"I say we carry her up the hill. She'll probably wake up by the time we get there."

"Everybody wait a minute," Mike said. He was unfastening his skates, and the laces flashed in the moonlight. He began to run up the hill in his socks. "I'll get my dad," he told them, tripping as he turned to call over his shoulder. "Somebody take off their jacket and cover her up."

It was so cold they shivered just listening to his words. They all knew he was right, but not one of them, facing the wind, could imagine undressing in it.

"It was Gerald who did it," Dickie Domermuth said after the silence. "He should be the one."

Even as Dickie spoke, Gerald was unzipping his jacket, flinging his body out of it like a wrestler escaping a hold. He stuck the toe of his blade into the bank to stay steady as he lowered the jacket across Nicole. He went to take off his sweater, too, but Dickie caught his arm and said, "That's enough." For a moment the wind stopped above them, and they heard peace in the trees.

Then came the sound of grown-ups running, out of the houses and down the slick hill. It was more than just Mike and his father; most of the other parents came, too. Allie could see her mother's nightie flapping under her coat, and her father's robe belt dragging across the snow. They looked like a scattered army closing in for the kill.

"I didn't mean it," Gerald confessed to them, as he fell on his knees to the ground.

It turned out that Nicole had a concussion, which sent her to the hospital through the rest of the night and then gave her headaches for the next sixteen years, until she had her first child, when the pain seemed to leak out of her with the milk. After she and Gerald were married, she never mentioned the headaches to him in private, but if they had guests over and there was a lighthearted feel to the room, she sometimes went into a little routine to re-create what had happened back then.

"I was sitting on the crate with the other girls, innocent as a lamb," she said, tapping the salt shaker against the tablecloth to illustrate her position. "It was one of those frosty nights where you can feel the hair in your nose. I was sitting next to Allie Sprinkle, and she wouldn't stop shivering. She was one of those kids you just want to *slap* all the time, because they always look scared. I was about to tell her, 'Well, go back *in* then, for God's sake,' when all of a sudden this puck comes sailing through the air."

At this point Nicole usually chose the wine cork to simulate the puck's route. She aimed it at the salt shaker and let fly. Even when she hit the mark, there wasn't enough weight to push the shaker over, so she flicked at it with her fingernail, and salt scattered across the cloth. The guests laughed at this unlikely representation of Nicole knocked flat in the snow, but anyone who looked carefully through the candlelight could see Gerald wincing behind his smile. Someone always asked how the two of them ended up together, after such a bad start, but Gerald and Nicole always said they had no idea.

Usually, it was the accident itself that caught the guests' attention. But on a Friday night when they had some people from Gerald's office over for crab cakes and beer, one of the men said, "Allie Sprinkle. That sounds familiar. Would I know that name?"

"I don't see how," Nicole said, twirling her wineglass by the stem beside her plate. "This was a little town called Oxbow, up near Buffalo. By a butchery. Best barbecued wings you could ask for, but the air smelled like blood."

"Do you ever get back there?" someone asked.

"Not if we can help it," Nicole said. "Gerald's parents are dead, and we make mine fly down here if they want to see us." She was looking deep into her glass. Then she gave one of her famous smiles, as if to indicate she was only kidding, and swiveled in her chair to face Gerald. Ever since the headaches had left her, she found she couldn't resist making sudden movements with her neck. Sometimes Gerald caught her doing it, and asked her why, but she said she didn't know. She knew she would never have the courage to tell him she missed the pain he had given her, if this turned out to be the truth.

Nicole looked around the room at her guests, at their confident and capable faces; at the solid and pretty furniture she owned, and the silver tableware; at the ceiling above which her sleeping children dreamed of things they had yet to learn would not happen on this unmagical earth. She felt filled and blessed, and knew she should wonder what she had done to deserve any of it.

"Coffee?" she said brightly to the other end of the table, as she felt the mood of the party sliding toward the floor.

Across from her, Gerald looked up. He smiled at the woman he had nearly killed once, then loved.

"I'll get it," he told her. Before he left the room, he reached over to right the salt shaker, and he brushed the spilled crystals from the tablecloth.

The man who had asked at the party about Allie Sprinkle remembered, on his way home, where he had heard her name before. "It's the woman who took Laura's picture," he said to his wife, who was driving. "That woman Nicole was talking about, from their hometown? Allie Sprinkle. That's the name of the woman who took the portrait we had done of Laura, when we lived in Rochester."

"How do you remember these things? Besides, that's too much of a coincidence," his wife said. "It could be a whole different person with the same name. Besides, who cares?"

"Well, I do," her husband said. "I like things like this. I like it when it turns out that people knew each other somewhere before. It always makes me feel better, like the whole world is connected somehow. Just think about it," he continued, holding the dashboard as she cut a corner too fast. "If you believe in the Bible, we're all descended from Adam and Eve. If you go with the big bang, we all exploded from the same star, or crawled up from the same batch of ooze. Doesn't that make you feel better about the world? To imagine that everybody's related to everyone else?"

"It doesn't really make me feel anything," his wife told him. "Besides, you've been drinking."

"It always makes me feel better," he said again. They were home.

He remembered bringing his daughter to have her photograph taken by Allie Sprinkle. Allie worked where she lived, a house on a side street in a town whose name he could not quite recall, although Nicole's *Oxbow* seemed to ring some bell. *A. Sprinkle* was bolted in black above the mailbox.

When she came to the door, Allie looked small against the shadows of the foyer behind her, like a child herself. But once they were in the studio, which had been converted from an upstairs bedroom, she inhabited twice as much space as her body required. The air around her was charged with movement, not only of her arms, which flew around Laura's face and hair, but also of an energy that was almost visible in itself, like the confettied light thrown off by sparklers on the Fourth of July.

The portrait they ordered of Laura resembled a piece of art from an earlier century. Her eyes were locked in the camera's hold, and they contained a cast of — could it be mercy? — that neither he nor his wife recognized from before the photograph, and that they hadn't witnessed since. His wife went so far as to suggest that the negatives had been altered. They loved the picture for the beauty that was their child, but they were each secretly afraid of it, and they each learned a way of walking through the living room without looking into those eyes.

He became intrigued by the idea of the Burkes and Allie Sprinkle having known each other as children, and by his role as their connection later in life. In the strongbox that held the family's papers, he found the sheet of contact proofs Allie had given him, and he ordered an extra print of Laura's photograph. With the order he enclosed a note to Allie, telling her of how her name had come up at a dinner party in Maryland. She sent the picture but did not respond to the note, and as the years passed, as Laura grew up to look less and less like the wise child watching him from above the piano, he found it easier to look at the face in the filigreed frame. Soon after the dinner party, he left the firm where Gerald Burke worked, so he had no way of knowing that in the month following his message to western New York, a letter arrived at the Burkes' home in Silver Spring, addressed to Nicole (Rueger) Burke. In the return address corner of the envelope was a design logo composed of an old-fashioned bellows camera, the name Sprinkle, and the legend *Shooting Kids Since 1990*.

The letter had been tucked, under the load of the day's mail, into a newsmagazine; Gerald found it that night as he turned the pages. He was in bed, and Nicole was in the bathroom. When he heard the bathroom door opening, he stuck the envelope back in the magazine, feeling his heart beat beneath his Orioles shirt. Nicole was damp from the shower, and she leaned over to kiss him, smelling of shampoo and cream. "Just a minute, honey," he told her, and he carried the magazine into the bathroom.

He held the letter up over the sink, reached for the nail file in the toothbrush cup, and slit the seal with a sweep.

"Dear Nicole," the letter started. "It's been a long time, but I don't believe any of us could ever forget Everett Street. Or each other, even if we wanted to.

"I understand you have a son and daughter. Congratulations. Although I'm still amazed you would marry Gerald, when that puck was meant for me."

As he read this, Gerald felt a crawling sensation on the backs of his hands, but when he looked beyond the paper into the mirror, he saw that he was smiling. With relief he noted that Allie had added "Just kidding" in the margin of that sinister line.

"The next time you're in Oxbow, I'd be happy to photograph your children. My work is taking pictures, and kids are my specialty.

Enclosed is my card. In the meantime, my best to Gerald, and I hope the headaches have gone away.

"Sincerely, Allie S."

Gerald studied the signature closely, the way the *S* towered over the other letters, the way the *A* of *Allie* resembled a star. He put it back in the magazine and hid the whole surreptitious package in the basket of periodicals by the toilet. He returned to bed and made love to his wife with such attention and energy that when it was over and they looked at each other before switching the light off, he was not surprised to see suspicion in the face she turned to him.

That was November. At the beginning of December, Gerald took Allie Sprinkle's note and business card out of his briefcase, where he had been keeping the envelope since the day after it arrived. Answering the phone, she did not seem to hesitate when he said who he was, and for a moment he was afraid they might have had some contact in the past twenty years that he had forgotten since. "I intercepted your letter to Nicole," he told Allie, "by accident. But then I didn't give it to her, because I wanted to make it a surprise. The photograph. We're coming there for Christmas this year" — it had not been easy to convince Nicole to go back home, after so many years away, until he promised her a trip to Florida in the spring — "and I was wondering if I could get you to take a picture of our kids." Whenever he lied, his throat closed up, and he had to keep clearing it, hoping the sounds wouldn't put her off.

Allie's voice did not sound familiar, yet Gerald could, as they spoke, envision her clearly at the other end of the line. But then he realized he was picturing the small, sharp face in a stained snowsuit hood, turned up to the winter sky while the other girls watched hockey and called boys' names to the stars.

He remembered the time his father, who owned a Chevrolet dealership, sold Mr. Sprinkle a new car. It happened fast: one Sunday the two men met at the sidewalk, taking a break from cutting their lawns, and Gerald's father followed Mr. Sprinkle to the Plymouth Fury in the Sprinkles' garage, popped the hood, and started talking as he pointed. Gerald, who was watching from a tree, saw that Mr. Sprinkle, who was a packer at the Feible Meat Company, didn't understand what Gerald's father was saying. Mr. Sprinkle had an accent, and he gave little smiles of embarrassment as Gerald's father tried to explain things, gesturing at the motor with his cigarette. It was a hot day and Gerald felt the back of his shirt sticking to the bark. He had brought a soda up there, but after a few sips he didn't want it anymore; there was no place to set the can down and he couldn't toss it full, so he poured it out on ants in the branches, not exactly realizing that they would drown but, when they did, watching them closely before he let the can fall to the ground.

After dinner that night, while he was doing his homework in the next room, Gerald overheard his father telling his mother about the conversation with Mr. Sprinkle. His father used the word *chump*. "Too bad the flocus valve had to blow like this," his father was saying, and Gerald could tell that he was helping himself to the last piece of pie, eating it straight out of the pie dish in blueberry forkfuls. "That flocus valve will sure do it every time." Then Gerald heard the sound of his father's laughter blending with blueberry swallows. Gerald had not yet learned very much about cars, but he knew there was no such thing, in any model ever made, as a flocus valve. The next weekend, the Fury was gone, and Mr. Sprinkle was driving a new Nova from Burke Chevrolet. In the tree, Gerald watched Allie and her parents pull out of their driveway. Allie was in the back seat, and she saw Gerald and smiled and pointed at his name ornamenting the trunk, *Burke* in shiny chrome across the backside, and he knew that she meant with the gesture to thank his father for taking care of hers.

On the phone, Gerald and Allie arranged a date and time for

Gerald to bring the children to be photographed. "I live in the Ketchums' old house now," Allie told him. "Remember? Behind the middle school."

He thought of the house with the backyard where they sometimes had to chase home-run balls during kickball games. Mrs. Ketchum (whom they referred to, of course, as Mrs. Ketchup) used to sit on her back porch, sewing, and when a ball came rolling from the field onto her property, she acted as if she were about to have a heart attack. Nobody was ever willing to go get those balls except Allie, so they always let her play.

Two days before Christmas, Gerald set out with his family for Oxbow early in the morning. Because of the holiday traffic, the trip took most of a day. The kids spent the time fighting, snacking, and sleeping in the back seat, and Nicole napped for much of the ride, too, so Gerald was alone with the radio and the road. At the Thruway, when he rolled down his window for the toll ticket, he let in the cold air from outside, and his family woke up to complain. His son spit gum out the window, and his daughter performed a marriage ceremony between two of her dolls. "Do you, Jason, take her, Margo, to be your awfully wedded wife?"

Finally, they came to the exit for Oxbow and headed into town. The air smelled of exhaust and gravel, and ahead they could see the old stockyard from Feible's drawing near. When they came to Four Corners, Gerald was both dismayed and thrilled to realize how little had changed since they'd last been here — could it be six years? Yes, because their daughter had been in her infant seat, crying at the cold. As it had then and as far back as Gerald could remember, Costa's Snack Shoppe stood between the beauty parlor and the bank. Across the street, lights on the Christmas tree in front of Grace Lutheran blinked pastels across the snow.

From the back seat, their daughter asked, "Why did you guys get married?"

Nicole murmured over her shoulder, "Because we loved each other, honey," and, rolling up the window, looking into the mirror, Gerald saw with pride and pain that the baby knew better. They were leaving the center of town, moving out Cherry Avenue and past the veterinarian's office, where all the families in Oxbow took their dogs to die. Nicole had worked in the vet's building the summer after they graduated, and Gerald picked her up there when he was done with his job painting classrooms. Once, on a Friday after the vet and his assistant had both left for the weekend, Nicole and Gerald had sex in the examining room, on the padded table where the animals lay on paper sheets to receive their shots. The table was narrower than what they were used to, and as they moved, their heads and shoulders slid over the edge, but they managed to keep their balance until they were finished, when they slipped off sideways, Gerald hitting the floor first to cushion Nicole's fall. Nicole laughed and Gerald swore, and after they got up, she was still laughing and he swore again.

"What?" he asked her roughly. He had banged his shoulder blade on the way down.

"I can't help it," she told him, dragging their sanitary sheet off the table, rolling it up but avoiding the wet part, stuffing it in the full can. "It feels kind of out of control, doing it in this room. Usually I only come in here if he needs somebody to hold down their paws while he puts in the needle." She took a cloth from the cabinet and wiped the vinyl slowly, as if each motion required thought.

"He puts the needle in, and at first the dog tries to get off the table, but then it stops trying and goes kind of still. If you watch the eyes, you can see the life go right out of them. The eyes stay open, so it's not like sleeping, but — " Nicole made a *that's-all-she-wrote* gesture with her hand — "Well, you can see the light go right out." She had her head down and he was worried she might be crying, but when she looked up again he saw she was only hungry. "Let's *eat*," she said, grabbing his hand, and he tripped, following her, because she was moving so fast.

Now they wound their way down their old street, which curved like an arm around Everett Pond. The afternoon had settled into dusk, and teenagers were skating, girls in pairs or triples beside the banks, boys gliding in dreamy circles as they patted their pucks. It had snowed only a few times so far this year, and the pond's shoreline was congested with slush and weeds. The ice itself was ragged; they could see bumps in the gray surface, even from the car.

Still, though it was not as beautiful as they remembered, Nicole and Gerald held their breath together, as if they had come too suddenly on a scene from a mutual dream. "Hey, maybe they'll let me play," their son said from the back seat.

"Of course they will," Nicole said, but Gerald could see that the boy was, in fact, afraid of this, so he told him, "You're a little young yet," and his son flashed him grateful relief in the rearview mirror.

That night Gerald didn't wake up to hear the hockey game, but Nicole told him about it in the morning. It had gone on past one o'clock, because there was no school. On Christmas Eve the rink was quiet, and most of Everett Street went to midnight Mass. On Christmas night the game started up again, and this time Gerald heard the familiar sounds through his sleep, the scrape of blades and the rings of laughter looping the empty trees.

He got out of bed and went to the window. Ice glittered on telephone wires. The flickery bulbs suspended above the pond had been replaced by floodlights, which illuminated the whole rink, even the corners, where it used to be you could hide, if you wanted to leave the game for a few minutes to be alone with your heartbeat and the stars. The girls didn't sit on a crate to watch anymore, but stood in a circle, some of them smoking cigarettes with their backs to the boys, all of them talking while the action passed by. They wore their daytime clothes under their coats and jackets, instead of pajamas and gowns. Occasionally they said something to one of the players, or admired a shot with a flirty hoot, but it was a tired admiration, and Gerald saw that the girls might just as well have been hanging out at Costa's, laughing over pop and French fries, for all they cared about the game. He closed the curtain with a sick sensation and the feeling that he had been fooled.

The appointment he had made with Allie Sprinkle was for the next morning at ten o'clock. After breakfast, Nicole's parents went out on errands, and Gerald stretched and said he thought he would go over to the Hello Dolly, to see if anybody from the old days might be around. The Hello Dolly was the diner next to the Oxbow branch of the public library, which was so small that the smell of books clung to you when you left it, like cigarette smoke from a bar.

"The day after Christmas?" Nicole said. She was arranging herself beneath the afghan on the sofa, and Gerald knew there was no danger of her wanting to join him at the diner. When she returned to Oxbow and saw someone she recognized, she crossed the street or aimed her eyes straight ahead with the look of a woman who had too much to think about.

"Some of the guys used to hang out for coffee," Gerald said. "Like Usiak and Dickie and Bob Lattimer. Maybe they won't be there, and either way, I'll only be a while. Hey, how about I swing by Costa's on the way home, and pick up some wings for lunch? The old recipe."

"Yuck," said the children in unison. Nicole's smirk turned into a smile. She would never admit how much she craved the tart taste of her childhood, but he knew he had offered exactly what she missed most.

He kissed them all good-bye, which surprised everyone, including himself. Then he went out. As he drove, everything felt smaller and darker than the way he remembered it, and the air held more weight, as when a storm headed in. There was bagged garbage at the end of each driveway, and he thought of the night he had told his mother to go to hell when she asked him to take out the trash. Instead of getting angry, his mother had cried, the rims of her eyelids reddening behind her glasses, and Gerald spent forty minutes with her at the kitchen table, apologizing until he believed she forgave him and everything was all right. When he finally stood up to kiss her hair and take out the big green bags bursting with Lucky Charms boxes and SpaghettiO's cans, she held onto his hand for a few seconds, not letting him get away.

"I know you think you love Nicole," his mother had told him, "but she isn't good for you. Listen to me, Gerry. I promise you: I know." His father was in the next room, and she whispered the last sentence. Gerald nodded so she would give him his hand back, but he hadn't really listened. Only now, as it crossed his ears like the voice on a tape he had just replayed, did he hear what his mother had said.

He passed the junior high, where he saw boys slightly older than his son building an igloo on the playing field. It made him smile until he saw, jutting from the snowbank they scooped from, a six-pack of blue-canned Pabst. In front of the house he still thought of as Mrs. Ketchup's, he sat for a moment and watched the window until something — a hand? a face? — moved by the curtain, and then he got out and, feeling feverish, went to the door. He raised the knocker and tapped it gently beside Allie Sprinkle's name.

When she answered, he had to squint into the light she brought with her as she opened up to the outside, and he felt the panic that comes from being seen clearly and not being able to see back.

"You made it," she said, reaching her arm out, and he stepped forward to hug the warm shadow before he realized she had only meant to shake hands across the distance between them. But it was too late to check his momentum, so he followed through, drawing her shoulders toward his coat and giving a kiss to the hair by her ear.

"But where are your kids?" she asked, leaning to look beyond him at the empty stoop.

"They couldn't come." Gerald stamped his feet on the mat and watched his lie take physical shape in the form of white breath. "They both got sick at the last minute. I figured I'd keep the appointment, anyway." He had not yet lifted his eyes entirely to meet hers. "I'll pay for it, don't worry. Like when you pay at the doctor's for not canceling in time."

Allie's smile was stronger now — he could feel it touching him — and he allowed himself, at last, to look at her. He was shocked to see that her skin was darker than he remembered, and appeared slightly tough, the way it would if life were a sun she had been exposed to in amounts that weren't good for her.

Yet (and he realized that this was what should have surprised him, but it did not) she was beautiful. For the first time, Gerald understood what it meant for someone's features to *grow into themselves*; her eyes were the right size, finally, for all the sorrow she stored in them, and her mouth was worn to a fine crease by laughter and — who knew? — perhaps love.

"Well," she said with a shy shrug, reading all of this in his face. "Come in."

She took his coat and hung it on the banister knob. "I hope you don't expect me to take *your* picture," Allie said, as she led him down the hallway to the kitchen, where water was whistling. "Because I should warn you, something bizarre happens when I put grown-ups in front of my camera. They all come out looking like Gerald Ford."

"Even the women?"

"*Especially* the women." She laughed, inviting him to join her in it. It was the sound he associated with winter nights at the pond, but before he could even realize this completely, Allie set a cup of tea down in front of him and said, "You know, maybe it's because I knew I'd be seeing you, I went over to the old neighborhood the other day. I haven't been there in years, you know? Not since my mother died. Not since the house was sold. I think a Puerto Rican family moved in — have you met them?"

"No," Gerald said. He remembered Allie's mother, a thin woman who, in her thirties, had lost all her hair. After that she wore a kerchief, and behind her back, the kids called her Hanky Head. "We haven't been outside all that much."

Allie seemed to consider this, as if it were important information, before she continued. "Anyway, it was supper time when I drove over, just getting dark, and the little kids were still out on the rink in their double runners. But the weird thing was, their *mothers* were out with them. Holding the kids up and catching them when they fell. Remember how the parents never came near us when we were out there? Nobody taught us to skate; we just did it until we learned. So what, if you fell? The older girls would pick you up. They were our babysitters. The pond was like sacred territory, just for us kids."

Listening, Gerald dribbled some tea down his chin, and instead of handing him a napkin Allie reached over with her own and dabbed at the wetness. This contact, even through paper, made him pull away without meaning to, and she said, "Sorry.

"The parents knew to stay away," she went on, getting up to throw the napkin in the trash. "At least, until that night."

He knew right away, of course, which night she meant. She was talking about the accident: about those moments when he sent the puck with a clean crack into the shadows, lost it, then heard and saw the hard black circle knocking Nicole Rueger on the side of her pretty head. In the months that followed, he had watched the scene often behind closed eyes. He began with receiving the pass flat at the edge of his stick from Mike Usiak, feeling the puck sit there on the wood for a few seconds before he hauled off and slapped it like punishment, no holding back. Then came the images of Nicole lying on the ice, her long hair splayed out beneath her, one leg bent behind her at the knee; Nicole coming home from the hospital, using her parents as crutches, a white bandage where she used to have bangs.

But what was most vivid to Gerald about that night was not anything about his victim, or what happened after she fell, but what it felt like to hit the puck the way he had, as hard as he could, one solid stroke and a single motion, letting everything go. Afterward he asked himself, when he could stand to, if he had known it was possible he might hit one of the girls. The puck had not gone anywhere near the goal he would have scored in. Was there a wish involved? Had he — God help him — even aimed? He didn't think so, but he couldn't be sure, and the not being sure was what kept him awake so many nights when he should have been sleeping.

Of course, he would never tell Nicole that. When, because his mother made him, he went to visit her at her bedside the day after she came home, he kept his head lowered, and he even, briefly, touched her hand, a gesture unusual for any twelve-year-old boy, but remarkable in him. By the time she was well enough to go back to school, he began picking her up in the mornings so they could walk together, apart from the other Everett Street kids. Before then he had always walked with Mike and Dickie, and they had plenty to say, none of it kind or clever, about his new habit of walking with a girl.

When they kissed for the first time, one January afternoon on the way home — they'd stayed late, he for detention and she for cheerleading, and it was already dark as they came to the pond — it felt to both of them like what was supposed to happen next. It was a quick kiss, little more than lips overlapping, but they both knew what it meant. They were officially a couple; he had consented to his fate. Nicole snipped her face and Gerald's from the old class photograph of Miss Huberty's second grade, and she taped the pictures to each side of the locket her parents had given her for her hospital homecoming.

"I know," he said to Allie now, referring to that night. He could feel, in his chest and throat, the desire to tell her about the joke Nicole had made out of the accident over the years, knocking over the salt shaker with her fingertips. But before his voice found the first word, he discovered that he did *not* want to tell her. Instead, he turned the impulse into a cough.

Allie nodded, and though he understood that she was trying to communicate something, he could not yet guess what it was. There was a plate of cookies on the table between them, but instead of taking one she only pressed a finger into the crumbs. "I always wondered what would have happened, if I had been the one," she said, and Gerald believed he heard a tremble in her voice. "Instead of Nicole, who got hit. You know?"

He did know, perhaps more than she did; but he also knew that to admit it would be a mistake. He closed his eyes at the thought of the puck having taken a different route, fallen to gravity sooner, found Allie Sprinkle as its mark. The vision stirred a sweet wailing in his gut as he heard the apocalyptic approach of a town truck coming through to spread salt on the street. Before he could open his eyes again, the backs of Allie's warm fingers were laid against his forehead, the way a mother checks for fever in a child. He had never been touched by her before, and he knew he should be startled, but it felt — what was the word he wanted? — more *ancient*, or *familiar*, than Nicole's touch ever had.

Allie blushed when he looked at her and let her hand drop, and recklessly Gerald reached out to cover it with his own. But she retreated, pulling away a loose fist from the question in his clasp. "I haven't seen you since the night of graduation," she said. "Remember how hot it was, under those rented robes? When we all walked into the gym by homerooms, it was the best feeling of my life. It was like those nights at the pond, before the accident. I could sit there and close my eyes, and feel love floating around in the air like snow."

Gerald watched as he listened, resisting the temptation to touch her lips with his fingers. Allie seemed to be saying something he had always known, but which he had never heard before, in his own voice or any other. "Remember when Emil Marsh brought in those cocoa cookies his mother made for the bake sale in third grade, and everybody made fun of them because they looked like turds? Emil was trying to laugh, but I could see him swallowing. It made me so sad, I felt like screaming. Same with Lynn Harder, the time she wore that skirt with the dog her grandmother sewed on it. Girls used to wear poodles like that. Her grandmother probably thought Lynn would love it, and she probably did. But we were too old to think a dog on a dress was the best thing. By then, we all knew it was queer.

"The only time nobody ever made fun of anyone was during the hockey games. Then we were all just out there together, laughing in the cold." Allie was staring into her teacup. Steam slithered from the surface, and Gerald imagined it was this warmth flushing her face.

"What have you been doing?" he asked finally, wincing inside at what an idiot he'd become.

"You mean this morning? Or for the past twenty years?" Allie smiled, and Gerald saw that instead of the fearful sarcasm with which these words might have been uttered by someone else, her question contained only a generous grace.

"Well," he said, "I guess either."

She shrugged; the gesture was not to show her indifference, he saw, but to buy time while she decided how to answer him. "I went to Buf State for three years, and then right before I was going to be a senior, my father had his first heart attack. My mother needed me. I mean, she didn't *ask* me to stay home, but I could tell that's what she wanted." Allie looked down, and Gerald pictured Mrs.

Sprinkle's Hanky Head bowing with gratitude for this daughter she could count on.

"So he died the next year, and I was working at Costa's, and combined with my mother's sewing and my dad's benefits, we could keep living in the Everett Street house. I took a night class in photography, and my teacher thought I was good, so he taught me a lot of extra things and helped me set myself up. In business, I mean." Allie paused to blow across the surface of her tea, though it could not still have needed cooling off. From the way she said "my teacher," Gerald wondered if the "extra things" he taught her concerned photography, or love. When the silence continued, he knew.

"Anyway," Allie said, shaking herself out of the reverie, "that was a long time ago now. Almost fifteen years. I lived with my mom until she died, and then I bought this house. It just seemed right, somehow. Mrs. Ketchup's. Sometimes, in the summer, I swear I can hear her rocking in that chair on the back porch."

"Is she yelling at us?" Gerald found himself smiling, remembering Mrs. Ketchup's warbly yet terrifying voice.

"No," Allie said, also smiling. "Her ghost is friendly. It doesn't talk."

Then neither of them knew where to go in the conversation. Gerald thought he should probably offer to leave, but he didn't want to. His tea was gone, but Allie had most of hers left. "What about children?" he said, not exactly sure what he meant by it. Allie looked puzzled, too.

"What about them? You mean, my photographs?" she said, and he nodded, though it was not what he'd had in mind. "Well, it came about kind of accidentally. My brother's wife — you remember Timmy? they're living in Syracuse — had twins, so I took a bunch of pictures of them as a final project in my photography class. My teacher entered one of them in a contest, it won, I got my name in the paper, and people started calling to see if I'd take pictures of their kids." She shrugged again, this time in an *I-don't-know-how-it-happened-but-I-sure-am-glad* kind of way. "Now they come from all over the state, sometimes farther. Last year I even had a family from Georgia come up. They were also visiting Cooperstown, but they said their main reason for making the trip was because of me." Her tone chimed with modest pride, and Gerald had to close his eyes to get his bearings. He was thinking of so many things at once that if someone had asked him what town he was sitting in, he would have needed several seconds to figure it out.

"Well," Allie said. "As long as you're here, would you like to see the upstairs?" She was already rising, and Gerald stood hastily, banging his knee on the table. It had not sounded like an invitation to her bedroom, and he felt relief and disappointment warring in his chest. Yet what could she want to show him? On the steps, he made sure not to follow too closely, in case she stopped without warning and he could not help himself from reaching up for an embrace.

She opened a door at the top of the hallway and led him inside. Again, there was too much light coming in through a wide window, and he beat his eyes fast a few times to adjust to the snowblink and sun. On the far side of the room was a rolled backdrop, with stools of various heights anchoring the canvas where the roll met the floor. In the center of the room, a collection of cameras and other equipment — umbrellas and meters, reflectors and lights — surrounded a tripod that looked almost like a human figure, tall and skinny, beckoning to them as Gerald and Allie stepped through the door.

Allie went to the window and covered it with a cloth screen. It was then, as the room became dim enough to examine, that Gerald saw the children looking out at him from the walls. They were black-and-white photographs of faces, all with eyes focused straight at the camera. Some were smiling; others only stared. Even the faces of the unbeautiful children riveted him with a force far more powerful than beauty. All of them knew who they were, but they did not yet know who they *would* be, and it was this freedom that Allie had embalmed on her film.

Gerald went toward the faces and touched some of the frames. Allie was watching him, and when he drew his breath and held it, she moved closer. But when he reached a hand out, she pulled away.

"I didn't mean it like that," he said. He could feel his voice, emerging, scrape his throat. "I just — " He couldn't finish.

"I know." She patted him on the back, the gesture used to console or to say *try again*. "You'd better go home, Gerald." Outside, the salt truck screeched, sounding like the duck-and-cover drills they'd learned as children.

"Bob Lattimer's father still driving that thing?" Gerald moved to the window to lift the screen and look out, though his vision was blurred.

"No," Allie said from behind him. "Bob is."

Gerald turned to her again, showing a smile he knew must look as foolish as it felt. "Couldn't you take my picture?" he said, already knowing the answer but trying to believe she might change her mind.

She smiled back, her lips rising to the corners of well-worn grooves. "No."

"Please? I'll pay you double. I mean it. I want you to." He knew that both of them could hear the urgency in his voice, and though it embarrassed him, he was helpless to hide. "Allie — " He reached again for her, grabbing air. The lust in him was not for her body, or even for her. It was the desire to have that night and his life back, and it was the fiercest thing he had ever felt.

"Gerald, *no*." Allie went over to the wall to straighten one of the frames he had slanted without realizing, then motioned for Gerald to precede her out of the studio. Behind her, she shut the door.

"Could I just stay a little longer, then? To talk?" he asked, when they reached the bottom of the stairs. But he saw that Allie was pretending she hadn't heard him as she handed him his coat.

They went outside. The morning had turned warm, windy, and he felt too hot in his heavy sleeves. The sky and the snow seemed the same shade of gray; in her front yard, Gerald bent over to pick up a handful of slush, and he tried to shape it into a ball, but it fell apart in his fingers. Still, he tried to toss it so that the melting fragments would shower around Allie in a festive rain. When this didn't work, he gave the stupid smile again, then winked streaks of wetness from the edges of his eyes.

He took out his billfold, but before he could open it, Allie pressed his fingers closed around the leather. "Don't, Gerald," she told him. "I won't take it."

He started to answer, but then he knew not to, and he got in his car and began backing out of the driveway. In the cold, watching him, Allie tried hugging herself, but as he pulled away, he could see that it wasn't enough.

He had not been about to give her money. He had only wanted to show her pictures of his kids.

He drove the streets without being aware of steering, back through Four Corners, past the Hello Dolly and the Feible Meat Company, past the funeral home. Though it had turned brighter outside, the air still felt heavy, as if something not in the forecast was headed his way.

In junior high, which began the year after Gerald had struck Nicole with the puck, the girls all had to wear gym suits, which they bought from the Little Folks Shop. Mr. Neander, Sue Neander's father and the man who would, a few years later, back out of his driveway on a foggy October morning in his Impala and hit and kill Craig Domermuth, Dickie's little brother, who was riding his bike to school, ordered the suits specially at the beginning of every year.

The boys got to wear whatever they wanted in the way of gym shirts and shorts, and the classes were boys and girls together, so half of the court or field was always in uniform and the other half wasn't.

What was it that happened to Mr. Neander after Craig Domermuth died? Of course Gerald remembered hearing everything about it, how Sue's father, when he realized what he had done, tried to drive the car off the boy's body; later, they said this was probably what killed him. After school that day, all the kids went by Sue's house to find out if there was anything left to see. Mrs. Neander was out at the end of the driveway, running a hose on the street. She must have been standing there for a long time already, because the pavement was soaked and the water reached as far down as two houses on either side. When she saw them all watching her, she lifted the hose a little, without seeming to mean to, and the spray came toward them, making them all stumble backward to avoid getting wet.

Their retreat made Mrs. Neander cry. "Please," she said to them across the stream that sounded like summer, "please." But none of them knew what she meant. Mr. Neander never went to jail or even had charges pressed against him, because it had been so foggy that morning, and there were reports that Craig had been riding his bicycle very fast. Sue came back to school the following week, and everybody held their breath the first time she and Dickie Domermuth passed in the hall. But they were all disappointed. There were no screams or slaps between them, no apologies and no truce. Maybe these had been exchanged when no one was looking. More likely, though, it was easier just not to admit what had happened. It was over and done with, was what the sermon at the funeral seemed to say.

But this was all still ahead of them, still to come after they learned to drink beer in the stockyard, after the first girl in their class got pregnant and had the baby, after nobody could force them to wear gym suits anymore. The girls' outfits were striped blue and white, one-piece cotton suits that zipped up the back and showed every burgeoning bump of soft bodies coming to the fore.

One hot afternoon in April, they were playing softball. Gerald stood in right field, and Allie Sprinkle was in center. When the bell rang and they began to go in, Allie walked ahead of him, and Gerald squinted at the slow shape in front of him, to make sure of what he saw. A brown red stain spread from between her legs and up the seat of her gym suit, which clung and gathered in the clenched place between her thighs. He did not perceive what it was, at first, and when he did — in that sudden way things make sense so that we can never, after that moment, remember what it was like *not* to understand them — he wanted to catch up to her and hand her his windbreaker and tell her not to ask any questions, just tie this around your waist.

But he didn't. It was impossible to translate what he knew he should do into an action, the same way it had been impossible to hold back on that sitting puck. Instead, when he saw Nicole coming in from left field, he called her over. "Do something," he said, pointing forward at Allie with his eyes. Nicole looked, and he saw a cruel smile take hold of her lips.

"*Do* something," he said again, as Allie kept walking, oblivious, wearing her womanhood for everyone to see. She was getting close to the rest of the class, the girls in their gym suits with their secrets and smiles, and the boys throwing the softball back and forth between mitts, except for the one boy who always carried the bats and bases to and from the equipment room, balancing the wood on one shoulder with the rubber mats in his other hand. Gerald always wondered why this boy was responsible for it all, why they didn't each take a piece of the game back with them to make it fair; but nobody ever offered to help, and Mr. Carmody didn't make them, so it was always the same boy who carried everything, and he never complained.

Allie Sprinkle kept walking, passing some of the pack. Gerald watched as first the boy with the bats noticed the menstrual stain and looked immediately down at the ground, as if he wanted to give back what he'd seen. Then some of the girls caught on, and the gasps and laughter made the whole class look, and Nicole ran ahead of Gerald to find her friends, and he saw Allie come to understand what must be happening and to feel the wet shame widening between her legs.

Somebody said, "She must've fell on the floor at Feible's," causing a fresh wave of hilarity to float across the field.

"Come here, Alice," Mr. Carmody said, but she wouldn't. "I said come HERE," he said, and instead she continued walking sideways across the field and through the bushes by Mrs. Ketchup's house. After lunch she came back to school wearing the gym suit blouse tucked into a long, old-lady skirt that had been cinched at the waist with a velvet sash. The mocking started all over again when she appeared in this costume, tardy to Earth Science, and as she moved to take her seat, Allie kept her gaze fixed on Gerald's face. He tried not to look back, but he couldn't help it. Now, he remembered what he had known in the moment their eyes met, and in the next — because he was not yet ready to know it — forgotten: although she looked like nobody any of his friends would ever admit wanting to be, Allie's face held a peace they had all lost without realizing, which they would spend the rest of their lives seeking and failing to retrieve.

As he stepped into the house, scraping his shoes on the stoop to get the slush from Allie's yard out of his shoes, Gerald could tell that everyone was home. The children were playing a new video game. Nicole's parents had returned from the pharmacy and the salon. He could hear them all in the living room, talking at the same time. Nicole was still on the sofa, a thumb holding her place in the book while she watched what the children were doing.

She raised her eyes as Gerald came to the doorway, and from the angle of her brow, he saw that he had let her down again in the way only he could, without even knowing. It was the look she used to get along with the headaches, halfway between an accusation and an appeal. He shrugged his coat off and threw it across a chair, and only then did he realize that his hands were empty, and he knew even before she did what his wife was going to say.

"Well?" she asked, and everyone else in the room paused to listen for his answer. "I thought you were going to bring me back some wings."

Oregon

TWENTY YEARS EARLIER, Elizabeth had made a long-distance phone call to her friend Deborah in Maryland. Elizabeth lived in Vermont, and as she dialed Deborah's number, which she felt embarrassed to know by heart (because surely Deborah would have to open her own address book, to locate Elizabeth), she looked out her kitchen window at the broken snowplow. It belonged to her next-door neighbor, who fixed cars for a living on his front lawn.

The neighbor's name was Wily Cobb and the plow had been broken since the winter before. All summer it sat on the strip of dead grass between the two yards, and children from the neighborhood played on it, climbed it like a jungle gym and used it as the safety in TV tag. (When you got touched by whoever was *It*, you had to shout out the name of a television program to unfreeze yourself.)

When Deborah answered the phone down in Maryland she sounded sleepy, and Elizabeth apologized, but she didn't offer to call back later because she wanted to talk now. She had something to tell Deborah. "I dreamt you had a three-month-old baby," she said, imagining how Deborah must look on the other end of the phone, her dark hair unbrushed but beautiful on the shoulders of her nightgown. The nightgown would have no holes or stains on it, as all of Elizabeth's did. "A three-month-old girl baby. Her name was Abigail."

Deborah was silent, and Elizabeth wondered if she had gone away from the phone. "Are you there?" she asked, wanting to add, *I am paying for this call, please say something.*

"You're unbe*liev*able," Deborah said. Was that a toaster Elizabeth heard popping up in the background? Maybe Deborah had started eating breakfast, which Elizabeth had never known her to do. Or maybe someone else, who did eat breakfast, was also in the room. "I can't fucking believe this," Deborah said.

"What?" Swearing always made Elizabeth nervous, no matter who did it or in what tone. She traced her trepidation not to anything in her childhood experience, like a reproving parent, but to a restraint and modesty she believed she had been born with. This quality made her blush, but she had long ago learned to allow it the air it demanded in her soul; otherwise, it threatened to poison other parts of herself she wished to hold onto, like her humor and glad grace.

"Glad grace" was a phrase from a poem by Yeats. In college, when Elizabeth had been afraid she might be in love with Deborah, she copied out the poem and made a watercolor to go with it, for Deborah's birthday. In the line that went, "But one man loved the pilgrim soul in you," she simply left out the word *man*. Deborah came into Elizabeth's room where Elizabeth waited, pretending to be writing a paper. Deborah held the unwrapped gift in the doorway, and across the room she said, "It's beautiful, Liz. Thank you."

Elizabeth was not sure what to make of Deborah's words — were they a signal of some kind, a response? — and so she didn't answer. Instead, she looked down at her notebook. Behind the oily curtain of her bangs, she felt her forehead growing warm.

"But I want to make sure of something," Deborah said, coming into the room to sit, her small weight at the end of the bed making loose papers slide toward her on the comforter. "I love you, too, but as a friend. If that's what you meant by this, then I'm sorry for wondering anything else.

"But if you meant something different, like love in the sense of—*you* know—well, I wanted to tell you, I'm interested in boys. Men." She gave Elizabeth a smile so forgiving, and so aware that there was really nothing to forgive, that Elizabeth felt her heart stretch a little as she realized that this kind of love was surely more important than the other.

After graduation, Elizabeth moved to Vermont with Sam, who had been a fraternity brother of Deborah's most steady beau. When autumn came and they began to heat their rented house with a wood stove, Elizabeth came to see that her friendship with Deborah was very much like a fire. She, Elizabeth, was its tender, the one who made sure there were always live coals in the bed. She made the first phone calls and sent the first letters, kept enough oxygen circulating so the flame wouldn't go out.

Deborah was the kindling. She was the spitting spark, the burst of warmth and light that comes from touching a funnel of newspaper with a match. She was the bright heat that attracts everyone who enters a dim or chilly room. They come to warm their hands by it, and might be caught daydreaming in the force of the crackling glow; but if someone like Elizabeth isn't paying attention, the flame will begin to sink.

When Elizabeth made the phone call to Deborah that March morning, the fire between them was still burning, but burning low. Nobody had stoked it since the December holidays, when they sent each other presents (Elizabeth always said she wasn't anything; Deborah was, as she put it, "technically a Jew").

That day, Elizabeth waited until Sam left for work before she picked up the phone. It still struck her as unfair, and made her feel a little guilty, that her boyfriend was still with her, while Deborah was alone now. But maybe the sound of the toaster, in the background of the connection to Maryland, meant that something had changed down there.

"Is somebody in the room with you?" Elizabeth asked.

Instead of answering, Deborah said, "I just can't fucking be*lieve* you had that dream." She paused. Elizabeth was getting used to hearing *fuck* again from her friend. "I *am* pregnant," Deborah said.

"You are?" It seemed to Elizabeth that *pregnant* took longer than the other words to travel through the wire. "Are you kidding?"

"Of course not." Deborah sounded insulted. "I would kid about that? Yeah — three months. I wasn't even going to tell you, but you surprised me by having this dream. Especially the three-month part."

"Three-month-old *baby*, I said." Elizabeth turned away from the window, because suddenly there was too much distraction outside — Wily Cobb refilling his birdfeeder, the sun bouncing off the snow's crust. "You're talking about a three-month-old *fetus*." Then she realized what Deborah had said. "What do you mean, you weren't going to tell me?"

"Well, I had an appointment. For tomorrow. There's this doctor a friend of mine knows." Deborah's voice was deliberately casual as she waited for Elizabeth to catch on.

"What do you mean?" But Elizabeth already understood, and she also knew why Deborah would hesitate or even decline to tell her. "Don't," Elizabeth said, before Deborah could try to reply.

"I knew you would feel that way." Deborah sounded resentful and triumphant at the same time. "How can you be so against it when you're not even Catholic?"

"I'm not against it for everyone." This wasn't true, but over time Elizabeth had found the words to make her friendships easier, when the subject came up. It had nothing to do with politics or religion; the simple truth was that she had more faith in infants than she did in adults. Why was that so impossible for people to understand? She tried not to sound panicked. "Is it Tony's?"

There was a silence before Deborah answered, "No."

"Oh," Elizabeth said. "Well, is it someone — you could be with?"

Deborah said "No" again. "I have no choice," she went on, and Elizabeth could hear her friend chewing, the sound of dry toast crunching across the line.

"Yes, you do." Elizabeth closed her eyes, and immediately she could see the baby from her dream of the night before. She had been holding the baby against her own shoulder, rocking in a chair in the middle of a field. She could feel the soft brush of the baby's hair against her lips as she turned to kiss its forehead. In her dream, Deborah's daughter smelled like soap and champagne.

"I think I'm going to puke," Deborah said. Already, the toast was making gagging sounds in her throat.

"Call me back," Elizabeth told her. "Call collect, if you want to."

Deborah did not have the abortion. Instead she had the baby, a girl, and she named her Abigail, after the child in Elizabeth's dream. "She wouldn't be here, if it weren't for that dream," Deborah told Elizabeth, when she called from the hospital to say that her daughter had been born. "I swear to God, Elizabeth, if you hadn't called that day, I'd be getting ready to go on a date right now." The baby had arrived on a Saturday morning in September, and by the time Deborah telephoned Elizabeth in Vermont, it was six o'clock. Elizabeth and Sam were sitting on the porch steps, splitting a beer and watching the neighbor kids jump from the snowplow into a big leaf pile, when the telephone rang.

"I don't know who the date would have been with, but I know I'd be getting ready," Deborah continued, and Elizabeth could hear her friend shifting against the hospital pillows. "Instead I'm just lying here with this little *thing*." From the tone of Deborah's voice, Elizabeth could tell she was saying thank you. Elizabeth sent Abby a blanket she'd knitted herself, and at Thanksgiving, she went down to Maryland to meet her goddaughter while Sam spent the weekend with his parents in Maine.

"What does a godmother do?" Elizabeth asked, sitting around with Deborah and the baby after a dinner of soup and crackers and boxed pumpkin pie. They had on a football game in the background because both of them were accustomed to these TV sounds on Thanksgiving Day, but they were still sitting at the table, looking at each other and at the baby while they talked.

"I should know?" Deborah tried to put a bottle in Abigail's mouth, but it was not what the baby wanted. "You already saved her. How could you ever top that?" Her daughter squirmed against Deborah's chest.

Elizabeth took the baby from her. Abby laid her head on Elizabeth's shoulder and settled in.

"See, she knows," Deborah said, adjusting her sweater. "She knows I was going to kill her. She knows who she owes her life to."

"You weren't going to *kill* her." Elizabeth lifted a hand to cover Abigail's ears, as if the baby could make sense of anything. "She wasn't a person yet. You just weren't sure." She leaned down and sniffed. "I think somebody needs a change," she said, making a song of the words.

A silence thicker than usual settled around them, and Elizabeth recognized, with a small shock, that Deborah wanted to say something, but wasn't sure how. She had never known Deborah to hesitate. "Listen, could we make a pact?" Deborah said then, trying to sound casual as she cut fork paths through her pie. "That we won't ever talk about it again? I feel shitty enough, looking at her and thinking what might have happened. You're the only one who knows, Liz. If you could promise never to bring it up, I'd — well, I'd be forever grateful." It was a phrase out of the kind of book neither of them would ever read, and they both realized this and smiled. Elizabeth held two fingers, index and middle, aloft in the air, which now smelled of full diaper.

"To my grave," she said.

It was the last time they ever talked about the circumstances of Abigail's birth in front of her, because the next time they all saw each other, at Deborah's wedding, the baby was five years old. Elizabeth and Sam had separated, and Elizabeth had moved to California to be away from him and from New England, where she had begun to feel depressed even in summers. *Depressed* wasn't exactly the right word; she was petrified. Not in the sense that she felt terror, but the opposite: hers was a numb body, a stone globe without grooves. For a while she tried to chip into it, reach some nerve, but this cost too much, and when a company near San Diego offered to pay her well to work long hours, she signed on. When she left Sam and Vermont and the house with the wood stove, the snowplow still sat broken on Wily Cobb's front lawn. Kids had stopped playing on it, and the grass rose around the plow's decayed wheels, grew into the chassis and twined itself through the gears.

Though she had no idea what moved her to do it, Elizabeth took a photograph of the old plow before she left. When she got to California, she put the picture on a bulletin board in her kitchen, with other souvenirs that reminded her of where she had been, and of what she had valued in her life: a picture of herself and Deborah on skis, taken a moment before they fell into each other and went down laughing; ticket stubs from a summer Shakespeare festival in Canada, where Sam had played Horatio; a picture of herself and Abigail on that Thanksgiving visit, Elizabeth's lips brushing the baby's fine hair as they had in the dream that resulted in Abby's being born.

The man Deborah married adopted Abby and gave her his last name. He had a job in Washington and enough money and a good enough heart to buy Abby whatever she wanted, and then some. Still, Elizabeth sent her goddaughter presents on every birthday and at Hanukkah, to keep them connected; to remind Abby that she, Elizabeth, existed in the world. Abby always sent back a thank-you note with a scribble from her mother at the bottom, and as the years passed, the gift and the note became the only exchanges between the two of them, Elizabeth and Deborah, who would still say they were best friends, though they had fallen out of touch.

Twenty years after Elizabeth's dream, Abby called her from college. She was in her second year at Boston University, and she had met her godmother only three times in her life; she remembered only two of those times, and only one with any clarity.

It was the third, most recent visit that made Abby think of Elizabeth when she needed help. They had seen each other two years before, when Abby graduated from high school. Elizabeth asked if she could come to the ceremony, and though Abby was impressed that Elizabeth was willing to make such a long trip for her — and intrigued by the prospect of getting to know, in person, the friend who sent her the presents and who had dreamed her name — she also felt apprehensive. Would she be expected to hug, to kiss Elizabeth, to make a fuss over this woman she knew mostly through the mail?

But as it turned out, she *wanted* to do these things. They greeted each other as naturally as if they were related by blood and glad of it. Deborah hung back at the airport when they picked Elizabeth up, waiting until her old friend and her daughter embraced before going forward herself. After the commencement, for the rest of the weekend, it was Elizabeth and Abby who seemed the intimates, who spoke as if they had a history together — details to catch up on and secrets to trade. Deborah served them coffee and then left to do laundry or to talk to her husband, who was preoccupied with work he'd brought home from the office.

Only once, on Sunday morning, did Abby walk in on what she'd expected to find all weekend — her mother and Elizabeth sitting close to each other at the kitchen table, talking not in whispers but not loud enough to be overheard either, shutting up when Abby entered the room.

"What were you saying?" Abby pulled a chair out and sat down with the women. If she had not just graduated, she would not have asked, or even joined them at the table; but as it was, she felt older now, and entitled to know what went on in the wider world.

"Oh, nothing," Deborah told her. "Girl talk. I don't have to tell you about *that*."

Elizabeth seemed to realize that this would only frustrate Abby further. "Your mom was just saying how proud she is of you, and I agreed."

Of course, Abby knew there was more, but she also knew that she was not likely to get it out of them. The only thing to do was accept the compliment and be grateful to Elizabeth for giving it. When they brought her to the airport for her flight back to California, Elizabeth reached into her pocket before she got into the ticketed passengers line, and she handed Abby something small and flat, taped over in Kleenex and labeled with an *A*. Inside was a key.

"That goes to my apartment," Elizabeth told her, kissing the hair around Abby's forehead. "You're welcome any time. Hold on to it." Though Abby had no idea how to find anything in California, and though she would have to look up Elizabeth's address in her mother's book to find out what door the key fit, she recognized what Elizabeth was offering — herself, her home — and it surprised Abby into wanting to cry as she said good-bye. She stood with her mother as they watched Elizabeth put her bags on the belt and walk through the metal detector, then down to the gate where she would wait alone to depart.

It was on a Wednesday in November of her sophomore year that Abby called Information in San Diego to get the number she needed. She started dialing, then hung up and went over to the bureau, where in front of the mirror she brushed her hair. Then she picked up the phone again and completed the long-distance call. She was sitting on her bed in her dorm room, and though it was late afternoon, she had not yet turned on the lamp. Through her window she could see the headlights of cars carrying people home from the city, and beyond them, a few flakes of snow falling into the Charles. Elizabeth didn't answer, and only when she heard the machine pick up did Abby remember that in California, it was two o'clock in the afternoon. She spoke her message, regretted it for a few seconds, then went out to find her roommate at the pub where they didn't check IDs closely and beers were two for the price of one.

When Elizabeth came home that night and played her messages, she repeated Abby's twice before she picked up the phone and dialed the number Abby had left. As it rang, Elizabeth looked at her watch, then winced, seeing that it showed ten-thirty. She was about to hang up when Abby answered, sounding sleepy and, Elizabeth thought with a flash of alarm, drunk.

"I'm sorry to call back so late," Elizabeth said. "I forgot about the time."

"'Sokay." Across the country, Abby struggled to sit up in her bed. "I didn't mean to bother you," she said, knowing even in her equivocal consciousness that this would bring her the response she was hoping for.

"It's no bother at all," Elizabeth assured her. "I'm glad you called. Honey, of course you can come out here. Just tell me when to meet your plane. Do you need money for a ticket? Are you all right?"

"Don't be so nice to me," Abby said. Something on her end of the line made the mouthpiece move, and Elizabeth could tell that her goddaughter was crying. "I'm not a good person. I've really fucked up."

"It doesn't matter," Elizabeth told her. Standing in her California kitchen, looking at the sliding doors that opened onto the patio, she saw her long reflection in the dark glass and knew that this was what her life had been leading to. It was funny how you knew, when the moment came; you had no warning, but when it was there in front of you, calling you over, there was no way you could have any doubt.

"Please don't tell my mother," was the last thing Abigail said.

Waiting for Deborah's daughter in the airport, Elizabeth was sure she knew what kind of trouble Abby was in. She knew it the way she had known to dream that Deborah would have a baby, all those years ago. It did not seem uncanny to her, or anything to be afraid of; she believed that somehow, by a confluence of love and intuition and historical molecules, she was attuned to the fertility cycles of Deborah and, now, of her daughter.

And yet when Abby stepped through the gate behind all the other passengers on her flight (it was like seeing Deborah, and Elizabeth made a noise in her throat without realizing, as she raised a hand to catch Abby's eye), and pitched herself at her godmother's body, mumbling "I'm *pregnant*" into Elizabeth's shoulder, as if she half-hoped the sleeve might obscure what she'd said, Elizabeth felt stunned. She was so expecting these words that when she heard them, the sudden symmetry of the situation — time folding back upon itself to make a perfect fit at the edges, over the intricate layers of twenty years — made her breathless and blind for an instant, and she reached for a chair. Sitting, she could see and breathe again, and Abby hadn't seemed to notice her lapse.

"I'm sorry," Abby said. When she had separated her face from Elizabeth's shoulder, Elizabeth smelled liquor, and now, looking into Abby's eyes, she saw that they were bloodshot as well as afraid.

"You shouldn't be drinking," Elizabeth told her, raising her hand to move a piece of Abby's hair to one side.

Abby pulled back, more in reaction to Elizabeth's words than to her touch. "Why not? I can handle it." She spoke with her mother's defiant inflection.

"I mean because of the baby," Elizabeth said. Around them, a flight to Denver was beginning to board, and people kept brushing against them with carry-on bags.

"Well, I'm not *having* it," Abby said. Her expression then betrayed the fear that a terrible mistake had been made. Elizabeth saw that she'd inherited not only her mother's black curls, but the same habit of pulling the longest ones straight in her stress. "That's why I came out here. I thought you would help me." Her fingers fiddled with the strap of her knapsack, which contained all she had brought. In a lower voice, less sure of itself, she added, "I thought that's what a godmother was supposed to be *for*."

"Look, let's get out of here," Elizabeth said. She stood up and put her hand out to take Abby's bag, but Abby held onto it and slung it over her rumpled shoulder. Walking beside her, Elizabeth was reminded of the TV news pictures from her and Deborah's college days, soldiers hauling their belongings numbly onto the bus. *You have no idea*, she wanted to say to Abby, but instead she asked, "Are you hungry?" and when Abby nodded, Elizabeth took her for something to eat.

She had come to California on a Wednesday night, a week after she first contacted Elizabeth by phone. Her idea was that she would terminate — that's what she called it — on Friday, spend Saturday recovering, and take the last flight back to Boston on Sunday. This she told Elizabeth over breakfast on Thursday morning. There were two weeks left before the Thanksgiving break, during which she could catch up on any schoolwork she'd missed. Elizabeth had taken Thursday and Friday off from work, and they both slept late. It was after ten as they sat at the table. Sun lit up the red jar of jam.

While Abby presented her plan, Elizabeth listened to it all before she said anything. The coffee she poured for both of them was decaf, but she didn't let on. When Abby took a sip to show that she was finished saying her piece and was prepared for a response, Elizabeth looked down at her plate and said, "I'll take you for the abortion if your mother says it's okay."

"*What*," Abby said. She had been lifting a piece of toast to her mouth, and she started to smile, thinking it was a joke. But when she saw that Elizabeth meant it, bits of bread flew out of her lips as she hurried to protest. "But that's the whole point of my coming here — so she wouldn't know. Look, I don't need her permission. I'm old enough. I could have gone somewhere in Boston to do this, it happens all the time.

"But . . . I didn't want to tell any of my friends. I didn't want them to know who the — *father* — was, it's a long story. And I didn't think I could do it alone." She waited for Elizabeth to say she understood, and to give in. Elizabeth knew this would make things easier for Abby, and in some ways for both of them, but she couldn't do it, and she raised her mug to have an excuse not to speak.

"Oh, God, I can't be*lieve* this." Abby rapped her forehead against four fingertips.

"Can we just talk about this for a minute?"

"There's nothing to talk about." Abby got up and squeezed the back of the chair as she spoke. "Look — Jesus. I'm nineteen years old. I'm in college. I was stupid, I did a dumb thing and got caught, but does that mean I have to drag it around for the rest of my life?"

She coughed on something and when it didn't subside, Elizabeth handed Abby her own glass of juice. Abby gulped and handed it back, empty, and muttered, "Thank you."

"Abigail," Elizabeth said.

"What."

Elizabeth got up and went over to the bulletin board, where she kept Abby's baby picture. With every step toward it, she told herself that she had not committed to anything by these movements across the room. She could turn around and come back to the table. It could still be undone — until she reached for the photograph, and took it down. The corners had curled through the years, and the colors had faded, but it was still easy to discern the comfort this infant felt, leaning against the warm and steady heart of her godmother. Elizabeth brought the photograph to the table and propped it gently beside Abby's plate.

"So what," Abby said, but she sat back down.

"This is why I want you to think about it." Elizabeth sent a quick prayer (though she did not think of it in terms of that word) across the country to Deborah, asking to be forgiven. But she would have no way of knowing if it had been granted, before she went ahead and did what she needed forgiveness for.

"Your mother was thinking of — the same thing, when she was pregnant with you." To her surprise, because they tasted so sour and scary coming out of her mouth, the words in the sunny kitchen sounded empty and clean.

Abby looked straight ahead at Elizabeth, and then down again at the photo. "How do you know," she said. An eyelash dropped onto the image, and she lifted the picture to blow it aside.

"I wouldn't be telling you, if it weren't for what you're in now." Elizabeth felt her face growing hot; her own voice sounded distant to her, and for a moment she wondered if this could be Deborah's telepathic way of punishing her for betraying what was Deborah's alone to confess. "But I thought you would want to know, before you made a decision like this."

"How do you *know*, I said." Abby was looking at her again, and Elizabeth thought she could see a different, more dangerous quality of anger in her goddaughter's eyes.

"Because I talked her out of it. That dream I had, where your name came from? I didn't even know your mother was pregnant, when I had it. Something about the coincidence, or whatever you want to call it, must have made her think twice." Elizabeth pressed her lips together as if she might take the words back, but it was already too late.

After a moment Abby said, "So what? Did you ever have any dreams about a baby *I* might have?"

"No, of course not," Elizabeth said.

"Well, then." Abby stood up again, leaving the picture where it was. "I guess that means that *my* life is up to *me*." She tried to be sarcastic, but her voice tripped on a catch. She turned away, but not before Elizabeth saw that her calm was crumbling. "Fuck it. I want to go back to the airport. Where should I call for a cab?"

"I'll drive you," Elizabeth told her. "I don't want you to go like this, though. I don't think I made myself clear."

"Oh, I think you did." Her goddaughter smiled in a way that made Elizabeth shiver, though it was eighty degrees. Abby crossed the room to the potted ficus plant sitting in the sunlight. She poured her remaining coffee over the plant. "Listen," she said. "You don't know me. And I don't know what kind of sicko kick you just got out of telling me that dream, but if you knew my mother at all, you'd know a dream's the last thing that would ever change her mind about anything. She doesn't believe in superstition."

"It's not superstition," Elizabeth told her. Then, before she knew what was going to come out next, she added, "It's God."

"Oh, yeah, *right*."

"Abigail," Elizabeth said, "I don't know why you'd think I would ever want to hurt you by making something like this up. I love you. And I never said your mother didn't want you, especially after you were born. But think about how *you* feel, now, with your own baby — "

"It's not a baby!" Abby shouted. At the front door, the postman bent his head to peer through the frosted window glass as he put the mail in the box. When Elizabeth waved to let him know everything was all right, he waved back and walked away.

"I'm sorry you don't believe me," she told Abby. She felt her lips trembling. "But it's true. And the only reason I'm telling you is so you don't make a mistake."

"Fuck it, I said." Abby went into the guest bedroom, leaving Elizabeth to hear the harsh sounds of yanking and zipping. She came out again with her knapsack bumping against her knees. "Can we just go?"

They drove to the airport without speaking. Abby turned on the radio without consulting Elizabeth, and she flipped through the stations until she found something slow and soothing, a Schubert sonata that made them both want to close their eyes.

"I'm surprised you like this kind of music," Elizabeth said. "Your mother was strictly rock and roll."

"I don't," Abby answered. But she made no move to change the dial. Her tone was grudging as she continued, "I didn't know you went to church."

"I don't."

"I mean, that you're religious."

"I'm not."

"Then what was all that crap back there about God?" Abby turned her face to look out the window. She let the breeze whip her hair.

"I don't know. It just came out." This was true; Elizabeth remembered the shock of feeling her own mouth wrap itself around *God*. "I don't know what I meant by it. It's not like I think of an old man in the sky, pulling strings on us like puppets. Or some giant game board where every move is already plotted out."

"Then what?"

Elizabeth looked over sharply, expecting to see a smirk on her goddaughter's face. But there was none. She realized that Abby was asking because she really wanted to know what Elizabeth believed. "Well," she said. "You'll probably think this sounds stupid, but I guess I think of it as love, or something. Maybe I think of it as hope." Her hands on the steering wheel relaxed as she heard these words.

After a moment Abby asked, "How come you never got married?"

"I don't know. I never met the right person." Elizabeth's mouth watered, a symptom that surfaced only when she lied, but there was no way for Abby to know this.

"Well, then," Abby blurted, "Are you gay?"

"I'm not anything." It was the same answer she used to give when someone asked about her religion. Though she always waited, nobody ever urged her to say more.

They drove to the music for another few miles.

Abby murmured into her collar, "I suppose you think you saved me back then. By convincing my mother not to go through with it."

Elizabeth remained silent.

"Yeah, well. Thanks for nothing," Abby said.

And why could Elizabeth not let it go at that? We have all told secrets and felt sorry afterward, all known ungrateful children, all given up a friendship at the natural end of it, when there was no reason to hold on. And yet Elizabeth did not consider Abby's flight that day to be a departure from her life. She still sent birthday and Hanukkah gifts, even when they were not acknowledged anymore. She still kept the picture of herself and the baby Abigail on her kitchen bulletin board. When, at parties where people didn't know her, she was asked if she had any children, she said, "No, but I do have a goddaughter."

Two years after Abby had come to California for fewer than twenty-four hours, Elizabeth received a wedding invitation. The honor of her presence was requested at the marriage of Abigail Berman to David Gray. Though the wedding would be held in Cape Cod, the envelope was postmarked from Maryland and addressed in Deborah's angular, assertive hand. She'd tucked a floral stationery card in with all the other pieces of tissue and paper, and on it she had written, "Dear Liz — Where's all the time gone? I refuse to believe we've known each other more than twenty-five years. If we were married, it'd be our silver anniversary. I gather you and Abby haven't been in contact for a while, and I've been awful about writing, I know. It's scary, how life slips away. But if you can forgive me, I'd love to see you at the wedding — can you believe our baby's getting married? You're more than welcome to bring a guest. Is there someone in your life? If there isn't, I'll find somebody here to fix you up with. The guys Walt works with are always getting divorced. Just let me know. In case you're afraid you won't recognize me after all this time, I'll be the one with mascara stripes running down my face. (Some things never change, thank God.) All love, Deborah." Beneath her signature she'd added, in a more urgent script, "Please come. Isn't it about time?"

Elizabeth sent back the RSVP card after marking a check in the space next to *Will attend*. At work she put in for a week's vacation, a few days on either side of the wedding, which was scheduled for the last Sunday in June. She called up Sam, whom she had seen a few times when he flew to the West Coast on business, and arranged to visit him and his wife and their children for a few days, after which she would drive down to the Cape.

She was tempted to invite Sam to go with her to the wedding, because he had known Deborah and because his wife was the type who would have understood, but in the end she didn't. She was afraid that she would want to leave the reception suddenly — to flee — and she needed to be free, if this turned out to be the case. On the morning of the wedding, she kissed his whole family good-bye, and the children begged her for a promise to come back through Vermont again, on the return leg of her trip. Elizabeth told them to visit California sometime. "Maybe we'll do that," Sam's wife said. Backing out of their driveway in her rented car, trying to hold them in her gaze as long as possible, Elizabeth ran over a chipmunk in the road. At first, glancing behind her, she thought she had killed it; then, getting out to look more closely at the carnage, she realized with relief that it had already been dead.

The wedding was being held in Hyannis, where the groom's grandparents had a home. It took Elizabeth five hours to drive there from Vermont. Traffic was tied up on the Sagamore Bridge, and looking around her at the tired families, Elizabeth wondered if any of them were also headed to Abby and David's wedding. She saw a baby in the back seat of a Saab vigorously chewing the polyester braid off a Barbie doll's head. In the front seat, the baby's mother was biting the skin at the top of her thumb. Elizabeth drew even with the Saab's open windows and said, across the space between them, "Excuse me. Did you know she's eating the doll's hair?" She smiled as she spoke, to show the woman that she wasn't a random nut case — that she had the best interests of the child, who might choke, at heart.

The woman looked behind her, but let the child keep sucking the synthetic threads. "It's a *he*," she told Elizabeth, before electronically raising her window and turning her face to the front. Elizabeth understood the woman's rebuff. She, Elizabeth, had tried to pass herself off as a fellow parent, and the real mother had caught on. Elizabeth let the Saab cut in front of her, and in a way nobody else would see, she gave it the finger. Her dress was sticking to the driver's seat, and she wished she'd had the sense not to change into her wedding clothes until she reached the Cape and found a bathroom. It was too late now, though. She leaned forward over the steering wheel and hoped for a breeze.

At the synagogue the guests were already being seated, and Elizabeth started to join the line behind the ushers, but then she felt a hand clamp her shoulder and turned to encounter Deborah full in the face. The shock made Elizabeth take a step back as Deborah laughed. "You made it!" Deborah said. Her features were bigger than Elizabeth remembered them, or maybe it was just that she had never seen them so close. She was wearing a blue dress and silver jewelry, and her body looked as petite as it had in college, except that its smallness now spoke more of deprivation and dieting than a metabolism fueled by exuberant youth.

"Honey, look who's here," Deborah went on, grabbing her husband by the arm and showing him Elizabeth, who lifted her hand in a half wave and said her name to help him out as he groped through his memory to place her. "Well of course he knows who you *are*," Deborah said, letting her husband go and linking her arm through Elizabeth's. This contact of their flesh made Elizabeth think she might collapse, but she held her breath and the impulse passed.

"Abby will be so thrilled to see you," Deborah said. "She told me not to bother you, you wouldn't want to come all this way, but I knew you wouldn't miss it." She was looking around vaguely, sending a blind smile — she didn't have her glasses on — to any and all whose attention might turn to her.

"You mean Abby doesn't know I'm coming?" Cold teeth bit Elizabeth's spine. She had taken the wedding invitation to be an offer of reconciliation on Abby's part, even though they hadn't written or spoken since that day two years ago, and now it occurred to her that Deborah alone might have been responsible for including her on the guest list. And maybe she had only wanted to inform Elizabeth of Abigail's marriage, without really expecting that Elizabeth would come. *I can still leave before Abby sees me*, she thought, but then the music started and she was forced into a seat.

During the ceremony, most of the people watched the bride and groom, but Elizabeth kept her eyes on the back of Deborah's head, on the warm black hair she herself had asked permission to brush on the morning of their graduation, when Deborah was plucked out of the diploma line as soon as the dean spotted the "Fuck Nixon" sign affixed to her mortarboard.

At the altar, the rabbi spoke of commitment in the face of crisis, tolerance in the face of anger, love in the face of fear. He directed Abby and her new husband to cherish each other and to welcome, with open hearts, any children God chose to send to them. When it was time to break the wineglass, Abby and David lifted their feet over the cloth, and Elizabeth wondered if she was the only one who could see that Abby's heel came down first, making the bigger sound.

She hid herself, blending in with the other guests, until the congregation began to disperse. Deborah and her husband were swept away in a cloud of relatives, and Elizabeth saw her chance. She left her gift on the table and began to sneak out of the synagogue, but again someone caught her arm. She turned with a cry, anticipating Deborah, but found Abigail there instead. "I'm sorry," Abby said, seeing she'd startled her godmother. "But I have to talk to you." The crowd was spilling out into the hall. "I'm supposed to spend a few minutes alone with David, but he's throwing up in the back," Abby whispered. "Can we go in here?" She was already opening a door to the bride's dressing room. Elizabeth followed, her own nausea stirred.

Abby motioned toward the sofa, where a dress and a man's suit were laid out for the honeymoon trip, but Elizabeth shook her head and remained standing. "I can't sit down in this thing," Abby said, laughing as she fingered her billowed skirt. "I'd never get up again." Then she coughed, but Elizabeth could tell it was only the fake sound of stalling. "Listen," Abby continued, "I don't mind you coming, but I had to catch you before you said anything. To my mother, I mean. Or David. Neither of them know about — " She faltered, again clearing her throat.

Elizabeth nodded. "The abortion," she said.

Abby winced at the word. "Well, actually, I didn't have one." She looked down. "I should have told you. Written you, or something. But — well, I just didn't." She lifted her chin in that familiar tilt of defiance.

"What do you mean? You had a miscarriage?"

"No."

"Well then — " Elizabeth halted. "You didn't *have* the baby?" she said, dreading to admit the pleasure of this possibility as it passed through her.

Abigail nodded, biting her glossy lip.

"Oh, my God." Now Elizabeth moved to sit down, almost without realizing. "What happened?"

Abby shoved the honeymoon clothes out of the way and perched on the sofa next to her godmother, in the attitude of someone who has been waiting to confess. "I signed up for JYA," she said. "Junior Year Abroad? My mother thinks I spent the spring semester in Germany and the summer traveling on the Eurorail. When really I was sitting in this — *place* — in Worcester, Massachusetts, getting fatter every day. Just waiting. It was affiliated with a church, the home, but they didn't try to shove God down our throats. They didn't try to make us keep our babies. I think they were just glad we hadn't — you know." She would not repeat the word.

"Some of my friends actually did go to Europe, so I showed my mother *their* pictures, when they got back. I told her I took them all — the photos — which is why I wasn't in any of them." Abby made a face at how easy it had been to deceive her mother, but there was no triumph in the smirk.

Elizabeth asked, "What was it?" knowing Abby would understand what she meant.

"A girl. Six pounds, five ounces. Lots of black hair, like me. Like my mother." Her words were barely loud enough now for Elizabeth to hear. "She was adopted by some people in Oregon." *Oregon* emerged through lips shaped by reverence, as if she might have been pronouncing the name of heaven, or another place she had heard of with longing but never been to see.

"Oh, Abby." Elizabeth's hand went up to Abby's cheek. She meant only to touch it briefly, but Abby reached up to press Elizabeth's palm to her face and kept it there, like ice to a swelling. Under her fingers, Elizabeth felt the bride's flesh trembling. "And you never told David either?"

Abby shook her head. "I just couldn't. I mean, I thought I would, but I was never sure how to explain . . . I told him I was a virgin, the first night we were together, so after that, what could I say? I didn't think I'd end up *marrying* him. Jesus. Anyway, it's better this way." Again her chin rose resolutely. "You're the only one who knows. And — " She dropped her chin a little — "I don't want you to tell. Anyone. Ever."

"Abby — "

"Please. I'm begging you."

Before Elizabeth could respond that Abby had no need to beg, the door to the private room opened and a photographer burst in. "Say *quarter-pounder-with-cheese!*" he called out, and Elizabeth felt her goddaughter blush. When the flash went off, Elizabeth experienced — simultaneously in that moment — the next twenty-four hours of her own life: returning to California on an earlier flight, watering the plants on the patio, calling out for Chinese, and going to bed early so as to be the first one at the office in the morning. She would have a lot of work waiting. People would ask how her vacation had been, and she would smile and say, "Great!" Someone would suggest having lunch next door at The Lemon Tree, and would ask kindly if Elizabeth had any pictures of her trip. Elizabeth would pick out a few she'd had developed during her visit with Sam and keep her narration brief: "My old boyfriend and his family. We used to live together in Vermont. This is his wife, these are their kids. Yes, we get along fine — we were always more best friends, really, than anything else." Maybe she would show the picture of herself and Abby, cupping waists in the bridal room. But no: that picture hadn't been printed yet.

After setting them in his sights for a final shot, the photographer told Abby, "We need you outside, Mrs. Gray," and offered his arm to escort her back to the music and laughter.

"Go, sweetie," Elizabeth said, kissing the lace at her goddaughter's temple.

"Are you staying, then?" Abby asked, and it was clear what she hoped to hear.

"No. I need to catch an early flight back. I just wanted to see you, see your mother. Find out about — " Elizabeth trailed off, aware of the photographer listening. She gestured toward the west and finished, "Oregon."

A crease of pain crossed the bride's white forehead. "Thank you," she whispered, before the photographer steered her away.

In her rented car, Elizabeth reached for the heat controls — it was an automatic motion for her, being back in the East — before she remembered it was June. Turning off the vents again, she realized suddenly why she kept the picture of Wily Cobb's old snowplow on the bulletin board of the kitchen in her southern California home.

It was never cold where she lived now; she didn't want to forget how it felt.

The next time godmother and goddaughter saw each other was also the last time, four years later. Elizabeth still lived in California, but Abby and her husband had moved to Colorado. They had a son, whose picture they sent to Elizabeth every December on a secular holiday card. This winter ritual was the only communication between them, except for the note Abby had sent after the wedding. "Dear Elizabeth, it was wonderful to see you, thank you so much for coming, thank you so much for the gift . . ." and at the bottom, under her name, she'd printed in bold black letters THANK YOU, as if translating all of her previous words.

Four years after Abby's wedding, Elizabeth was forty-nine, and in the spring people started coming to her house to interview her. The two women and a man were filmmakers doing a documentary on death. (They called it a "life processes project," but Elizabeth knew better.) They had gotten her name from the doctor who gave her her treatments. "He told us you were a remarkable woman," the director had said, when she first called Elizabeth to see if she was willing to be involved. "We asked him if he had any patients who didn't seem to be afraid of their cancer, and he came up with your name right away." Elizabeth's mouth twisted at the thought that this particular doctor believed she would ever show him anything she might be feeling. Though she could tell she was being flattered because this woman wanted something, she didn't care. Since she'd left work right after New Year's, she didn't see many people, and sometimes a day would go by without her speaking. This was her own choice; she could still get around, still walk and drive — she had whole months yet — but she didn't feel like it. Occasionally she'd met someone from work for lunch at The Lemon Tree, but after the day Elizabeth hadn't made it to the ladies' room in time, they stopped calling.

Elizabeth didn't mind. The more her illness progressed, the more above the world she perceived herself to be. Not in a moral sense, but a physical one — as if she were floating away, a bit at a time. It was the floating that made things not matter. She was grateful she understood this, though she was not sure how she had come to learn it. Maybe we're all born knowing it, she thought, and we just don't realize unless we need to.

The first taping session was on a Wednesday evening. The cameraman showed up first, sweaty from coaching his son's Little League practice; then came the director and her assistant, a graduate student from USC whose loose-fitting sweatshirt did not conceal her oversized chest. (Elizabeth wondered if the director, whose name was Suna, had told the assistant to be especially discreet about her clothing when they were taping a subject whose cancer was in the breast.) Elizabeth served cookies and iced tea. "We'll start with some background," Suna told her. "Facts. You know, the easy stuff. Get you used to the camera." She asked Elizabeth where she came from. Elizabeth talked for the next two hours about her childhood in western New York, a place near Buffalo called Cheektowaga. She talked about her mother, who, when she appeared in Elizabeth's dreams, always stood behind an ironing board; her own legs held the board upright, and starch sprayed from her fingertips. She talked about her brother, Evan, who'd died in Vietnam the day Elizabeth lost her virginity (and the oddest part of that coincidence was that after the sex, before they got the news about Evan, the boy had looked down at Elizabeth's bitten face and told her, "You look like you just got back from Vietnam." She left this part out of the story, though), and about the way their father taught them Morse code and on summer nights went down the street with a flashlight to send them twinkling messages: *Hi kiddos, Finish your homework, What are you doing out of bed?* Though Suna stopped taking notes after fifteen minutes, and reached for a cookie every time she started to yawn — she ate nine — Elizabeth kept talking. She didn't care that none of what she told them would end up in the documentary; she just liked hearing herself say all of it out loud.

When she paused to take her medication, the director got in a question. "Do your children live around here?"

"I don't have any children," Elizabeth said. The words once held a taste for her, but the cancer had replaced it.

The director and her assistant looked at each other; the cameraman took his face away from the viewfinder. "Dr. Nugent told us you had children," Suna said. The tone of her voice implied that Elizabeth was lying.

"Well, he was wrong." Elizabeth laughed a little, choking down her pill. She had the terrible feeling — in fact, nothing had pierced her in precisely this place since the diagnosis — that they were going to pack up and leave. Once, in the restroom at work, she had overheard two women talking about a mutual acquaintance who had just died. "At least she didn't have any kids," one of the women said, and the other replied, "That's the only good thing about it."

"I do have a goddaughter," she told the documentary people. "I've known her all of her life."

"Well, do you think we'd be able to talk to her? Does she live around here?" Suna still looked doubtful, but Elizabeth saw that she hadn't lost yet.

"She lives in Colorado. But she's planning a visit." This wasn't true, but (Elizabeth reasoned) it could be. If she told Abby she was dying — oh, God, *dying*! — surely her goddaughter would come.

Abby phoned the same afternoon she received Elizabeth's letter. She called as soon as the rates changed; for Elizabeth, it was just after six o'clock. "Why didn't you tell us?" Abby asked, and Elizabeth tried to believe she had not had to work herself up into sounding stricken.

"Oh, I would have, sooner or later," she said. "It's not so bad yet. I was waiting for the full dramatic effect, like maybe when my hair fell out. But the thing is, they're making this film *now*." She paused as a sudden sharpness dug at the bone beneath her chest, cutting into her breath. "They were wondering if you could come out," she continued, when the pain gave up its grip. "I guess they want to interview you."

"Really?" Then Abby must have realized she sounded too interested, because she pulled back her tone a bit. "Well, of *course*, Elizabeth. I mean of course. It would be an honor. But really, I just want to see you." She didn't add *one last time*, although Elizabeth heard it. "I booked a flight already. The documentary is — you know, incidental."

"Well, it may be. But bring something flattering to wear," Elizabeth said.

There was the sound of play-farting in the background, and Abby reprimanded her son. Then she said, "Maybe Mother could fly out, too."

"No," Elizabeth said quickly. "Listen, it's my turn to ask *you* to keep a secret. I don't want her to know I'm — well, you know. Sick." She was so far beyond *sick* now that the word held no meaning for her, but it was better than the more precise one.

"Jesus. Why?"

But Elizabeth could not explain that she would never be able to say good-bye to Deborah. She might not ever speak to her again, let alone see her, but it was far better than saying good-bye.

Abby was scheduled to fly in on Monday evening. In the afternoon, Suna conducted a private interview with Elizabeth — *private* meaning that only the cameraman, but not the big-breasted assistant, was also present. "I hope you don't mind Jared's being a man," Suna said, gesturing to the camera, and Jared stuck his head to the side to flash them a Neanderthal grin.

"It's okay. He probably can't help it." Elizabeth gave him a wink back; she liked him more than she liked either of the two women. He did not flinch from the word *cancer*, and he had taken the time to look at the photographs on her walls.

"I'd like to ask you some personal questions," Suna said. "Some female things." She looked down as if in deference to her topic, but Elizabeth saw that she was referring to her notes. "I was wondering," the director began, dropping her voice conspiratorially, "if you see any irony in the types of cancer you have."

"Any irony in my cancer?" Elizabeth repeated, feeling foolish because she didn't understand.

"I mean, the fact that your own body is, essentially, attacking you in the uterus and the breast." Suna pushed her glasses up on her face. "I was wondering if you made any connections with that?"

"I'm still not sure I — "

"Look, I don't mean to be crude. But have you ever heard of angry womb syndrome?" Suna drove her pencil so hard into her notebook that the point broke, and in the shards of flying graphite Elizabeth saw that the director had come up with a way to use the circumstances of her life to the film's advantage, if Elizabeth would only cooperate. "It's when women who haven't had children get sick in parts of the body associated with childbearing and motherhood," Suna said, rummaging for a pen. "Some people believe it's the womb's revenge for not having been used in the way God intended."

"Wait a minute." Elizabeth held a hand up in front of her face, as she had seen people on television do to stop cameras from rolling. "When were we ever talking about God?"

"I was just speaking metaphorically." Suna tapped her pen impatiently on the pad. "Or maybe that's not the right word. I didn't mean anything." She seemed only now to sense that she'd offended.

"You don't have children either, do you?" Elizabeth said.

"Well, no. But I'm — " This time Suna interrupted herself.

"I know. You're young. You're not dying. Except, maybe, metaphorically." Elizabeth smiled as the director blushed, but they both knew it was not a cruel smile or an embarrassed blush; each felt, for the first time, safe with the other.

There was a long silence. "Hey, am I still supposed to be shooting?" Jared said.

When Abby arrived, Suna and Jared were out having dinner, and at the door Elizabeth gave her goddaughter a hard hug. She ushered her into the living room, which resembled a studio set.

"My God." Abby set her bag down and did a slow pirouette. Elizabeth thought she was reacting to all the film equipment, but Abby added, "It's just the way I remembered it. Everything about that day is kind of branded into my mind. The way the sun came in over there, at the kitchen — Jesus, is that the same ficus?" She sat down gingerly at the edge of the sofa, fingering its arms.

Elizabeth was about to say, "Listen, we don't have much time," when Abby reached into her bag and drew out a plastic photograph album. "I brought you more pictures of Nathan. I told him I was coming to visit my godmother, and he asked me did you know God. Then we figured out that you must be his *great*-godmother."

Elizabeth took the book and flipped through the pages, which showed a child who had received the thick hair and sharp brow of his mother and grandmother. (Although thinking of Deborah as a grandmother made Elizabeth want to fold up and cry.) "He's beautiful," she told Abby as she handed the album back, realizing too late that she had been meant to keep the photographs. Abby brushed a stray hair of Elizabeth's from the cover before tucking it back in her purse. She seemed nervous, but Elizabeth didn't know whether it was she or the cameras that made Abby shift in her seat.

"Listen." Elizabeth leaned forward and clasped courage between her hands. "I was thinking about what they might want to talk to you about. Now, I would never ask you to say anything you wouldn't want to say, otherwise, but — "

" — but there's something *you* want me to say." Abby finished for her and settled back, relieved that she only had to listen.

"Well, not exactly. Well, kind of." Elizabeth gathered her breath. "They'll be here soon." She could still stop herself from speaking, but she knew she wouldn't. It was like that moment years earlier when one instinct defeated another and she told Abby what Deborah had entrusted to her confidence two decades before. "It seems like what these people are trying to figure out is how my life has been special — or *meaningful*, maybe, is a better word. At first they thought I had children, which would have made me automatically worthwhile. I think they would have left when they found out I didn't, but they felt sorry for me." She let her lungs fill with breath. "When I told them about you, they perked up a little. I think they're expecting you to give them an answer. What I've done with my life. What I'll leave behind, besides — this." She gestured around herself and Abby's eyes followed, until she realized that Elizabeth was pointing at nothing in particular.

"The way I look at it," Elizabeth went on, "I never had a baby, but I *am* responsible for two lives being in the world. Yours, and — " She paused again, waiting for Abby to fill in the blank, and when she didn't, Elizabeth used the code known only to the two of them. "Oregon."

Abby startled in her seat, and Elizabeth detected the tin scent of fear. "Don't worry, I know we can't tell them about Deborah," she said. "What your mother was planning when she was pregnant with you. I want you to know that I would never betray that again." She emphasized *again* and saw that Abby took note of it.

"Good," Abby said.

"But Oregon," Elizabeth continued. "That's up to you, if you wanted to."

Abby frowned, as if she did not comprehend at first. Then she stood up and immediately sat down again, losing her balance in the cushions. "You want me to tell the movie people about *that*?" The apparent absurdity of it made her sputter. "Are you kidding?"

"Of course not." Elizabeth's chest went cold.

"My mother doesn't know. My *husband* doesn't even know." Abby made a noise of disbelief at the roof of her mouth. "And you want me to announce it in front of thousands of strangers." She looked at her godmother as if she had never seen her before. "I can't believe you would ask me to do this, Elizabeth. I can't believe you would use me this way."

"Use you?"

"What else would you call it? You want me to dredge up the most painful thing in my life, what I fight every day to forget, just so you can get on some goddamn PBS show that nobody's going to watch anyway?"

Elizabeth's hand went up to her throat. "It's not like I'm trying to be famous or anything," she whispered. "I just — " The truth of it came to her suddenly, and she spoke before she knew what the words would be. "I just wanted people to know I was here."

The fury on Abby's face cracked into something softer, and she covered her eyes. Elizabeth felt hope, remembering the day Abby had waited, in this same way, to see if Elizabeth would relent and help her get an abortion. When Abby was ready to look at her again, Elizabeth smiled. In a quieter voice, Abby asked, "Isn't it enough that *you* know? That *we* know?"

"I know it should be. But it isn't." Elizabeth had miscalculated the amount of time they would have to speak privately; she rose from the ottoman as she heard Suna and Jared outside. The sound of their approach made her think of boots in the forest, the loud stealth of war. She opened the door for them and they brandished leftovers, cartons of Chinese food and two fortune cookies, which they offered to Elizabeth and Abby. Elizabeth unfolded hers to read, "Among the lucky, you are the chosen one!" It made her laugh, though only briefly.

Abby took her cookie apart and shook the crumbs on the table, but no slip of paper fell out. "There's no fortune in here," she said. She tried to sound lighthearted, but clearly it bothered her. Elizabeth handed hers over.

"We must have gotten each other's," she said, and Abby's face flushed with chagrin. Elizabeth heard Suna groan because this usable moment had not been captured on tape.

During her interview, Abby sat up straight the way her mother had taught her and told Suna that Elizabeth had been a very important influence in her life.

"How has she been important?" Suna pressed. "Can you give us some details?"

"Well—she flew out for my high school graduation, and my wedding. She always sent me great presents. And actually, she gave me my name." Abby bit her lip, squinting into the sharp light, and Elizabeth could see that her goddaughter was struggling. She closed her eyes, knowing that the documentary, when it aired finally, would be about somebody else.

"Anything more you'd like to tell us?" Suna was still trying. "Anything you'd particularly like Elizabeth to know during—well, let's be honest here, what may be your final visit?"

Abby was rubbing her fortune between her fingers. She folded it into tiny pieces, as if to make it disappear. When she lifted her eyes to look at Elizabeth, she asked with them to be forgiven. "Just, you know, that I'm going to miss her," she said.

At the end it was Sam who sat with her, helping her to the bathroom and letting her grip his hand when the pills couldn't hold back the pain. In between he flipped channels with the remote or stroked the hair behind her ears, a sensation she'd loved since she was an infant, when her brother, forced to babysit, used it to get her to go to sleep.

"Well, Hermione, you certainly let me down," Elizabeth said one day after a lunch of gelatin and Coke, lifting a heavy hand to her heart. *Hermione* was the name Sam had given her right breast, thirty years ago; *Ludmilla* was the left. It had taken Elizabeth a long time to overcome the modesty she felt in letting Sam see her naked, but then she enjoyed the freedom of their bare bodies under the sheets. She had only endured the actual sex — what would have happened if she told him she thought of Deborah, the whole time he was touching her? — but she remembered the warmth of his breath with a tender dart. Sam used to speak in pretend-Russian to Ludmilla while he was making love. It made them laugh so hard, those harsh-sounding nonsense Slavic syllables, that sometimes he couldn't finish.

They tried to laugh now, but it hurt Elizabeth. From his backpack — for he still carried a backpack, though he earned a briefcase salary now — Sam drew out an envelope of photographs, including some from her trip to visit his family and others he had taken custody of long ago, when they'd broken up. To find them, he'd had to dig through seven boxes in the attic, and he would have given up before that if his wife hadn't made him keep looking.

"I thought I'd never see you again, after that trip," Elizabeth told him.

"Well, you were wrong, weren't you?"

Several of the photographs — the ones Sam's youngest children had been allowed to take, though they were barely big enough to handle the camera — showed only the torsos of bodies, or a sliver of face under fractured sky. "Why on earth would you keep these?" Elizabeth asked, holding up a shot of unidentifiable arms linking.

Sam shrugged. "Because my kids took them." It was the first time he'd ever given her a look that suggested she wouldn't understand,

and it so chilled her that she picked up the next photograph in the pile and began talking before she even saw what it was.

"Look at this one," she said. "Oh, God — that old snowplow. I saved this one, too. Whatever happened to Wily Cobb? I know he must be dead by now. But how?"

"Car crash," Sam told her. "Head on with a Beamer, the people from Boston who bought our old place. He never knew what hit him. God, that's — " He was about to say something like "the way to go," but he caught himself, and he tangled himself up in apologies which Elizabeth tried but failed to push aside.

He opened a book to read to her, but she made him stop after one line of Yeats: *When you are old and gray and full of sleep*. She closed the page on a penny and told him everything. Can one person ever know it all about another? He listened without speaking, though at times he seemed to wince at something he realized he should have known. When she was finished, she waited for him to say something. His face was filled with it, and she wondered what it would sound like in words. He turned his head from her, and through his fingers he let out a small burp, which he'd managed to hold in all that time. "Oh, God, Liz, I'm sorry," he said, going white, but she was laughing, this time from deep in her belly and without the pain.

"Bless you," she said, barely getting it out around her mirth.

"That's for a sneeze, silly."

"I know." She lay back on the pillow and closed her eyes, and within minutes Sam had fallen asleep next to her. The room smelled of roses somebody had sent her, and Sam's skin. Elizabeth watched him and gently rubbed spit from the corner of his mouth with her little finger. When he woke up it was dark out, and she could tell that for a single panicked moment, he forgot where he was. Then he pulled the shades and went to call his family from the living room.

"I think today was a better day," she heard him say.

Deprivation

THE BABY HAD BEEN CRYING for nine hours. Since four o'clock in the morning, through all of Nina's beseeching and ministrations — re-diapering, trying to feed, shuffling around the house while rocking him up and down, sitting in front of the TV, holding him like a football, showing him every stuffed animal she could find, putting him down on his back, putting him down on his stomach, putting him in the baby swing, bathing him, and singing — he kept it up, not a rhythmic squall, which would have worn him out eventually, but a continuous mewling she thought might go on forever. Curtis left for work at the usual time, around eight thirty, after kissing both of them and wishing Nina luck. He told her he would call around lunchtime, but when one o'clock came and went without the phone ringing, she cursed him and turned on a soap opera. This was something she had told both herself and Curtis she wouldn't do — start watching daytime TV while she stayed home with the baby — but it was an emergency, she told herself. If Norton didn't stop crying, she didn't know what she would do.

The baby was named Norton after the character on *The Honeymooners*, Curtis's favorite show. In the five months since the birth, Nina had regretted, often, capitulating to this request.

She had been thinking more along the lines of Kevin or Eric. But somehow Curtis had convinced her that people would think it was cool, and funny, to have a child named after the Art Carney character. There would be no other Nortons at school, he pointed out to Nina. Now she thought of this more as a reason to have nixed the idea. Her son would suffer — this she could already tell, when strangers asked and learned of the baby's name. They tried to cover it up, but Nina could tell they believed she had bad judgment. And she didn't, really — Curtis just got to her, one night while they were watching a rerun and Ed Norton was particularly kooky, and she thought that giving the name to their son would make him independent and original. So: Norton. Luckily, he wasn't old enough yet to know what a stupid name he had. For all he knew, he *was* a Kevin or an Eric.

On the soap opera, a serial killer was on the loose. Three citizens of Shadow Bay had already been murdered, the last victim having been the wife of the doctor who had just been reinstated at the hospital after going through drug rehab. The dead character's name was Madeline. That's a nice name, Nina thought. Why couldn't we have had a girl? But then Curtis would probably have talked her into *Trixie*. While she was watching the TV, Nina put Norton in his playpen and just let him cry. She turned the sound up and knew she was being a bad mother, but figured she would start dealing with it again at two o'clock.

Madeline was lying in her open casket in a tasteful white suit, with her family and friends around her. Every time someone came over to say good-bye, or to touch her hand, she just lay there; but when the character of Cerise was by the casket, Madeline came back to life. Cerise was psychic — she could always tell when something bad was going to happen, and she read tarot cards. Her brother had been the murderer's first victim.

But even though she was used to her own intuitions, Cerise

freaked out when she heard Madeline whisper to her from the coffin. Nothing *quite* so psychic had ever happened to her before.

From her silk pillow, the corpse of Madeline said to Cerise, "The killing is not over. I'm telling you, Cerise, because you understand these things."

In her shock, and making sure to whisper so none of the mourners noticed, Cerise asked, "Is *anyone* safe?"

The corpse shook her beautifully coiffed head and said, "All of Shadow Bay is in danger. Please, Cerise, warn everyone. There is more evil on the way." Then, as somebody else came up to the casket, she returned to the still and silent dead person she was supposed to be. The credits rolled and the program was over. Nina cursed.

She called Curtis at work. He developed software that made it easier for people to manage their to-do lists, and even though most of his work was in the office, they made him wear his long hair in a ponytail, in case any clients ever dropped by.

"He's still crying," Nina said.

"How come?"

She imagined putting his ponytail down the waste disposal and flipping on the switch. It was an image that had come to her before. "I have no idea, Curtis. Do you think if I had any idea, I'd be calling you? Don't you remember him crying this morning before you left?" But she knew he had slept through most of it. He had once slept through a Patriots game, *at* the stadium.

"Nina, babies cry." She could tell he wanted to get off the phone, which probably meant there was a supervisor nearby. But she wasn't about to let him.

"They don't cry for *ten hours straight*, Curtis. And if you're so laid-back about it, why don't you come home and take care of him? I just need to get out of this house. I need to hear something besides this goddamned sound."

"Nina," he said, in the patronizing voice that made her fantasize about cutting the ponytail off while he slept, "you know I can't come home right now. I'm out here earning a living. But why don't you call a babysitter? Pay her extra if he cries the whole time."

A babysitter. It hadn't occurred to her. She didn't know what her chances were, on short notice, but she said she would try.

She was lucky. She got Angela Civetti on the phone just as Angela walked in the door from school. "I need to run a few errands," Nina said. "It wouldn't be long." Angela said she could be right over. "Great!" Nina said, then thought she should tone it down so as not to make the teenager suspicious. "I really appreciate it, Angela. See you soon." *Watch*, she told herself, *Norton'll shut up as soon as Angela gets here. Like when you take your car to the shop and it's stopped making the clunking noise.*

But that didn't happen. When Angela arrived, the baby's cheeks were red and swollen from crying all day, and he was still at it. "He's been a little fussy," Nina said, "but maybe you can get him to sleep in the swing." That she had tried this strategy several times already, without success, she didn't tell the babysitter. "I should be back in an hour or so," she said, trying to gauge how long would be too unfair to ask of a sixteen-year-old without sufficient warning about what she was in for. "Oh, and help yourself to the cake on the counter. It's from my husband's birthday."

Too late, she remembered that Angela Civetti was the *bulimic* babysitter. Nina had had to call the plumber once when she clogged up the toilet with thrown-up food. But she couldn't take the offer back now.

Though she knew it was probably all in her head, it seemed that she could hear Norton's crying until she was at the end of the driveway. It had snowed fourteen inches during the weekend and Nina hadn't been out to drive since, so she had to adjust and pay attention to the slippery road. She went to Walgreens and wandered the aisles, picking out things she would need sooner or later: mouthwash (soon), a birthday card for her mother (the end of the month), a can of formula, and a set of colored plastic keys for Norton — as if that might be the magic thing he needed, what he'd been crying for all along.

When she returned home she found not Angela but Curtis, bouncing a screeching Norton on his knee. "What are you doing here?" Nina said. "It's not even four."

"I told them I had an emergency at home," he said. He was still wearing his work clothes — brown corduroys, a yellow button-down, and a tie with tumbling circus bears. "After you called, I felt crummy for being a jerk." He turned to look at her for the first time since she'd come in and collapsed, still in her coat, on the couch. "Hey, what happened to my cake? I was looking forward to a piece."

"Oh, God." Nina went into the kitchen and saw the empty cake plate soaking in the sink. She made a note to herself to look up the plumber's number as soon as Norton stopped crying — if he ever did.

"Do you think we should call the doctor?" Curtis laid Norton down and twisted off his tie.

"Wait a minute. Just let me try something." Nina reached into the Walgreens bag and pulled out the plastic keys. She shook them in front of her son's face, but it only made him cry harder.

"Hey, I like those," Curtis said. "I think I had one of them when I was a kid."

"Well, the doctor's a good idea," Nina said, going to the phone. "At least the timing's good — they have call-in from four to four thirty."

The nurse was so sympathetic it made Nina want to cry. "He'll be fine, honey," she told Nina, after determining that Norton's temperature had been taken and that it was normal. "It's probably colic. I don't usually recommend this, but if he's really been crying for that long, I'd give him some Benadryl. It should put him right out. He needs to sleep, if he's been awake this long."

"Thank you so much," Nina said. She wanted to stay on the line with this calm and comforting woman, but she knew other people needed to get through. She went into the bathroom and got the Benadryl, and with Curtis stroking Norton's forehead, she squeezed an eyedropper full of the pink medicine into her son's mouth. "That should do it," she said, and sure enough, within fifteen minutes their son was asleep, and Curtis and Nina called out for a pizza.

Within three hours, Norton woke up again. They were lying on the two couches in the living room, both facing the TV. Curtis had tuned in to a TV program about cops, and Nina found herself drifting to the sounds of sirens and the voices of police officers as they pulled people over or chased them through yards. Then it was a baby crying and she jerked awake, having to catch her breath. "Shit!" she said, afraid of something she couldn't remember.

Curtis had already gotten up and gone into Norton's room. The baby was squalling on his back, his fists clenched and his face red, and Nina followed Curtis around the room as he changed the diaper and put on fresh clothing. "He has to eat," she said, and they had another few minutes of quiet while Norton sucked down the contents of a full bottle. Then he began crying again. Nina sat in a chair and stared at the floor. She pressed her hands against her eyes until she saw little explosions.

"I'll take him out," Curtis said.

"In this weather?"

"Well, I'll have the heat on. You know how the car calms him down." He began pulling on his own jacket and boots while Nina dressed the baby and wrapped him in his alphabet quilt for good measure. "I'll drive till he falls asleep. Don't wait up," he said grimly.

With the baby gone, it took a full half hour to get the sound of his screaming out of her head. She turned off the TV and picked up her book, which she had chosen from the library shelves because it was skinny, and the only way she could read anything, these days, was in short shifts. *The Stranger*. She opened it to the first page. "Maman died today." The words caused her eyes to swell with hot tears, not because of her own mother, who was alive and well and serving her fellow mankind as an emergency medical technician in Mamaroneck, but because she herself was a mother now, and someday her son might read these same words and feel a burst of tenderness toward her, of the kind she had felt toward him since shortly after she knew he was growing inside her. Then she grew sad thinking of the pain Norton would suffer when she died, then sadder still when she realized that *he* would die, this fresh baby becoming an old man someday, if he was lucky; she couldn't bear the idea of him leaving the world she had so recently witnessed him enter, so she shook the thoughts away and focused on the story. Meursault, the main character, was at the beach in Algiers, and the sun was so hot it made his eyebrows drip, as cymbals of sunlight crashed upon his forehead. He couldn't tell whether the Arab man was coming at him with a knife. "The sun was the same as it had been the day I'd buried Maman, and like then, my forehead especially was hurting me, all the veins in it throbbing under the skin. It was this burning, which I couldn't stand anymore, that made me move forward." When she had finished reading about the murder, she put the book aside and looked at the clock; Curtis and the baby had been gone for nearly two hours. She was just standing up, not knowing where her next step would take her, when she heard the car in the driveway and they were home.

He was still crying. "Did he sleep at all?" she asked Curtis, whose hair was hanging loose on his shoulders — she could never get him to wear a hat.

He shook his head. “I drove all the way to Worcester,” he told her almost in a whisper, as if it were his own voice and not the baby’s on the verge of giving out. “I couldn’t stand it anymore. Did *you* sleep?”

“No. I couldn’t. I’m reading this weird book.” They both looked at Norton, still bundled in his carrier in the middle of the kitchen floor, his mouth open so wide they could see his tonsils throbbing in his throat.

“You go to bed,” she told Curtis. “It’s my turn.”

“Do you think the emergency room, if he doesn’t stop soon?”

She considered. “The nurse said it was just colic. I’ve read about it, they cry for no reason. He has to get tired soon. Doesn’t he?”

Curtis said he didn’t know and lifted his feet to let his boots fall off in thuds. He kissed in the direction of Nina and padded down the hall to the bedroom, where he shut the door.

She unswaddled her son and took him back into the living room with her. She tried the swing and the TV. She tried singing, and offered him more formula. Every attempt seemed to make him cry harder, though she knew that at a certain point — which he had reached long ago — this was impossible.

She propped him against a cushion of the couch. She thought she could feel every nerve in her body trembling. Norton watched her as he wailed, but he could have no idea what it meant to see his mother pick up another cushion and, breathing aloud, draw it close to his heaving face. She held it softly over his mouth and nose, just for a moment, long enough to muffle the crimson shriek. Then she took the pillow away, pitched it across the room, picked him up and began to rock.

It didn’t help. He kept on crying.

In the morning, Curtis came out still wearing his T-shirt and boxers. “I’m staying home today,” he told Nina.

"Oh, God, thank you."

"It's not for you. I feel lousy." They had to shout at one another over the sound of their son. He went to the kitchen to make coffee.

"Lousy as in sick?" She left Norton on his back on the living room floor, and came toward her husband.

"No. Lousy as in no sleep." He leaned against the counter with both hands, looking out the window. "I'll go out with the snow-blower today, as long as I'm home."

"Oh! Maybe you could take him out in the backpack. He loves it with the lawn mower, maybe the snowblower would work the same."

Curtis looked at her with what she would have interpreted as hatred, if she didn't know better. "If you think so," he said without enthusiasm. "But won't he be cold?"

"I'll bundle him up again." Norton's crying had gone way beyond giving her a headache, to the point that she thought she might vomit. She began packing the baby into his snowsuit while Curtis went to get dressed.

It was cold outside, though the sun shone against the snow. Nina jiggled Norton on her hip while Curtis adjusted the backpack straps, and then she lowered the baby in. Curtis winced as his son's screams hit the back of his head. He went to the garage, pushed the snow-blower out, and turned it on. In the house, Nina nearly wept from the relief of hearing a different noise.

From the living room window, she watched as they came into view, and she could feel her jaw actually drop as she saw that Norton had not only stopped crying, but was smiling and slapping at the air with his mittens. Tears and snot still streaked his face, but he was happy.

She rapped on the window and Curtis looked up. She pointed behind him and he craned to see his son, then turned back to her and gave a thumbs-up. She went to bed and tried to sleep, but her heart was racing, so she got up and opened her book.

The judge was asking Meursault what had caused him to kill the Arab man at the beach. Meursault thought for a moment, and then he replied that he had shot the man because of the sun. Everybody in the courtroom laughed, but Nina understood perfectly.

It took Curtis almost an hour to clear their driveway and the sidewalk in front of the house. When he turned the snowblower off and came in to warm up, Norton started crying again. "Damn it," he said to Nina, who had finished the book and was folding baby socks on the sofa. "I was afraid of this."

"Maybe you'll have to blow the Donahues out, too," she suggested. She thought she was joking, but Curtis blew on his soup and took a glum swallow.

"Maybe I will."

They took turns trying to nap, but it was impossible. After lunch Curtis put on his wet clothes and took the baby on his back again, and again Norton cheered right up. Nina checked to make sure they were out of sight, in the neighbors' driveway, before she turned on the TV. The killer was back at it in Shadow Bay, and she watched the whole hour with the drone of the snowblower safely in the distance. At two o'clock she turned off the TV. The theme song from yesterday's cop program began running through her head, and she found herself whispering the words. What *was* she gonna do when they came for her? Then she laughed at herself and loaded the dishwasher.

It was close to three o'clock when her boys came back. Curtis had cleared two more driveways and part of the cul-de-sac. Sure enough, as soon as he'd turned off the snowblower, Norton began crying again. This time Nina fed him two droppers of Benadryl, and within ten minutes he'd fallen asleep.

Curtis and Nina sat next to each other on the couch, both slumped and exhausted. Curtis said, "Maybe I shouldn't tell you this, but while I was out there I had an image of burying him in the snow, if he didn't stop crying. I know that sounds terrible."

"It does." Nina spoke quietly. She was tracing the pattern of the pillow with her finger.

"But it made me see how these things happen. I feel like I understand, now, how people can do such awful things to their kids." Curtis put his feet up on the table and went to wrap his arm around her, but she leaned away. It was a barely noticeable movement, but they both noticed it.

"What's the matter?" He flipped a tendril of his hair back over his shoulder, to get it out of their way. "You mean *you* never thought of anything like that, with all this crying?"

"Of course I haven't. What kind of a mother would I be?" But she didn't want him to answer her. Instead — because she didn't know what it would mean if she stayed away — she let herself move back toward him, forcing herself to snuggle into his side.

"A normal one, I think," Curtis said, but she was already falling asleep to the dream of a glittering Algerian beach, an Arab with a knife, the sun beating down to blind her as she lifted the revolver and, with little thought about what the Arab might have done to deserve it, fired.

Shirley Wants Her Nickel Back

WHEN SHE LEFT in the mornings, her husband and baby were still asleep. It was four o'clock, black and silent, a time when it felt illegal to be awake. She laid her clothes out the night before so she could dress in the dark, just jeans and a sweatshirt, sneakers and socks. And earrings — though no one would see her alone in the dawn-lit car, she felt nervous leaving the house without the familiar weight in her ears, as if gravity weren't enough.

She tiptoed out of the bedroom praying *Don't wake up*, and making toast in the kitchen, she held the lever so it wouldn't make the ding, and she washed the toast down with milk which she drank from the carton. She drank it this way in the mornings because there were no witnesses, and because it saved dishwashing later. She did it also because there was a sweet sneakiness in doing something she knew would make Jimmy sick to see. Then came guilt in replacing the milk now soiled with her spit, but that never stopped her from doing it the next time. The milk and the guilt were her secrets, nurtured by night.

Every marriage has secrets, her mother had told her once. *You don't have to tell everything. Listen to me.*

After Norine brushed her teeth at the kitchen sink, she shrugged her parka on over her shoulders, listened one last time, with her breath held, for the baby's sound, then zipped up and stepped outside, backing into the day. It was January in northern New York, not far from the Genesee River, and by noon the town might be warm under winter sun; but at this lightless hour she shivered on her way to the car, blowing on her hands through the frayed fingers of her gloves. The gloves were a joke in this weather, falling apart at the seams, but she couldn't bring herself to buy anything new these days except food and diapers, and an occasional magazine if she could justify it by clipping coupons.

The bills they owed sat on top of the TV. Every time she cleaned house, she dusted around the papers, the fancy letterhead with *Attorneys-at-Law* in polite black cursive, and beneath it the columns of figures ending in a total that made her want to throw up or cry. On top of that there was the money they were supposed to pay the Henzel family, and although the amount hadn't been determined yet, Norine knew the sum would be ridiculous — laughable, even, if somebody hadn't died.

Damages. The lawyer's word for *money* buzzed a rough mantra through Norine's mind. *Wrongful death*. Jimmy kept saying they would work out a system, set aside so much a month. But together they earned only enough for rent and groceries. Her Christmas tips had taken care of the overdue oil and electricity, but that cash was gone now and Norine knew it was just a matter of time before they started getting phone calls and mail notices they couldn't ignore. Jimmy didn't seem to worry about it, though Norine wanted him to. He had a way of shrugging as he said "It'll work out" that made her feel like slapping him back into the world.

Usually the engine sputtered at least a few times before catching. But something must have been on her side today, because even though it was cold out, it turned over on the first try. Her beams cast the only light in the quiet dark. She made it to the distribution center in the length of time it took Don McLean, on the "All seventies all the time" station, to sing *American Pie*. She had the final words in her head — the ones that described the Father, the Son, and the Holy Ghost making their getaway — as she got out and began loading her pile of newspapers into the car. The papers were heavy this morning, with a lot of ad inserts, and she swore when she saw them.

Someone finished the song's verse behind her, and she was startled to realize that she had not only been thinking the lyrics, but singing them out loud.

"Hey, Willie," she said, picking up speed because she couldn't stand him. Every morning Willie Mooney had food in his mustache and grime on his jeans. Just looking at him made her mouth go taut. He had parked next to her at the loading door, and they were pulling at the same pace.

He imitated the sound of her swearing and said, "What would your mama say if she heard that? Nice mouth on the minister's daughter." He sang his last three words in the tune of a tattletale: "I'm telling God."

"Go ahead," Norine said. "Like he listens to you."

"Without a doubt," Willie said, but she saw a streak of panic in his blink. Then he laughed at something privately, low in his chest. They dropped their papers in alternating rhythm, a duet of slaps. Willie stopped working, lit a cigarette, and smiled at her around it. Norine felt the hair rise on her hands. "Things getting any better?" Willie asked, blowing smoke out of the side of his mouth so it wouldn't hit her. "I see where your husband got a job. That's a good sign, ain't it?"

"I suppose," Norine said, slamming her hatchback on the last of her load. On the road again, moving toward the beginning of her route, she sent all the air out of her lungs and let it hang for a moment in the closed space around her, until she had to gasp to take it in again. There was no sign of the sun yet. The black outside her windows made her feel small and chased.

She took a cassette tape out of the glove box and pushed it into the deck. The tape was of an all-girl band Norine and her two best friends used to sing with, and drive to, on weekend nights when they were in high school. Even though Norine and Trish and Melanie all knew better, they liked to think of themselves as hotshots, like the girl singers, and they liked to pretend that they were the queens of Sackettsville — that the *us* the three of them made together was something special, to which other people would no doubt want to belong.

But now Trish was working for her boyfriend in Colorado, and although Melanie had not moved, she and Norine were no longer friends. For a while after graduation, Norine had thought of them as friends who didn't call or see each other, until she realized that this was the definition of people who were *not* friends.

Who could she turn to, if she were to leave? When she'd begun asking herself this after the accident, she had no answer. The impulse stagnated inside her chest.

The last house on her route sat on the blind turn before the bend in the road. The safe thing to do was park on the other side of the street, where there was a shoulder, and walk across to deposit the newspaper. But on a cold day like this one, it was tempting to drive up to the box, on the wrong side of the road, stuff the paper in from the driver's-side window, then gun it back to where you belonged.

When it was still dark out, you could count on seeing the headlights of any car coming around the curve. But after dawn, you took your chances with a head-on. In the first few weeks of doing the route Norine parked dutifully and crossed, after flipping down the sun visor to touch the photograph of Carl she kept fastened there with a paper clip. But she never saw a car pass, and the mornings grew colder, and so she began doing it the fast way, feeling the word

Please beat in her heart until she was driving in the right direction again, toward home.

She hesitated only a moment now, approaching the corner, before pulling up to the box. She shoved the paper out the window but in her rush she dropped it, and she swore. It would take longer to fold a new paper than to pick up the one that had fallen, so she leaned the door open with a creak and bent down to get it. When she lifted her head back up, at the same time putting the newspaper in its place, she saw — through lids already slitted, her mouth opened to a scream — another car coming around the bend. In that blind instant she imagined the swift pain of the crash, the crunch of metal and the windshield exploding in a glass shower.

But at the last minute the other car swung wide, out of her way, and barreled beyond her, sending gravel from the opposite shoulder to rain on her rooftop like hail. The driver's window was open, and as the car sped by Norine heard the man call her a foul name. She couldn't see who it was because she was still ducking, and she stayed low in her seat until she was sure he had passed and wasn't returning, before she yanked her car into gear and pressed the pedal to the floor until she was safe on the right side of the road. She was trembling. She was done.

The crash — the real one, the one that hadn't been escaped — was another thing she imagined in the daytime and dreamed about at night. Holding Carl to her breast at the corner of the couch, lulled by the rhythmic lip pulls and the drowse of his lashes as he fought sleep, or sometimes as she dusted or as she reached for a plastic bag from the roll above the carrot bin in the produce section of the A & P, she saw it in front of her — eclipsing her baby's face or the row of vegetables — the slice of the truck's grate into Mary Jo Henzel's flesh, and she heard, instead of Carl's sucking or the grocery's mellow din, the scream Mary Jo must have swallowed or the one that was thrown back in her throat as the glass broke around her, a shattered chrysalis in the street.

Norine had been asleep when she got the phone call. She was pregnant, just beginning to show, and she was still getting used to being married, because it had only been three months. That morning she and Jimmy had eaten cereal together, as usual, before heading to work — Jimmy as a junior agent at Genesee Mutual Insurance Company and Norine behind the desk and phone of a dentist, Dr. Payne, whose name Jimmy had never stopped getting a kick out of, to the point where Norine had to tell him to please stop, the joke was tired, he'd run it into the ground.

After work that night, Jimmy went out for beers with a friend from the insurance agency. It was a Thursday, and Norine was late getting home after listening to a long root canal in the room behind her desk station; when the patient finally emerged, looking numb and stunned, Norine wanted to apologize as she took the woman's check, or give her something in return to make up for the assault her mouth had suffered, but there was no adult equivalent of the plastic dinosaurs they gave to children, and Norine knew that whatever she offered would not be enough. She thought Jimmy might be home already when she arrived, and when she saw the dark windows of the apartment she swore and sat in the parking lot for a minute, summoning incentive to enter the empty hall. She went to bed after putting a plate of chicken in the oven for Jimmy, and fell asleep watching *Cheers*. When the phone rang she darted awake, squinting in the light of the lamp she hadn't turned off, hearing the TV's fuzz.

It was Daniel Veltman, saying he was sorry to disturb her so late. Then his voice shed its sympathy as he told Norine that her husband had been involved in a serious accident. Later, she remembered being struck by the fact that he'd said "your husband" instead of "Jimmy," though it didn't register at the time.

"Is he dead?" Norine asked. She wasn't awake yet and the information hadn't seeped through, but this seemed like the right thing to say.

"No." There was a pause, and she closed her eyes against the light and against what he would tell her next. "But somebody else is."

And when she went to the hospital, where Jimmy was having his eyelid stitched, she had to pass, at the nurses' station, the sister of the woman who had been killed. She did not know it was the sister until the next day, when she saw the photograph of Mary Jo Henzel in the newspaper and recognized the resemblance. But Norine overheard enough of what the woman said to the nurse and to Daniel Veltman to realize it was the same accident that had brought them both to this place. The woman wore a baggy sweater over a nightgown, which she had tried to tuck into a pair of jeans, but the gown's bottom trailed over the waistband, giving her an absurd flannel tail. Norine heard her keep asking, "What time did it happen? What *time*?" and Daniel Veltman said he couldn't be sure, somewhere around twelve thirty, and when she persisted and he finally said, kindly but with a squeak to his voice, "Does it *matter*?" the woman looked at him and laughed, and pushed hair aside from where it was caught in damp strands behind her eyeglasses, and said, "You're right, I guess. It doesn't."

If Norine had been friends with the woman, if she'd known her from work or church or from her childbirth class, she would have gone over to fit an arm around the sweatered shoulder, and helped lead the tight body to a chair, and fed it coffee or a candy bar from the machine.

But not only had they never met before; Norine's husband had been driving the truck that killed someone this woman loved. And Norine knew without being told that Jimmy had been drinking, and was guilty. She felt that these simple truths should make her hate the man responsible, even if he *was* her husband, but when the woman looked at her and Norine saw the beam of instinctive accusation in her eyes, she turned away and moved with swift steps down the corridor, to where Jimmy was bleeding and waiting.

They would not let her take him home. "What about bail?" she asked Daniel when he and another officer led Jimmy, handcuffed and limping, from the emergency room.

It was Jimmy who told her, "No, Nor," and she wasn't sure whether he meant *No*, they wouldn't be able to raise the money or *No*, he did not want to be let go. As they made their way to the exit in an awkward chain of arms, she held her breath and hoped that the other woman would be gone from the hall. She looked ahead, searching for the big sweater, and when she didn't see it, she said "Thank you" in her murmured exhalation, and Jimmy said, "What?" and she told him, "Nothing."

She followed them down to the police station, though inside they wouldn't let her see Jimmy, and as Daniel walked her to the door, he asked, "Do you guys have a lawyer?" She shook her head and he added, "Because you're going to need one, now."

His glance kept dropping to the bulge inside the waist of her sweatpants, and even though he was being nice to her in the face of things, she felt her hand drop to cover the baby with a protecting palm. He seemed to understand the gesture, and took a step back. He'd been two years ahead of Norine in school, and the first time she ever noticed him was the day he retrieved her mitten from the top rung of the icy jungle gym where Artie Bruner had tossed it. *Daniel Veltman* — though now was not the time to think of such things, she couldn't help remembering how his name always made her think of felt and velvet mixed together, a smooth comfort like the piece of her childhood blankie she kept in the nightstand drawer. It was an irony because Daniel was the opposite of smoothness, with his beard of acne scars, his uniform's shirt missing a button at the stomach, and his short hair scraggly at the ends. He looked more like an apologetic mailman than a police officer, and she heard his small "I'm sorry" follow her into the night.

Jimmy had done the most bone-headed thing possible, according to his lawyer, Harry Fritts (he sang bass in the church choir, and flaunted a public thus harmless crush on Norine's mother, who had enlisted him for the case). "They ask you how many beers you had, and you *tell* them? You tell them you know you got into that truck drunk, and the accident was your fault?" The tone of Harry's voice suggested that he might have heard stupider things in his life before this, but probably not. It suggested that he had never met a bigger doofus than Jimmy Ploetz.

"I wanted to tell the truth," Jimmy mumbled. "I thought that was the right thing to do."

"This isn't Sunday School. You get that, right?" Harry said, and Norine saw that out of the respect and perhaps lust he had for Norine's mother, he was holding back. But then he couldn't resist adding, "Don't blame me if you spend the next ten years in jail, okay, Jim? I could have gotten you off."

It was easy to see that Jimmy's confession, during his interrogation at the police station, would not have vexed Harry so much if he didn't understand it as the only thing standing between his client and freedom. Harry said he could have gotten the Breathalyzer thrown out by exposing the fact that a test taken on the same machine, earlier the same evening, registered a reading so off the charts that it would have meant the guy who blew it had to be unconscious or dead. He also said he'd question the findings of the blood-alcohol count they'd done at the hospital, raising the fact that since Jimmy had diabetes, his glucose levels could have affected the readings.

But Jimmy had confessed, like a bonehead, so now he was going to have to suck it up, Harry said. Then Daniel Veltman came to the rescue. Before the preliminary hearing, Jimmy and Norine were waiting in a room with Harry Fritts when a knock came at the door. Mr. Fritts opened it (just a crack at first; he never explained why, but Norine finally figured out he was afraid of somebody getting in with a gun — there'd been some threats), and a man with a file stuck a folder into the crack and said something had come up. Norine and Jimmy did not look at each other. They knew it would be bad news.

But when the man had gone and the door closed behind him, Mr. Fritts tossed his own folder across the table, letting all the papers spill out. Norine moved to collect them, but Mr. Fritts held up a hand and said "Never mind, honey — we got 'em."

"Got what?" It was Norine who asked this; Jimmy stared at the floor.

"Not *what*. *Who*. The cops. I don't fucking *believe* this. Now, don't tell your mother I said that." Mr. Fritts raised his hand as if to clap Norine on the back, then seemed to reconsider because of the baby, and hit Jimmy instead, on the shoulder of his borrowed suit. "You are one lucky son of a bitch." He spoke in an excited surge. "The cop who responded that night? That little guy out in the hall, with the zits? Well, turns out he's saying now he forgot to read Jimmy his rights, before he got the confession. If he didn't read him his rights, it doesn't matter if he says he's the Boston Strangler, they can't use it in court." Jimmy, in his chair, came back to life for a moment; he frowned and opened his mouth as if to say something, but Mr. Fritts, perhaps sensing danger, cut him off.

"You kids go out and celebrate. Okay? It's on me." He took out a clip of money and handed Norine a fifty-dollar bill, and Norine took it because she knew that part of his exuberance came from knowing that Norine's mother would think he'd had something to do with this turn of events, which could only be described as a miracle.

Outside, Mary Jo Henzel's sister leaned against the courthouse and smoothed a gum wrapper between her fingers. She had not made any sort of noise when the dismissal came from the judge, and when Norine realized this, she was surprised, because in movies and on TV, when something happened to excuse the defendant, the victim's family always jumped up and vowed to take revenge.

But Sandra Looby didn't say anything as Norine and Jimmy came down the steps. She just kept twisting the gum wrapper, and when they were all on the same level, she put the wrapper into her pocket and smoothed her hands along the sides of her hips, as if wiping them clean or dry.

Jimmy stopped short and Norine bumped into him. Jimmy put his hand out. Norine saw that Sandra Looby recognized her from the night at the hospital; she nodded at Norine, and Norine felt horrified, shrinking in shame, breathless with the punch of it.

"I'm Jim Ploetz, Mrs. Looby. I guess you know that. I don't know if I should be talking to you like this. I mean, not in a legal sense, but — well, I know you must hate me. You should. Do you want me to — " He made a waving gesture toward the sky, as if offering to fly away.

"I don't see how that would do any good." Sandra Looby's voice was surprisingly young sounding, like a teenager's. Yet the eyes locking Jimmy's looked older than she could possibly have been, and Norine saw how thickly the makeup had been applied beneath them to hide the half-moons of sleeplessness and stress. "I'd like to do something to you," she said to Jimmy, "but I wouldn't know what. I could shoot you, I guess. My husband has a gun. Or I could run you over with my car. I suppose that would be like — what do you call that? Poetic something."

"Justice," Norine said.

Sandra just looked at her, and Norine felt herself blush. "M. J. lived with me," Sandra continued. "They didn't get along very good, her and my father, so my husband fixed up the back bedroom — we used to keep junk in there — and we let her stay with us, in exchange for babysitting and cleaning and that."

Jimmy made a noise that could have been translated as "Oh," or "I see," although everything Sandra was telling them had already come out in the news.

"She was fifteen, just," Mary Jo's sister went on, "but she had a fake ID that put her at twenty. She was a lousy babysitter, she hated kids, and as far as the house went, forget it. We'd find things all over, in places where she shoved stuff instead of cleaning it up. Like one time I stepped on something under the baby's rug, I thought it was a toy or something, it turned out to be a dried turd." She paused and looked sharply at Norine, as if daring her to react. Norine, realizing just in time that she had no right to show any disgust to this woman, managed to keep from making a face.

"Why are you telling us this?" Jimmy asked. It was a very different picture of Mary Jo than the one the TV news had presented.

Sandra Looby shrugged, looking surprised by his question. Then she laughed a little, showing a crooked front tooth. Norine wondered for a ridiculous moment if she could get Dr. Payne to fix it for free.

"I don't really know," Mary Jo's sister said. She reached out to touch Norine's pregnancy without waiting for the usual tacit permission. Under the weight of the other woman's hand, Norine understood that Sandra felt entitled to this gesture. "But, like, they made her out to be such a saint. If she was sitting there in that courtroom, she would of cracked up. Look," she said, moving her face closer. Norine's instinct was to pull back, but Jimmy held his ground. "M. J. walked that way every night, late, coming back home from The Glow Worm by herself. I always knew she'd get hit someday. I mean, how could she not? You can't pull that shit forever. No shoulder out there, she always wore black so she wouldn't look fat, and she drank Seven-and-Sevens all night, which the boys bought her. My husband picked her up once on his way home, said she was bouncing all over the road." The sister paused again and squinted, as if trying to assess the effect this information might be having on Jimmy.

"Are you saying it wasn't my fault?"

She laughed again, and this time Norine saw that the tooth was damaged, beyond saving, at the root. "Of course not. Just that it would of been someone else, if it hadn't of been you." She lit a cigarette quickly and blew the smoke away from Norine. "I think I remember you from high school," she said to Jimmy. "I seen you around in the halls. Didn't you used to wear weird pants or something? A couple sizes too small?"

Jimmy reddened. "I didn't have working papers to buy my own clothes yet. I had to wear what my uncles handed down."

"But the day of his first paycheck," Norine spoke up, "He bought some Levi's that fit."

"Well. I don't remember you *that* good." The sister stubbed out her cigarette. "Look, you don't seem like assholes. I'm going to sue you, though. Sorry. My lawyer says even if you don't have the money now, I can get it in little pieces from your paychecks for a long time. Attachment, I think it's called."

Norine felt herself and Jimmy both staring dumbly — in fact, these were the exact words that crossed her mind, *staring dumbly* — at Sandra Looby. "It won't be much," Norine said. "We're having a baby," she added, pressing herself along the curve under her coat.

"I know. But my sister's *dead*." Sandra Looby was not about to let Norine even climb onto the platform of the sympathy train. Down at the curb a car horn beeped, and the three of them looked at the driver, Sandra's husband, who made a violent *get-away-from-them* motion with his hand. "Okay, I gotta go," Sandra said. As they watched her descend the steps of the courthouse, Norine tried not to notice that a safety pin held up her hem.

"Shit," Jimmy said, after a moment.

"I know." They went down the steps themselves, Jimmy supporting her at the elbow. She asked Jimmy, "He lied, didn't he? Daniel Veltman. About reading you your rights?" She watched his hesitation — the hesitation of someone debating himself — and when he told her, "I don't remember," she knew he was lying, too, and inside her she felt the baby churn, and she was thrilled and at the same time saddened by this foreign, hopeful movement beneath her heart.

A few days later, after the news had died down and the change in their phone number came through, after the people at Genesee Mutual said they were sorry but they didn't think people would exactly be lining up to buy insurance from Jimmy right now, Norine found him standing at the living room window, watching the neighbors go to work. It was their six-month wedding anniversary, but neither of them mentioned it, and she wondered if he'd just forgotten, or if he felt as she did that there was nothing to celebrate. When Jimmy stepped behind the drape to avoid being noticed, the baby lurched again in Norine to remind her of two things: that she was not alone, as she had come to believe she was. And that despite what the court said, her husband was not free.

A week after bringing the baby home from the hospital she'd taken the paper-route job, so she and Jimmy could alternate staying home with Carl. Originally they'd planned to bring him to The Romper Room for day care while they both worked, but after the accident and Sandra Looby's lawsuit, it was a luxury they couldn't afford. Now, as she drove home still hearing the man's voice calling her a name after she almost caused a collision, she looked in the rear-view mirror and saw newsprint smudges on her forehead, where her fingers had passed in pushing the hair out of her eyes, and with it the image of crashing. The light in the sky was higher now, sun white on the windshield, melting ice off the hood. Usually through the living room window, when she returned from her job, she could see

Jimmy and Carl sitting in the rocking chair, watching *Sesame Street*. The routine was that Jimmy would hand Norine the baby and get up to shave for work.

He had been given a job at Guthrie's, short-order cooking and cleaning up. Sam Guthrie, who hired him, had been in jail once for a short time. Not for killing anybody, he was quick to say, but his crime was also influenced by alcohol, so he knew what that felt like, and he knew what it felt like to be locked up. Now that he was sober and a Christian, he tried not to judge. He started Jimmy at five-fifty an hour and raised it within two months. They got along; working side by side at the breakfast and lunch grill every weekday, they became familiar with each other's stories and with the smell of their blended sweat.

At first, Jimmy was afraid to be seen by customers, and he hid deep in the kitchen by the rear grill, beyond the view of even those sitting on stools at the counter. But gradually the regulars drew him out. There was a group of them who came in before going to their jobs at the moving company and the car dealership across the street. Jimmy had known some of them in junior high, and now he became their friend again, bumming cigarettes on his breaks, laughing at variations of the same jokes they had all laughed at when they were eighth graders, smoking by the four-square courts while they watched the girls play, hiding butts in cupped hands. Norine was never a part of that shiftless herd, and Jimmy left it when she picked him, in tenth grade, to reform and to love.

She was popular with her classmates and her teachers and this scared Jimmy a little, because he thought you had to choose. And he was afraid at first that she might be a Holy Roller, but her mother turned out to be like no minister he had ever known or even imagined. The first time he picked Norine up at her house, he wore a tie for the mother's sake, which he intended to remove as soon as they were back in the car and pulling out of the driveway. But Mrs. Ellis suggested he take it off as soon as he stepped in the door.

"I try never to wear anything I couldn't sleep in," she told him, as she held out a bowl of popcorn in which she had already greased her long fingers — Jimmy felt it when they shook hands. Mrs. Ellis herself had on sweatpants and a turtleneck. Her brown hair was tied up in a cloth band wrapped around a ponytail. She and her husband and Norine were watching *Police Academy* in the family room. It was Saturday night, and Jimmy planned to take Norine to see a movie at the mall, get something to eat on the way. But Norine made no move to leave the room, once she had gotten up to say hi to Jimmy and pat him down on the couch next to her.

"Do you mind — just for a little while?" she said, leaning forward to take a sip of her mother's Coke. "I thought this was going to be stupid, but I like it so far." Jimmy looked around him, without being obvious about it, while they all watched. It was a classy house, but comfortable too, and he did not feel nervous around her parents, the way he felt around his own. Mr. Ellis was quiet in his chair and laughed in low tones, but his wife's amusement rang through the room and became something Jimmy listened for more than the punchlines on the screen.

They ended up staying for the whole movie, and at the end of it, when Mrs. Ellis got up to eject the cassette, Jimmy leaned over to hand her the cover and said, his heart beating in his throat because he was afraid it might be the entirely wrong thing, "I thought you'd be writing a sermon or something."

"I finished it this morning," she told him. "I always have to watch a dumb movie afterward. It brings me back down to earth."

"If anybody knew what went on in this house on Saturday nights," Norine added to Jimmy, "my mother would be disbarred. Or fired. Whatever you call it, in a church." She laughed, and he heard that she had inherited her mother's generous sound.

"What's the sermon about?" he persisted, following Mrs. Ellis from the room, forgetting for a moment whom it was he had come to see.

"Oh," she said, dumping burnt kernels into the trash beneath the sink, "Fear. Love. Faith. Redemption." She picked a piece of white corn from between her teeth. "The usual." Jimmy felt himself blush in the fluorescence of her smile.

The title of the sermon was "Shirley Wants Her Nickel Back." It came, she explained to her parishioners, from a jump rope jingle she had chanted as a child:

> Shirley Temple, movie star,
> Loves to ride the trolley car.
> When the train goes off the track,
> Shirley wants her nickel back.

The sermon addressed the similarities between a trolley ride and the journey through life. How it was easy to have faith when God, the conductor, sped us along the predicted route. But what happened when the train of our destiny suddenly became derailed? Well — here the Reverend Ellis pulled her fingers into a fist — God would help us to see that the journey we'd bought the ticket for had, in fact, a different destination than the one we ourselves intended.

"But no matter where the train takes us, He's along for the ride. No matter what we've done, no matter what shame we carry, that's His promise to us — the covenant of His infinite mercy and His abiding love." Norine's mother paused, then took off her glasses and bowed her head toward her chest. "Let us pray."

Sitting in a church pew the next morning for the first time in his life, Jimmy looked sideways at Norine, wondering if he could take her hand. But before he could even begin to make a move, she reached over and laced her fingers through his. Next to her on the other side, her father looked down and frowned. Jimmy had no way of knowing that Norine's gesture was born of embarrassment. She had thought her mother's sermon was simple in the worst sense of the word, and trite. Life as a train ride — oh, *please*.

But Jimmy took her touch as a signal that she had been as moved as he was; that she wanted, in reaching for his hand, to seal the feeling between them. When she tried to remove her hand from his a few moments later, he tightened his grip to show her that he wasn't ready to give it back.

Norine was almost ten when her mother started minister school, thirteen when she graduated and began her job. Before that, Norine remembered a woman who was in bed when she left for the bus in the mornings, and was sometimes only getting dressed when Norine came home. She did not go out except to shop for groceries, at the store where she had all the aisles memorized and her routine timed, and to pick up the newspaper from the end of the driveway and the mail from the box by the fence. This had been the way things were since sometime between Norine's first and second grades. She did not recall the exact moment she realized that her mother never left the house anymore; it had not happened suddenly, but nobody seemed to challenge it, once it began. As she grew older, the memories of her mother outside — picking Norine up from school for a dentist appointment, climbing a stepladder under an apple tree in the fall — faded from full pictures to glimpses of movement and color that came when she was not expecting them, leaving flickering images she did not dare to trust. Inside the house her mother was cheerful, filled with laughter and love. This was all that mattered to Norine, and as she became accustomed to running errands for her mother on the way home from school, to accepting rides from her friends' parents and to her father's unreadable sighs, she forgot that her mother was different from other people, in that her world contained six rooms.

On the day during Norine's fourth-grade winter that her mother followed her to the bus stop after breakfast and waited with her until it came, Norine did not even allow herself to realize what had happened — that her mother had stepped outside — until the bus was pulling away, and she saw her mother's white smile and wave through the grimy pane. Nobody said anything that night and Norine was afraid to bring it up, but the next day her mother announced that there were going to be some changes around here, that she was going back to school. At first Norine was glad to think that her mother could do whatever she wanted, and would not need to make all those elaborate arrangements anymore. But as time passed she began to wish for the indoor mother again, because Norine had to share the new one with other people and places. She missed watching *One Life to Live* together every day, the feel of her mother's slippers under the afghan they shared on the couch. She was ashamed of herself for wanting her mother to go back to being sick, and she never let anybody know that she felt this way. She also missed being needed, until she found Jimmy Ploetz waiting for her in the blue jokes and cigarette smoke outside the school cafeteria. When he looked at her across the parking lot as the buses pulled into their going-home line (she could always tell when he was looking, though he moved his head when her gaze settled anywhere close to him), she felt that rare and intoxicating sensation of having been recognized.

The morning after the accident that killed Mary Jo Henzel, Norine went, by herself, to tell her mother about it. Jimmy was still in jail. It was Friday and her father was already at work when she arrived at the house, poured herself coffee, which she did not usually drink, and began to talk. As she spoke she watched her mother's fingers, which rested on the keyboard of the PC where her next sermon was taking shape as she listened to *Good Morning America* on TV. The skin looked raw red and puckered, despite the medical lotions she coated them with at night. Norine knew it was her mother's one concession to vanity that she was embarrassed about those hands. When she served Communion, she gave out the blocks of bread with her palms facing upward, as if she were receiving the sacrament herself, instead of bestowing it on the parishioners.

There wasn't very much for Norine to say; it was all out in a few sentences. She felt disconnected, as if she were giving a book report on another family's story, telling details of a drama without acknowledging it as her own. Her mother's eyes closed after the first words, and when Norine was finished, she waited for the eyes to open and for her mother to come over and tuck her into a hug. Reverend Ellis was known as a hugger; in the greeting line after each service, she hugged people instead of shaking their hands. (The congregation took this to be a nurturing gesture; only Norine guessed that it was related to the condition of her mother's skin.)

But after hearing Norine's story, her mother leaned back in her chair and said, "How is poor Jimmy?" and Norine wanted to scream *What about Mary Jo Henzel?* and she might have, if other houses weren't so close to them on either side. Instead she waited while her mother went to the bank to get bail money, and she turned off the TV because of the local news updates, which all showed the same foggy photograph of Mary Jo Henzel, followed by the announcement of Jimmy's name uttered through a newscaster's curled lip. She went up to her childhood bedroom, where she fiddled with pink pens from the white desk and walked around looking at the walls, at the posters she had hung in high school and earlier, boy actors from magazines like *Tiger Beat*, and ballerinas in arabesque over a promise Norine had believed once: *If you can imagine it, you can achieve it.* That was back when she assumed she would have a different kind of life than the one she ended up with. Who didn't? — she knew that — but other people at least seemed to have some idea about *how* the wrong life had happened to them. Where the train had gone off the track.

And yet she *did* know. She'd been supposed to go to college; that was the plan all along. Though her father had not been able to do so and her mother's degree was a shady one, conferred by some correspondence program she applied to in haste so that she'd have something to put on her application to the equally shady divinity school, they had always told Norine they wanted her to get an education. She thought she might become an English teacher, or a historian. She loved words, and she especially loved the way people spoke and wrote in olden days, as in the letters John and Abigail Adams sent to each other when she was keeping the homestead in Massachusetts while he helped forge the Declaration of Independence in Philadelphia. *My Dearest Friend*, they addressed each other in the letters, which were so reverent that Norine sometimes wanted to cry. The most memorable passages — the ones Norine had to shut the book on when she went to page through it again while she was pregnant — had to do with Abigail's sixth pregnancy and her premonition, which proved correct, that the child would be stillborn. She also worried that she herself would die in childbirth, leaving John bereft and her children motherless. Yet it wasn't all sad; Norine enjoyed reading John's catalogue of Abigail's faults — which she herself had solicited from him — including the observation, "You very often hang your Head like a Bulrush." And she was amused when they followed the custom of the times in avoiding explicit references to pregnancy in their correspondence, saying instead that Abigail was "in circumstances."

Norine couldn't even imagine what Abigail must have gone through, having to take care of a farm and all those children by herself, with the threats of smallpox and war so close by. When she read books about such people in history she was tempted to wish she had lived back then, so she'd have some sense of what she was made of. As it was, she had no idea.

The day Norine found out she'd been accepted to Buffalo State, and her father took her out to celebrate at The Breakfast Barn, just the two of them, and told her how proud he was of her, she looked down at her plate and mumbled that Jimmy Ploetz had asked her to marry him, and that she'd accepted. She did not mention the baby yet; they planned to do that together. She would never forget the shocked silence that came back at her across the table, or the affliction in her father's eyes when she finally raised her own to look at him. Wordlessly she begged him to argue with her, or even to insist, but he did neither, and it made it worse when Norine realized that he was holding back what he wanted to say because he thought this would make it all easier for her.

They broke the pregnancy news that same evening. When the test had turned up positive, she'd panicked and thought about taking care of the situation herself, without telling anyone. But one night while they were watching *Matlock* alone at her parents' house, she started crying — hormones, she supposed — and Jimmy got it out of her. She couldn't tell what he was thinking, at first. But a few minutes later, grinning like an idiot (though she tried not to think of that phrase as she watched his face), he said they should get married, and a few minutes after *that*, he began making his pitch to name the baby after Norine's mother. "It would work either way," he said — "Carl or Carla. Isn't that cool?" — and she tried not to realize that this idea had not just come to him; he had thought of it before. She had no intention of doing any such thing, but she agreed in order to stop his wheedling, and she agreed because it was a less pressing question, at the moment, than the one about whether she should marry him or not. So it was her own fault when he told her mother, before Norine could stop him, that she was going to have a namesake; after that, she had no choice.

When they sat her parents down and told them about the baby, her father went into the kitchen because something was stuck in his throat, but her mother was quick to get over Norine's change of course. She said she was thrilled with the idea of having Jimmy for a son-in-law. What she was really thrilled with, Norine knew, was the idea that it was her ministry that had turned him around. After joining the church, he'd cut down on his beer drinking and shaped up, even graduating on time, when that had seemed only a remote possibility before he met Norine.

"You can always go to college," Carla Ellis told her daughter. "Just because you don't start school when everyone else does doesn't mean anything; after all, look at me." That's when Jimmy told her the baby's name would be Carl or Carla, and Norine had to keep her mouth shut. Her mother beamed and said God was smiling on them all.

The morning after Mary Jo Henzel died, with her mother at the bank getting Jimmy's bail, Norine longed to stretch out on her old bed and sleep but she knew she would never want to get up if she did, so she went back downstairs, where she would be an adult because she had to. Before she left her room, though, she stood for a moment in front of the mirror, where she used to watch herself cry for the pure fascination of it; she could never quite get over how grotesque her face — any adult's face — could look, in the seize of tears. But she did not cry now. In the glass she saw the same high forehead, the same brown hair parted in the middle and the too-small green eyes but for which, she secretly believed, she would be beautiful. She turned sideways and folded her hands over her mound of baby stomach, remembering how she used to examine herself, in this same mirror, for bloating after she'd eaten an extra doughnut for breakfast or a slice of her mother's pie. But this fat, now, was different; this was alive. She patted her belly and turned away from the reflection. When she shut the door she heard something fall from one of the walls inside, but she did not turn back to find out what it was. Then she went to the bathroom and threw up for the first time in her pregnancy.

When her mother returned they went to the jail together to pick up Jimmy and pay his way home. He was rumpled and silent, and he looked neither of them in the eye. He slept the whole rest of the day — he had not slept at all in the cell, he told them, though it was more comfortable than you might guess — and the women kept their voices low in the kitchen and said many things without words.

Her mother left in the afternoon and told Norine she would be back the next day to keep Jimmy company while Norine took some time for herself to do whatever she wanted — get a haircut, breathe some air. The apartment held a strange vibration, like an echo without sound. Norine did not want to go anywhere or do anything, but in the end because her mother urged her she drove half an hour east on the Thruway toward Syracuse, listening to the road roll beneath her, trying to imagine that she was alone in life and could head wherever she wanted, and hoping to find something in front of her that she had not been expecting, something that would surprise her into being grateful for the miracle of her own breath. At the same time this magic would eliminate Mary Jo Henzel's death, and, while it was at it, decide for Jimmy that he would quit drinking again. By the time she had all of this figured out, Norine was afraid of what she wanted because it was impossible, and everything that seemed possible to her was what she did not want. She changed directions at the next exit and went home.

When she entered the apartment she found her mother and Jimmy sitting at the kitchen table, splitting a Genny Cream, and when they looked up at the sound of the door opening, they showed her expressions so guilty she might have caught them in a kiss. They fumbled around like lovers trying to hide the evidence, and Norine had to tell them to settle down. She tried to smile at them, but she could feel her brows wavering, and when Jimmy went into the bathroom she said to her mother, "How can you *drink* with him?"

"It's his last one," her mother told her. "He promised — this was his farewell toast. I've got someone coming over, from AA, to talk to him." Norine felt her face swelling with tears so heavy it was hard to breathe. Her mother came over to hold her shoulders while she cried, and Norine wanted to push the ugly hands away, but she did not have the energy or the nerve.

Finally, she fell asleep on the couch. Her mother offered her lap as a pillow but Norine refused, and her mother sat and watched her from the easy chair. When Norine awoke, her mother was gone and Jimmy held her, and it was dark outside. The TV picture was turned on but not the sound. Norine struggled to sit up, but Jimmy would not let go easily; she had to push him away.

"What day is it?" she asked, because it had been so long since she had thought about time. When he told her Saturday night, she felt herself already dropping into the deep cave of the weekend, and could not imagine crawling her way back out. She did not believe she would be able to sleep, because she had not slept the night before, and the night before that, she had awakened to news of death.

But she did sleep, and the next day she went grocery shopping, as usual, and to the pizza and video stores, making the motions of what had been her life, and it wasn't until the following day, when the news carried film of the dead girl's funeral, that she let herself remember what had changed in the world because of what her husband had done to it. (Her *husband*! She still couldn't get used to it, let alone to the fact that she would soon be a *mother*.) From that day forward she and Jimmy learned to look away from people and from each other, and in the month before Carl was born they stopped going to childbirth class, so that when Norine's labor came they had forgotten most of what they had learned, and Jimmy sat outside in the waiting room while Norine squeezed a nurse's hand to get through.

Now, as she returned with her heart still speeding from the near collision at the end of her route, no one was home. Something felt wrong even before she stepped inside the apartment. With a mother's certainty, she could sense that her baby was not here, that his breath and smell and pulse were absent from these three rooms, and for a moment she felt shock and chagrin at having entered the wrong house with her key; in the same moment she knew it wasn't the wrong house, but something wrong in the right house, which was worse. There was no real reason for panic, but she felt it nonetheless.

She snatched the phone up and punched at the numbers for Guthrie's. "Is Jimmy there?" she asked, before anyone could speak on the other end. "Did he come in early? Does he have Carl?"

It was Sam Guthrie. "Norine?" Sam said. "No. I haven't heard from him. He's due in at seven. Why?" His voice was confused, and then it picked up her alarm. "Did something— "

She hung up and swore, short and hot into the mouthpiece, the exhaled breath coming back at her with the rank smell of terror. She returned the phone fast to its cradle and felt her fingers vibrating from the smack. She yanked it off again and called her mother, who answered on the fifth ring.

"They're both here," Mrs. Ellis said. "Honey, what's the matter?"

"How did they get there?"

"I picked them up."

"Is he okay?"

"Of course. We're having coffee."

"No, I meant Carl."

"Oh. Well, of course. Why wouldn't he be?" Her mother sounded irritated.

"Don't you get mad at *me*," Norine said, and she was surprised to hear that her voice came out angry, when what she felt most was fear. "Listen, I'm coming over to get them." She hung up before her mother could answer, and went out to the car without putting her coat back on. She didn't realize it until she was halfway there, and even then she didn't feel the cold; she was insulated by a rage she hadn't seen coming, a fever taking sudden hold.

Her mother opened the door for her. "Look who's here," she said, in a cheerful voice aimed at the baby. Jimmy was already standing up.

"Can you drive me to work, hon?" he said to Norine.

"What do you think I'm doing here?" She yanked the zipper on Carl's snowsuit too hard, causing the baby to cry.

"Here, let me," her mother offered, but Norine shook her head. "At least take my jacket," her mother said, but Norine refused that, too, not trusting herself to speak. Her mother stood in the window as Norine backed out of the driveway, ignoring her mother's wave.

"You scared me," Norine said, hating the way her husband slumped next to her in the front seat like a scolded teenager.

"Why?"

"Why do you *think*?" Then she sighed, because he really looked as if he didn't know the answer. "You can't just take a woman's baby and not tell her where, Jimmy."

"But he's mine, too."

"I know." She slowed the car, realizing that she was finally about to bring up the question she'd wanted to ask him for a while now. Why did she need courage? Because — she realized later — so much depended on his answer. "Listen," she said, trying to figure out how to put it. For all her thinking about it, she'd never come up with the words. "Listen." Hearing herself stall, she took a breath and mumbled, "You didn't mean it that day when you brought up suicide, did you?"

He jerked his head to look at her and said, "*What?*"

"A couple of months ago. After a meeting. You came home and said you didn't know if you could keep going."

"Oh, God." He lifted his fingers to the side of his head and rubbed slowly, appearing to smooth out his thoughts. "That had nothing to do with suicide, for God's sake. I was talking about staying sober." He was silent for a moment, then added, "Why would you think I meant that?"

She didn't speak the words she heard in her head: *Because I think you should. Think about it, not actually* do *it. Somebody else is dead because of you.*

Instead she said, "But you'd tell me, right, if you felt that way?"

"Of course," he said, so immediately that she knew he didn't mean it. He sighed in the manner that always signaled an effort to appease her. "Look, Nor, I'm handling it. Guys in the program are helping me. So is your mother."

Norine's foot skipped on the accelerator. "Can't you talk to me sometimes? I'm your wife." She'd meant to say "I'm your *wife*," but the emphasis came out on "*I'm*." The car swerved slightly as she grabbed with her foot for the brake. "Be careful," Jimmy said, his hand darting up to grab the dash.

"Be careful? Be *careful*?" Norine repeated. Thinking about what he'd said, she made a sound that Jimmy mistook for laughter. Then he must have mistaken the laughter for invitation, because he hurried to engage her in talk, and to take advantage of the warm feelings he must have imagined seeping between them like heat through the open vents.

"Your mom was telling me about all that time she didn't go out of the house, when you were in grade school," he said. He was looking out his window at the strip of stores next to the Texaco where he had pumped gas in junior high. "How come you never told me that? I could totally relate."

Norine felt something digging into her stomach, but when she reached to adjust her seatbelt she realized it came from inside. "Well, it was way over by the time you met her. I figured, what difference did it make."

They were nearing Guthrie's, and ahead of her Norine saw a car pulled off the road. Coming closer, she saw that it was Willie Mooney's Oldsmobile, with a tire blown out, and he was trying to flag somebody down. She drove right by him, speeding up as she passed.

"Hey, you should have stopped for him," Jimmy said.

"Why? He's a loser."

"He's your colleague," Jimmy said, barely loud enough for her to hear him. He hated it when she acted in the way he called *high and mighty*. "Not everybody's cut out for college. It's not the be-all and end-all, you know." She knew what he was thinking: that maybe she thought her husband was a loser, too. "You and him have the same job, Nor."

"You and *he*," she said, also hating her own snobbery, but doing her best not to say what was really in her head: *Whose fault is it that I had to take that crap job, anyway?* Then she recalled Jimmy's choice of words and snorted. "Yeah, Willie Mooney's my *colleague*," she said, watching Jimmy next to her shake his head as if to say *I give up*.

She was gripping the steering wheel tight because in her head at that moment was not Willie Mooney but something else, the memory of a day during the winter of her fourth-grade year, a snow day, no school, when she and her mother sat on the couch and watched TV for six straight hours, through all the game shows and into the soaps, getting up only to use the bathroom and to look at the snow. Just as it was getting dark, Norine dozed and heard her mother go out to the garage, close the electric door that operated by a button, and start the car. She told Norine that the furnace wasn't working, and that they were going to sit in the car, where the heat was on, and warm up. Her mother was writing something at the kitchen table, and when she folded it over Norine saw her father's name on it. Her mother tucked her into the back seat of the car, and Norine had just fallen asleep again under the blanket in the back seat when her mother shook her gently and said, "It's working again, honey. Come back inside." It was the next morning that her mother took her to the bus stop in the cold. The note was gone from the table and Norine saw the ripped-up pieces of blue stationery in the wastebasket. She thought about fishing them out to put them together — she'd always liked puzzles — but something told her she didn't want to know what this picture would turn out to be.

As she pulled into Guthrie's, snow glittered on the road. The smell of gas, which wafted out from the stoves in the restaurant, made her want to gag. She parked and waited while Jimmy got his things together. She saw that he wanted to keep talking, but she drummed her hands against the wheel. He tried to kiss her cheek, which she turned away.

"Nor, what's the matter?"

Norine wanted to shout, "You *killed* somebody is what's the matter!" but she kept it in; his door was open. Through her window, she watched Willie Mooney get out of a Plymouth Horizon and wave at the driver as he made his way toward the Texaco. Even from this distance, she could see that the skin of his hands was gray with the same shadow of newsprint staining her own.

"Go on," she said, shooing Jimmy away from the car. She felt her nostrils flaring above her smile. "We'll pick you up tonight." He smiled back and went in to work. She had parked near the rear, but he walked around to the front entrance, gave her a thumbs-up, and pushed the door open with his shoulder. He seemed to stand straighter than she had seen him in a long time, more at home with the weight he carried through the world.

She went home, where there was a message from her mother on the machine. "Norine? It's Mommy. Can you please tell me what I did wrong?" Norine swore and smacked *Erase*. Then she called the police station, got connected to Daniel Veltman, and asked him to meet her at the old gas station behind the high school. After they'd hung up, she stood for a moment with her finger paused over the button that said *Memo* — the feature that allowed her and Jimmy to leave messages for each other — and pressed it, leaning her face forward so he'd be sure to hear it clearly. "I'm taking a trip, Jimmy. Carl's with me, he'll be fine. We both will." She hesitated, knowing there were a few seconds of time left on the tape. "Don't you dare hate me — you did this to yourself." After the beep sounded that told her the message had recorded, she realized how weary she was, and she considered erasing it, canceling with Daniel, and just lying down for a nap.

But instead she packed Carl into his snowsuit again, and got back in the car. At the drive-through bank window she took out everything left in the account, which was eighty-four dollars. At the Quik Mart she locked Carl inside and ran in to buy a package of Little Debbie's and a pint-sized carton of orange juice. These she ate and drank using the steering wheel to rest her elbows as she licked chocolate from the tips of her fingers. She did not taste the food, so although she could tell from their texture that the cakes were stale, it didn't matter. She took in the sugar and pulp until she felt full, but it was not filling the space she aimed for, and she pulled back onto the road with a belch, hating her own indelicacy, tasting acid and fat.

Carl fell asleep in his seat. Norine did not stop driving until she reached Old Post Road, where the Loobys lived, and where Mary Jo Henzel had died. But Norine didn't go down as far as the place of the accident, which was two miles further out, though she knew exactly what it had looked like that night — the underbrush growing right up to the edge of the pavement, so there would have been no shoulder, no escape — because she had driven this road often before the accident, and since then, she had seen it so many times in her mind.

She drove slowly, looking at names on mailboxes, until she saw L OBY, and then she braked. The houses were set back from the road and scattered, across yards now crusted with snow; Norine saw the marks of boots and aluminum saucers stamped on the Loobys' front lawn.

Nobody lived out here unless they had to. Old Post was a hick back road, a shortcut you took to the Thruway, if you'd lived here long enough to learn. Through a window, Norine saw Sandra Looby bend to pick something up from the floor — a toy? a sock? a piece of cookie? — and she yelled something, as if to answer a call from another room. Then she moved out of sight.

Norine made a three-point turn and headed back in the direction from which she had come. It would have been faster to drive straight down Old Post, but she refused to take Carl over that part of this road. Besides, there was no hurry. Instead she took the long way, having to stop at all the lights in town, pretending not to notice people she knew — people who went to her mother's church — driving other cars or dropping envelopes into a mailbox or walking their dogs.

At the broken-down Sunoco station, which had been out of operation for years now, she turned in to see that Daniel had beaten her there. They parked the way he had taught her, ever since they'd started meeting like this, with their cars facing in opposite directions so they could talk to each other through their driver's-side windows. Like we lazy cops do, he told her, making both of them smile.

But today, instead of speaking to him across those safe inches, she invited him to come over and sit in her car. He hesitated for a moment, then got out of the Crown Vic slowly, approaching her passenger door as he might approach someone he suspected of having a weapon. Norine giggled. "Get in, silly," she told him. When he did, he swiveled to look back at Carl, who began to fuss until Norine reached back to hand him a toy.

When he'd turned frontward again but still Norine remained silent, Daniel said, "Well?" He was tapping the tops of his trousers with his fingertips. Norine knew he wanted to touch her.

"I'm leaving," she told him, realizing that she said it less because it was true than because she wanted to get a rise out of him.

"Where?" His lack of alarm showed he didn't believe her.

She shrugged. "Just out of *here*. For a little bit, anyway. I don't know, maybe I'll be back." They both knew she would be, but he indulged her by playing along.

"I was thinking of sending a letter to your captain," she went on. The notion had occurred to her in a wild burst of inspiration during her drive. She did not intend to follow through on this, either, but she knew it would prompt a reaction. "Saying what you did for Jimmy. You must have gotten in trouble, I don't care what you say."

Daniel tried to whistle, but it came out in a squeak. "Whoa. Jesus. Don't even *think* about doing something like that, Norine." She liked how his voice sounded saying her full name, instead of shortening it the way Jimmy did. She could smell him sweating. "You think it would be better, somehow, if they know I *lied*, instead of thinking I made a mistake?" He shook his head and shifted in the Subaru's narrow seat. "It's over now. History. Just be glad we all got out of it okay." When she made a noise, he amended, "Well, okay, not *okay*, but better than it could have been." He stopped himself short of saying *better than we all should have*, but she heard it anyway in his tone.

"Besides," he went on, and she could tell he would think about regretting, later, what he was about to say. "I didn't do it for Jimmy."

She nodded, acknowledging that this was something she already knew. It was hard to look at him straight on, so she stared ahead through the windshield. After Daniel opened the door and stepped out, she waited for the sound of his car leaving, then realized he'd already gone.

It was beginning to snow, lightly, a few flakes here and there, and she thought that probably what she should do was go home, erase the message she'd left for Jimmy, and stop being such a drama queen; then she remembered that the weatherman had said it would probably turn to rain, and driving in the rain was a comfort to her, the rhythmic sound of the wipers dulling the unpleasant pulse in her brain. At the Thruway, she hesitated only a moment before choosing the line of traffic that would lead her west and then north.

Up here the country was bare and gray. It felt like driving off one planet and onto another without need of a bridge or passport, only a slight shift of altitude in the way you looked at things. Ahead of her were signs for towns whose names felt halfway biblical: Pope Corners, Lustra, Fort Galilee. In Lustra, at the side of the highway, she passed a group of people ice-skating, and pulled over to watch.

She had loved to watch skating when she was a kid. At the end of her street was a depressed ring of meadow the boys flooded, every Thanksgiving, to freeze themselves a rink for the rest of the winter. In junior high Jimmy had played in a few of the pick-up hockey games, but then he quit. He did not tell Norine why, but one night when he was having dinner with Norine's family, he confessed. "We couldn't afford to buy me skates, so I took my sister's old ones and painted them with black shoe polish. The guys could still tell, though. *Here comes Tonya Harding*, they said."

Norine had wanted to smile, but she was afraid Jimmy would feel offended. Her mother got up from her chair and came around to hug Jimmy from behind. For his next birthday, her parents bought him a new pair of hockey skates. It was just after they'd told her parents about the baby, and until then Norine had held out hope that her father might sit her down and tell her that baby or no baby, he wouldn't let her marry the wrong man for the wrong reason. The fact that the skates were from both her parents was what let her know, once and for all, that her father was not going to fight her on it. And when he gave in without fighting, she felt betrayed.

At the edge of the road now in the oddly named town, she didn't know how long she had watched the skaters, but it had been growing dark for a while. The snow fell steadily, forming a film on her car. When the last kids changed into their boots and sneakers and headed off with their skates slung over their shoulders, she fixed Carl a bottle and settled back against the headrest, listening to her son behind her making contented sipping sounds. She closed her eyes, then opened them when she heard another noise that sounded familiar, but that she couldn't quite place. Squinting through the trees at the side of the road, she saw a half-lit neon sign that said "Bowl-a-Drome." She thought she could hear pins crashing distantly and it made her want to smile, thinking of the crazy babysitter her parents used to hire to take care of her after school, when her mother went to minister class.

The babysitter, whose name was Robin, had told Norine that thunder was the sound of God bowling in the sky. Lightning meant he'd scored a strike. Norine loved her, although Robin never came back after the day she taught Norine how to use a Ouija board, and spelled out the message that Norine's house would burn down some night when everyone was asleep. Soon after that, Robin's father was arrested for fraud, and the family moved up to Maine. Sitting in her car these many years later, Norine smelled the fresh snow and wondered where Robin was now.

She pulled off the Thruway and parked in the bowling alley's lot. Carl seemed in danger of falling asleep and she knew this was a bad sign, because if he slept now, he'd be up all night. She listened to his breath for a while, watching the Bowl-a-Drome's red sign blinking against the sky. Tentatively she opened her door and put her foot down. The cold solidity was a comfort, and she stepped out of the car.

An ambulance whizzed by on the main road with its siren wailing, and it took a moment for Norine, after the sound faded, to regulate her breath. She glanced back into the car, but the baby remained sleeping. "I *told* her it wouldn't work without sugar," a young woman said to an older one who might have been her mother, as each tossed a bowling bag into the back seat of a Rambler. "It tasted just like paste." When they drove away, bits of wet gravel spat onto Norine's shoes.

Flakes fell in her bangs and she brushed the wet strands aside. It felt good to have the hair off her forehead; maybe, she thought, she should consider growing it out. She unbuckled Carl, who whimpered until Norine found the pacifier and handed it to him.

Inside the bowling alley, it was much lighter than she'd expected. She thought such lounges were designed to be dim, the better to hide how dingy both the place and the people were.

But here, the lanes themselves were illuminated not only by fluorescence overhead, but also along the edges by strings of chili-pepper bulbs, giving it all a festive look that made Norine feel better, despite her resistance to being cheered.

The bar area, too, was bright, and this she welcomed because she knew it would make it harder for Carl to fall back asleep. There were more people sitting around tables than at the bar itself, and they were all more or less watching something on the big-screen TV. It was a play-off game between the Dolphins and the Bills. Most of the audience rooted for Buffalo, yet there were apparently enough Miami fans to liven things up. The Dolphins went ahead by six and some guy yelled "Flutie sucks!" and somebody else yelled back "*You* suck, asshole," and then a woman sitting alone at a table noticed Norine with the baby and said, "Hey, everybody, shut up." Norine looked at the woman with gratitude and, invited by a nod, took the seat the woman pulled out for her. Norine assumed she was hooked up with one of the men at the bar.

"Cute baby," the woman said, and Norine blushed because although she loved Carl, she knew he wasn't really all that attractive as babies went, and at the moment he wore dried milk at the corners of his curled-down mouth, and an expression that made him look gassy. "I used to have one of those," the woman continued, and Norine said, "What, a baby?" and the woman laughed and said, "No, I mean that exact diaper bag, with the daisies. I had the baby too, of course. Except now he's nineteen. Hasn't been cute for about ten years now, maybe more. But you get used to the partying, and the coming home late, and the stealing from your purse, and—have I left anything out? Oh, yeah, the cursing. That's always fun to listen to. Of course, he gets you on the double standard, with that one. That's what he actually said to me one day, in high school—that I had a double standard when it came to language in the house. It was okay for Mitch and me to swear, but not Davy. I gave the 'as long as you're living under my roof' speech, all that crap. But I also said to him, hey, if you can use words like *double standard*, and tell me I should be *frugal*, why don't you try harder at school, and make something of yourself? You could be a lawyer or something. Know what he does now?"

Norine shook her head, feeling breathless just listening to the sentence fusillade.

"Works at the Valvoline," the woman said. "Over on Exeter? If that's where you go to get your oil changed, you've probably seen him. He's probably lubed and tightened your car up. For all the good *that'll* do him in the world." She sat back sighing, and under the table Norine glimpsed her unfortunate choice of leggings, fuchsia, tucked into a pair of knockoff L. L. Bean boots. Above the leggings, a too-small white turtleneck hugged her bosom and displayed old perspiration stains under the arms. Her brown hair fell to her shoulders in purchased waves, and though at first glance Norine had taken her to be close to her own age, she saw now that the woman's face showed a pattern of wrinkles, or what Norine's mother had, in a sermon once, called "experience grooves."

"I don't live around here," Norine said. This information seemed to make her new companion suspicious; she pulled her beer back toward herself slightly on its cardboard coaster, though she did not take a sip. "I was just out for a drive, is all," Norine added.

"In *this*?" The woman tilted her head toward the window, and looking out Norine could see that it was coming down hard now, swirling in the wind.

"It wasn't snowing when we left, at least not this bad."

"How far away you from?"

"About two hours. Down near Rochester."

"Well, you're not going to make it back there tonight. Why don't you just sit tight, have a few drinks and get a room at the Tree Top, let the guys plow, and in the morning you can go home." The woman nodded again, this time in the direction of the men at the bar, who were obviously not preparing to be plowing out anything anytime soon. She yelled something in a low tone to the bartender, who came over and put a red drink down in front of Norine.

"What is it?" Norine asked. It looked like cherry soda, but when she took a sip, she could tell it contained alcohol.

Without answering the woman said, "See, he has the right idea" and jutted her head toward Carl, who — despite the noise around him, or maybe because of it — had snuggled his head to one side of his booster seat and fallen asleep. "Just relax, for once in your life. It's a snowstorm, get cozy. You're among friends."

Friends — the word conjured up, for Norine, the image of herself with Trish and Melanie, and their high-school drives around town with the radio blaring. When she'd hooked up with Jimmy, they stopped inviting her along. *Who are my friends now?* she thought, taking another sip of the delicious red soda. *Well, Jimmy, of course. And Daniel.* But neither of them was a friend, exactly. They were both something more complicated than that.

She exchanged names with the woman. "I knew a Norine once," Paula said. "A teacher at the school my kid went to. She farted once in assembly and never lived it down. It's a pretty name, though."

"It comes from the same root as *honor*," Norine said. As she heard the words, she felt the need to duck her head to her drink. Before she could finish it, Paula had another one delivered to her.

"So why the road trip in a blizzard?" Paula herself was nursing her beer; the fact that she wasn't guzzling made Norine trust her more than she might have, otherwise. "It's not exactly sightseeing weather. Not to mention there's nothing up here to see."

Norine felt herself beginning to relax, as Paula had directed her, and realized what she'd been missing. She'd never been much of a drinker — she didn't hang out with that crowd — and now that Jimmy was in the program, she didn't bring home beer or wine. They couldn't afford it anyway, but even if they could have, she'd have kept it out of the house so he wouldn't be tempted. "I don't know what I'd do without you, Nor," he'd said, more than once when he'd come home from a meeting and described the trouble other people had with family members who drank around them, while they were trying to stay sober. "I'm the luckiest guy in the world."

When Paula asked what had brought her up north, all Norine could get out was "My husband" before the other woman nodded sympathetically, as if she knew what was coming next.

"He cheat on you?"

"No." Of this Norine was certain. She knew Jimmy would never risk losing her — or (it was almost too painful to admit) her mother, in that way.

"So what'd he do, then? Or is it just general misery?" Paula doodled on a cocktail napkin — nothing identifiable, just random marks to show she had been there.

Norine rubbed her lip, which felt fuzzy. Carl gurgled once, then settled back into sleep. She realized that she had never talked to anyone about the accident, except for the morning after it, when she'd gone to tell her mother. She felt what she knew to be a perverse thrill as she leaned forward and whispered, "He killed someone."

"*Wow.*" Paula had the sense to look slightly ashamed of the smile that came to her face when she heard this, but not ashamed enough to get rid of it. "How? Like with a gun or something? Or I knew a guy once who beat his wife to death with her hair dryer. The noise drove him crazy, he said."

"No. It was an accident." Norine turned Carl's seat away so he wouldn't be able to hear her if he woke up, though of course he wouldn't have understood, anyway. "He was driving home, and he'd drunk too much, and he hit a girl who was walking home in the road."

"Oh." Though Paula tried to hide it, Norine could see she was disappointed. It wasn't a *murder*, then, and likely there were not many juicy details. But her new friend summoned a valiant show of interest. "So what happened? They put him in jail, or what?"

Norine shook her head, once again enjoying the sensation of liquor humming through her blood. "We thought it would be like eight to fifteen, for manslaughter, but he got off on a technicality. The cop who arrested him said he'd made a mistake in procedure. Which wasn't true, but he had a crush on me in high school. The cop."

"Jesus." Paula whistled. "That's more than a crush, honey." She'd slowed down even further on her beer, and Norine didn't know what to make of it; was it related to the fact that she'd told Paula her husband had committed his crime after drinking? Somehow, it made Norine more determined to finish this second drink, and to order another. It had always been like this for her: whatever another person felt or did, she instinctively adopted the opposite attitude or behavior. The first time she noticed it was in sixth grade, when they were putting on *H. M. S. Pinafore* for parents and the rest of the school. Norine was only part of the chorus, but she still felt nervous about going onstage. Yet standing in the wings next to Kelly Wexler, who was playing Buttercup, she heard Kelly say, "I'm so scared I could puke," and instantly Norine's own nervousness went away. It was as if there wasn't enough room for both of them to have the same feeling. Later, of course, it happened with Jimmy and her mother. The more fond he became of the Reverend Ellis, the more her mother irritated Norine. Now, if Jimmy gave one idea about a decision involving what was best for Carl, Norine insisted in the other direction, even if she believed that Jimmy was right. She had no idea why she was like this, but she knew herself well enough to know that she *was*.

"That's more than a crush," she repeated after Paula, her tongue tingling as it began tasting the third drink. The sensation tickled, but it more annoyed than amused her; to distract herself from it, she began to talk. Recklessly, she told this stranger what she had not told anyone before: how she had begun dating Jimmy Ploetz because (though this wasn't a conscious motive) she thought her mother would disapprove, and because she thought there might be something in him — hidden — that she needed.

She was right about the hidden part. Jimmy was the first person, the only person, who saw that there were two parts to Norine: one that felt she was better than other people, and one that felt she was worse. They never talked about it directly, but she came to understand that being with him helped her see there might be a third option, somewhere in the middle, which was where she finally felt comfortable — where she wanted to live.

But by the time she started wondering if this was enough, and realized that her mother not only didn't disapprove of Jimmy but embraced him like a lost lamb (Carla Ellis had actually used that phrase once, to describe him), Norine was pregnant. "I found myself in circumstances," she told Paula, and giggled when her new friend looked confused.

And at first, newly married, she thought it might work out, after all. The truth was that she'd always planned on being a mother, just not this soon. Once she got used to the idea that it was so close, and so real, she loved the idea of taking care of a baby, of being that important to another human being. This baby would need her for the next twenty years, probably longer. Almost as long as Norine's own life so far. She painted the second bedroom and used some of her paycheck to buy an expensive crib. The women at her mother's church threw her a shower, and sitting among all those other mothers and the gifts they bestowed on her, she felt a sense of purpose she had not even tried to imagine until she felt that first shocking kick.

When Jimmy began going out for beers after work with guys from the office, and missing suppers at home, Norine let him think that her anger was because she didn't get to see him, but really her resentment was on behalf of their unborn son. "You're not going to do this after he's here, right?" she asked him, and Jimmy told her to take it easy: "I'm home all weekend, aren't I? And it's not every night. This is what they expect of me, Nor. I'm supporting a family. I have to be one of the guys."

Bowing her head closer to Paula's so that she could be heard over the bar's din, she proceeded to confess about Daniel Veltman — how one day he'd walked into the dentist's office where Norine worked, carrying two of his front teeth in an envelope because Willie Mooney had punched them out when Daniel tried to wake him up under the Millsap Bridge. After Dr. Payne did what he could for

Daniel and gave him a Percocet, Daniel was going to call the station and have someone come pick him up, but Norine offered to drive him home instead. When they got there — to the condo that looked as if he'd just moved in, though he told her he'd lived there three years — Norine, well, seduced him. She blushed as she said the word.

"You jumped his *bones*," Paula translated with a sly grin, raising her hand in a fist to show solidarity. "You *go*, girlfriend." She leaned her face in to receive more of the scoop.

But that was the end of it, Norine realized; the rest she couldn't say out loud. "It was just that one time," she said, hoping Paula would be content to leave it at that. On the TV above the bar, somebody scored, but she wasn't paying enough attention to find out which team it was. Instead she was remembering the night Carl was born, and how when the nurse laid him on her stomach she closed her eyes in relief, thinking about how Abigail Adams must have felt, giving birth to a lifeless child. In the weeks that followed, she couldn't look at Carl while holding in her head the knowledge that she'd thought about ending her pregnancy, so she developed a mental muscle strong enough to separate these two truths, and to keep them from hurting each other or herself. Jimmy became an afterthought. Mary Jo Henzel became a ghost. When Norine got out of bed every morning before the sun rose, what fueled her was the idea that she was doing it for her son.

When Norine faltered, Paula picked up the slack. "I cheated, too," she admitted quietly, looking into her drink. "With Hank over there." She nodded toward the end of the bar at a man with a beard and a Harley belt buckle, who seemed to be concentrating hard on scraping, with his index finger, the last drops of nacho cheese up from his plate. "I'm not proud of it, but there you go. Life's too short not to be happy, is what I think." She pushed hair back from her temples as if it were sweat from her brow, accumulated during the course of summoning this pearl of philosophy.

"But you don't look happy," Norine blurted, not planning the words before they came out. That was the beauty of alcohol, she saw now. You might be guilty of something, like saying something you shouldn't, but the liquor kept you from feeling ashamed.

Paula raised her eyebrows, and Norine expected her to respond in a way that showed she was insulted. But instead she made a "Hunh" noise, as if Norine's observation intrigued her. "I don't, do I?" she said, craning her neck to catch sight of her face in the mirror above the bar. Then she slumped down again. "Well, what the hell? What's *happy*? Jesus. Damned if I know."

"But you're with him now, right?" Norine nodded toward the Harley guy. "Isn't that what you wanted?" She was surprised to realize how invested she felt in whether Paula would know the answer to this question.

"Well, no." Paula shrugged, and Norine could tell that although she wanted to come across as someone it didn't make any difference to, the truth was that it did. "Mitch wouldn't take me back." It appeared that the words stung her throat on their way out. "That was the thing about Mitch — he kept me honest. Until I wasn't." She laughed hoarsely, as if she had made a joke, then cast her eyes at the dirty floor.

For a moment, Norine felt suspended, as if the air in the bar had suddenly frozen or thinned. She looked at her watch, but it had stopped shortly after she arrived in this odd little town. "What time is it, anyway?" It was dark outside, but in January, when it was snowing, that could mean anything.

"Almost seven," Paula told her, "but so what? You can't go anywhere."

"I have to get back for my job tomorrow." It was easier to say this, Norine realized, than to give the real reason.

"What kind of job you do?"

"Delivering newspapers." It was a relief to be able to say it, and not have to pretend she did something more important, the way she had to fake it with people at her mother's church. When they asked her what she was doing these days, she always said, "Freelancing."

But Paula had begun laughing, starting low in the throat and then opening up so that Norine could see all her fillings, and the men at the bar turned to see what was going on. "That's so funny," Paula said, barely able to get the words out as she pointed at Norine. "You're a *paperboy*!" The line threatened to cut her breath off as she doubled over in mirth.

Norine balanced herself at the edge of the table and said "You should talk," though even in her compromised state she could tell that it didn't exactly make sense. She felt shocked to the core. Who was this woman, with a bad perm and sweat rings under her armpits, to judge *her*? With as much dignity as she could muster, she wrapped Carl in his blanket and began carrying him toward the exit.

It was the way Paula had said the word, not the word itself. *Paperboy*. That word had made her laugh when Jimmy used it, the night before Norine had to get up for the first time, in the dark, to make her deliveries. "My wife the paperboy," he'd whispered, grabbing her carefully around the waist because her body was still tender from giving birth. "That turns me on." Norine laughed, because she knew it wasn't a bid for sex, which neither of them had felt like since before Mary Jo Henzel's death. He was just trying to make her feel better about the sacrifice she was making, and for the first time since the accident, she'd turned toward him instead of away.

An icy blast bit her face as she pushed the door of the Bowl-a-Drome open into the night, but she barely felt it, insulated as she was by the heat of her sudden resolve. If she left now, she calculated, she could make it home before Jimmy's shift was over, erase the message she'd left for him, and still be in time to pick him up. If she left now, she could plan on the way home how she would tell him about Daniel Veltman. How she would ask Jimmy to forgive her, and how she would vow that if he gave her another chance, he wouldn't regret it.

So what if he talked to her mother sometimes? Stumbling across the parking lot, she heard the question as clearly as if someone were speaking inside her brain. It was her mother's job to help people. What was wrong with that? And so what if Jimmy never read a book, except *If I Ran the Circus* and *A Fly Went By*, and so what if he looked blank sometimes when Norine used certain words in front of him, like *vindicated* or *qualm?* He kept her honest. *He kept me honest*. She aimed toward the car with her keys ready, hurrying as much as she dared.

She slipped a few times on the thin white snow, but managed to right herself. At the car she clicked Carl in and, pushing her bangs out of her eyes, remembered wondering, earlier, if she should grow her hair out. What silly things she spent her time thinking about. Maybe she would sign up for a class at the community college in the spring. Just because she hadn't gone off to Buf State for four years didn't mean she couldn't learn anything new, be excited about something, make life better for herself and for them all. She'd call in the morning for a course catalogue.

It was easier than she thought it would be, the driving — the car moved easily out of the Bowl-a-Drome's parking lot, and now she saw the sign for the Tree Top motel Paula had mentioned. Norine shivered. The idea of spending a night in a cheap room, in the middle of nowhere, gave her the creeps. Next to Jimmy was where she belonged.

Pay attention, she told herself, as she felt the car start to slide. *Concentrate on the road*. Her father had taught her how to drive, taking her out in the big Buick every Saturday and Sunday, and when she got her license they celebrated, just the two of them, at The Breakfast Barn. She thought now, thought hard, and remembered what he had told her about maneuvering a car in the winter: if you start losing control, turn the wheel in the direction the car is taking you, even though it will *feel* like the wrong thing to do. "It's just one of those things you have to memorize," he'd told her. "Do the opposite of what comes naturally. Instinct won't help you, then."

In the back of the car her son made a noise, and she saw in the mirror that he was awake. In the tiny moment she took her eyes off the road, the car spun out, and a torrent of words raced through her head, but not the ones she needed. *Every marriage has secrets. That's God bowling — see that? — He got a strike.* She was headed crazily toward the median, which was only a strip of pavement between the two sides of the highway. *I'm so proud of you, honey. Didn't you used to wear weird pants or something? If you can imagine it, you can achieve it.* The car kept sliding and she was trunk-first across the middle of the road, with traffic on its way toward her, and — *Don't you dare hate me, you did this to yourself* — she jerked the wheel against the skid before she remembered, too late and with a cry in her throat only the baby witnessed, that this was the wrong move.

Revelation

DO NOT FEAR WHAT YOU ARE ABOUT TO SUFFER. Anne found the note tucked into the flap of her purse where she kept her cell phone. At first she thought it was her own grocery list, or a receipt she intended to save; it was written on a scrap of white paper, in black ballpoint pen. The handwriting looked neither masculine nor feminine, and was a cross between printing and cursive.

The first time, it didn't bother her. She figured it had found its way into her bag by accident, dropped in the flurry of human traffic she navigated each day.

But a week later, she found a postcard in her mailbox, blank except for the same message in the same nondescript hand. Her name and address had been printed in block letters, and the stamp in the corner said *LOVE*.

She asked her friends what they thought, and several of them advised her to call the police. She did, thinking that they would ask to see the messages; but the officer she spoke to said that it wasn't enough to go on. If and when she received a third communication, he told her, she should call again.

She tried to forget about it, but she was on guard now. Every time someone brushed near her, she looked the person over, then searched among her belongings for a piece of paper with a scrawl. A month went by, six weeks. She was just starting to relax when, on a Friday afternoon, she got into her car after work and found another note tucked under her windshield wiper. *Do not fear what you are about to suffer*. She had been brought up on TV movies; she was afraid to turn on the car. But finally she did, and when it failed to blow up with her inside it, she drove straight home to pick up the first two notes, then straight to the police station.

The officer whose desk she sat at was a woman named Phyllis Jones. She took Anne's name and address and phone numbers, then sat back in her chair, out of which stuffing poked through slits in the green plastic. "Do you have any enemies?" she asked Anne. Anne couldn't tell whether Phyllis Jones was a cold fish or extremely bored, or both. She might have been asking if Anne wanted an order of fries.

"Not that I know of," Anne said.

"Anybody you can think of who might want to hurt you? Or at least scare you?"

Anne thought. She could feel the line between her eyes grow deep as it creased down the center. Phyllis Jones watched her thinking and added, "Anybody *you* hurt, lately, maybe?" Her voice became canny, as if she had figured it out.

"Well, I broke up with someone," Anne said. She was looking off to the right, as if remembering the scene of the rupture itself.

"When would this have been?"

"It was two months ago."

"And the notes started when?"

"Right after that! Oh, God! No, I can't believe it would be him — he would never do anything to hurt me."

"Hurt people hurt people," Phyllis Jones observed, and at first Anne thought, *I'm talking to a lunatic*. Then when she understood how to parse the sentence, she wondered if the officer had made this up or if it was a saying around the station house. "Are you absolutely positive it couldn't be him?"

"Well." Anne untied the scarf from around her neck. If she was going to consider Richard a stalker, she needed more room to breathe. "I guess not positive. But the notes are so weird. He doesn't talk like that."

"Like what?"

"Like the Bible."

"You know this is from the Bible?" Phyllis Jones squinted at the message on each of the three pieces of paper Anne had brought in.

"When I got the postcard, I did a search on the Web," Anne said. "*Do not fear what you are about to suffer* is from the book of Revelation."

"What's it talking about?"

"I don't know. I think death."

Phyllis Jones sat straight up suddenly in her stuffing-spilling seat. "Then it's a *death* threat?" she said sharply. "We take those things serious around here."

Anne began to feel panicked. She tried to calm down by reminding herself what she knew — that Richard, no matter how upset he had been over losing her, would not send her death threats.

But then, who would?

"Look, we know whoever it is has your name and address," Phyllis Jones said. "I want to talk to this guy. What's his name?"

"Richard Dover." She drew the name out as if, at the last minute, she might refuse to provide the whole thing.

"Write down his address." Phyllis Jones proffered her notebook, and reluctantly Anne jotted it down.

"Does he have to know I'm the one who sent you?" she asked. "I mean, what if he didn't do it." She knew this was wishful thinking, but she said it anyway. "Can you leave my name out of it?"

Phyllis Jones was shaking her head. "I don't see how. He's gonna wanna know how his name came up."

"What are you going to do?"

"I'm gonna show him these letters, and see if he has any reaction to them." Phyllis Jones slipped the pages in an envelope. "I think I'll be able to tell if he's seen them before."

Anne stopped herself from saying that she doubted this. Richard was an extraordinary liar, to the extent that he sometimes didn't realize when he was doing it. It was one of the things that had endeared him to Anne early on — his need to invent circumstances or history for himself, when he felt his own coming up short.

He had never lied to Anne, though. That was one of his rules. In the days following the breakup, she wished that he *had*, so there would have been some behavior of his to point to, when she told him he wasn't "the one." Instead she had resorted to those abstract and nebulous phrases ("Something feels off"; "It's not working for me"; "I do love you, just not the way you deserve") that made her cringe in thinking about them, afterward.

"Can I come with you?" she asked the policewoman.

Phyllis Jones gave her a look that indicated she'd been asked stupider questions in her lifetime, but not recently. "No, you go on home," she told Anne. "I'll call you when I get back."

"I have to tell you, I really think we're making a mistake here."

"Well, it's my job to find out." Phyllis Jones pulled on her uniform jacket and patted the gun at her waist. "I'll let you know what he says."

He knew someone would be coming soon. Anne might have let the first one go, but the postcard and the message stuck on her windshield would send her to the police. Of this he felt sure. He stood at the window, waiting, jingling the change in his pocket, remembering how she used to raid his pants for quarters, to use for laundry and parking. He pretended to begrudge it, but they both knew that she was welcome to whatever he had.

When the cruiser pulled up outside his apartment, he cleared his throat and got ready. He was disappointed that they had sent only one officer. She was a small woman who looked like a teenager dressed in a cop costume for Halloween.

He opened the door as soon as she knocked. She established that he was Richard Dover, then asked to come inside. She took note of the neat room — the magazines arranged on the coffee table, the CDs all stacked in their rack — and she felt doubt starting to rise. He offered her coffee but she declined, and she pulled the letters out of their envelope.

"Do these look familiar to you?" she asked, handing them over. He took them and sifted the pages, looking down and reading each one before patting them back into order.

"Yes. I wrote them," he said.

She could feel her eyebrows go up, despite her training and inclination not to betray a response. "You did?"

"Yes. I know where you got them."

"Well — why?" She had been so prepared for him to deny it that she needed time to regroup.

He shrugged. "I wanted to get her attention."

"Well, you did. She thinks they're some kind of threat. And we agree with her." She reached over to take the notes, as if not trusting him to give them back.

"They're not a threat. Not a threat at all," he said. "It's just a verse from the Bible."

"But what's it supposed to mean?"

He shrugged again, but he managed to do it in such a way that it didn't seem dismissive or rude. "Life is suffering. It's the Buddha's first truth. I've learned a lot about suffering in the past two months.

"I just wanted Anne to be aware of what can happen, and to not be afraid." He thought that maybe he shouldn't have brought up the Buddha. The officer probably wasn't interested. But it was all true.

"What are you, some kind of kook?" She folded the notes up and returned them to their envelope.

"No," he said. "I just wanted to get her attention," he repeated.

"I'm going to tell her you admitted to sending them. She'll probably want to press charges and get a restraining order."

He held his hands up at his sides in a gesture of potential surrender. "I'll be here."

She could feel him watching her as she went back out to the car. *What a creep*, she wanted to think, but she couldn't deny the piece of her that felt sorry for the man.

The woman wouldn't press charges. "You met him," she said to Phyllis Jones. "You can see he's not going to hurt me."

"Lots of people don't *look* dangerous," the officer told her, though she knew what Anne meant. "At least get a restraining order," she suggested. "So he can't send you any more notes."

"But I'm not scared anymore," Anne said. "I know it's him. Even if he writes again, I can ignore it."

Phyllis Jones said, "Well, it's your funeral. But if you're not gonna listen to me, I got work to do." She gave the envelope with the messages to Anne, who put it in her purse.

At home, she took out the envelope and tapped it against her fingers. She knew she should throw it away, but instead she went to the phone and dialed Richard, who was waiting for her call.

"My God, it *is* you!" he said. "I was afraid to trust caller ID."

"So I guess the police came to see you." She had decided not to make small talk, but to go straight to the point.

"I didn't know what to do, Anne. I didn't think you'd talk to me if I just called you up."

"I wouldn't. We agreed not to."

"*You* agreed. I never wanted that." There was a silence during which she could tell he was berating himself for raising his voice. "I just wanted to get your attention," he said, more softly. He was beginning to believe it himself.

"Richard." She was going to say *Don't do this*, but she stopped herself. "How are you?" she asked instead, after a pause.

"I'm good. I'm okay. I mean, no, I'm not, Anne, I'm terrible. Can we get together? Could I see you?"

"Richard, I don't think that's a good idea."

"Yes, it is. I promise. This is the last time, and after this, you don't ever have to set eyes on me again."

She was about to say she didn't mind setting eyes on him when she realized that this might count as leading him on. She agreed to meet him the following night. He wanted to go to their usual place but she was afraid of the feelings, so they picked a lounge they had never been to before.

He was waiting, already seated, when she arrived. He gave her a flower. "I know it's dumb," he said, twirling it by the stem on his napkin, "but I wanted to have something for you, to thank you for seeing me."

"You don't have to thank me," she said.

"Yes, I do. I'm sorry about the notes, Anne. I know that was weird."

"Well, it did kind of freak me out." She ordered a Diet Coke, wanting to stay clearheaded. He ordered a beer.

"It's just — well, I've been thinking about what you said that day." They both knew which day he meant. The drinks came, and they paused while the waiter delivered them.

"That was a terrible day. I don't think I want to remember what I said," she told him.

"You said you didn't feel *cozy* with me. And I was just wondering what in the motherfucking *hell* that was supposed to mean." He was still looking at her with the same grateful, slanted smile. She would never have guessed the words that had just come from his mouth.

"Look, Richard, I don't need you swearing at me." She took a short sip of her Coke, then looked up at him. "It doesn't become you."

"Oh, it doesn't become me," he said.

"Look, this was a bad idea. I'm leaving." She took out a couple of dollars and put them on the table.

"No! I'm sorry. *Anne*. Please sit down. I'm just nervous, seeing you after all this time. No more swearing, I promise."

"This was a bad idea," she repeated, then took her seat again.

"Here's what I really want to know." He wrapped a big hand around his beer and leaned forward. "Do you think if we just gave it a little more time, it could have worked? What if the exact thing that made you realize you loved me was going to happen the very next day? We never found out."

"Richard — "

"I mean, that happens to people. You look at them one way, at the beginning, and then suddenly you see them a different way and you realize you love them. That's what happened with me when I saw you in the hardware store that day, when you didn't know I was there."

"Richard." She couldn't look at his face; it was grotesque with his hopefulness. "It wasn't going to happen. That's why I ended it."

"But two years, Anne! How could you not feel cozy in all that time?"

"I can't explain it any better than that." She let her eyes slide around the room as she realized that he had begun to cry. "Richard, please stop. Listen. I'd better go."

She left him like that, snuffling, wiping his eyes with a cocktail napkin. When he didn't get up to follow her, she sighed with what felt like relief.

A week and a half went by before she found the note slid under her office door when she came back from lunch. *Do not fear what you are about to suffer*. She picked it up and rubbed her fingers over the words, which held for her a sweetness about them now, and a sense of nostalgia. She started finding them everywhere — in books she was reading, taped to the underside of her umbrella, in her mailbox at work. They came to contain a kind of comfort, and she collected them chronologically, beginning with the one she had mistaken for a grocery list in her purse. She kept them in a shoebox, and when the box ran out of room, she bought a pasteboard filing cabinet and stored the notes in that. There was something poetic and beautiful about the messages, and sometimes she arranged them around her just so she could read the duplicate lines of warning and wonder what they might mean. When they stopped coming, abruptly, in the middle of winter, she missed them. But she consoled herself with the ones that had already come to her, unbidden but, now, so dear.

Testimony

ALL THAT DAY as she waited for her sister to come home, Maxine remembered the goats. She did not know what it was that had nudged them into her mind — there was nothing remotely goat-like, or even countryish, about her sister's house or the neighborhood — but once the image presented itself of the white faces, the angular slit mouths emitting their treble bleats, she could not get rid of it.

They'd been given the goats the spring Maxine was eleven and Tillie nine. Tillie went by Tildra now; she corrected anyone who tried to use the nickname, even Maxine, which Maxine considered cheeky because she was here, after all, to do her sister a favor. But back then, in upstate Crete, New York, they had been Max and Tillie and didn't think twice about what they were called. Together they settled on the names Pete and Smiley for the two goats, which their father had waiting as a surprise in a pen he'd built behind the garage. Their father was an insurance salesman, not a carpenter or a farmer, and on the first night of the goats' residence with the Wrynn family, they escaped and died on Route 12. Mr. Wrynn, his lips set in a line, fastened the fence where Pete and Smiley had pushed through and told Max and Tillie that they would try again, but with just one goat this time. The new one they named Clover, and she lasted a week before dying of a deficiency of vitamin E.

Not uncommon, said their neighbor Fran Bardwell, who worked for the only vet in Crete.

"Then why didn't anyone tell us?" demanded Mr. Wrynn. Maxine thought of the way her father had been down on his knees in the goat grass, holding Clover's dead head. "I would have bought her vitamin E by the barrel." He leaned forward to look into the animal's vacated eyes. "Goddamnit." Although Maxine was young, she knew when her father believed he had failed. It was less an expression on his face or the way he held his body than an odor he gave off — something rancid and poisonous, his blood or skin souring on the inside of him, like milk turning in the quart. He often began projects with enthusiasm, like the time he started building a darkroom before he realized he couldn't bring running water into the basement, and the time he tried to help Sammy Lussier build a car for the soapbox derby and forgot to leave room for the seat. Maxine believed that the smell her father gave off, in the aftermath of these disasters, was the scent of his own self-disgust. Whenever she got a whiff of it, she stayed away.

By the time Tillie pulled into the driveway, Maxine had started her niece, Isabelle, on her five o'clock feeding. She thought Tillie would want to take her, so she started to get up and hand her over, but Tillie waved and whispered, "Go ahead, she looks comfy. Besides, I have to pee." Maxine kept the bottle in the baby's mouth and listened to Tillie use the bathroom and change her clothes. When she came out of the bedroom, she'd traded her heels for slippers and her receptionist's dress for a sweatshirt and jeans. It was a point of pride with Tillie that she had been able to get into her jeans a week after the baby was born. Max had always been the big-boned one, like their father; Tillie took after their mother's more delicate side. From the looks of the two sisters, you'd guess Max was the one who had recently borne a child.

Maxine's own version of pride would not let her show Tillie that the difference between their sizes bothered her. Since they'd been teenagers, whenever they shopped for clothes together, she held in her head the comments that wanted to break free, like *I am disgusting* and *My thighs make me want to barf.* She always bit her tongue after failing to fit into a pair of pants she'd selected, and smiled as if grateful when Tillie said she'd go look for the next larger size.

But the sisters were twenty-four and twenty-six years old now, and other things had replaced or at least joined clothing and bodies as subjects worthy of their concern. Tillie was a mother. Maxine had had a few bad years out of college, when she'd depended on her parents for money to augment what she made as a temp, and during that time she'd tried halfheartedly (some pills, some whiskey, but not enough of either) to kill herself, which her parents didn't know. Tillie, when she found out, called Maxine an idiot. "You of all people should be glad you're alive," she said. She was referring to the fact that Maxine had been diagnosed, in eighth grade, with a benign lump on her frontal lobe. The benign part was what she usually left out when she told the story, along with the fact that from the beginning, the doctor had referred to it as a cyst. Maxine herself used the word *growth*, knowing full well what it implied. She knew it was wrong, but she got so much out of telling people and watching their eyes grow wide: a *tumor*? On your *brain*? They always treated her gingerly, with more kindness, after they knew. Maxine wondered what other people used, once they were out of school and grown up, to get such attention and sympathy. Or maybe some people didn't try; she suspected that one was supposed to relish being an adult, and not look for ways to be taken care of, but she couldn't imagine feeling this way herself. Though they'd never discussed such things, she knew Tillie couldn't imagine it, either; and Maxine worried about her niece, who was only an infant now but who would, in a few years' time, be competing with her own mother for nurturance from the world.

Now Tillie stopped off at the kitchen to pour herself a rum and Diet Coke before flopping on the other end of the sofa to watch her daughter being fed. "How was she?" she asked Maxine, her eyes betraying an ecstatic wince as the first sip slid down. "I was going to call, but the goddamn phone never stopped ringing."

"Don't you get a lunch break?"

"Of course. But it's only half an hour. I mean, by the time I scarf down a yogurt and use the john — " Then Tillie's eyes narrowed as she watched her sister's face, and she put her glass down hard on the puckered cover of the *TV Guide*. "What?" she demanded of Maxine. "Why do you look at me that way? Okay, I know it, I should have called. But it was busy, Max. And I trust you. It's not like I didn't *think* about her or anything." When Maxine remained silent, Tillie stood up and reached to snatch the baby away from her. "Jesus! Screw you, Maxine. You can shove that holier-than-thou attitude straight up your born-again ass." With anybody else, she would have used the word *fuck* instead of *screw*. But there was still something in her that remembered she was the younger sister, and so she held back at the last moment, afraid to show how far she had strayed from where, in life, they had started.

The baby, having lost her hold on the rubber nipple, was crying. Maxine got up and walked over to the window. She was accustomed to the faraway, third-floor view she had from her attic apartment outside Boston, but here everything swam smack up against you, life-size, as if you were in a submarine too close to the reef. Tillie's neighborhood made her feel spooked, with its square plots and painted mailboxes, and all the houses in the development constructed according to one of two styles; directly across the street was the mirror image of Tillie's, and the houses on both next-door sides of her, 12 and 16 Woodhaven Circle, were duplicates of her number 14. When she was a child, Max had read a science fiction book about a suburban neighborhood she'd imagined looked just like this. In the book, all the children playing outside bounced balls in unison, and every jump rope slapped the pavement at exactly the same time. During this week she'd spent at Tillie's, Maxine felt as if she'd been living inside that book.

She turned suddenly from the window. "Hey, do you remember those goats?" she said.

Tillie was jiggling the baby, trying to pat out a burp. "What goats?" She spoke crossly, as if she hadn't noticed the change of subject or Maxine's conciliatory tone.

"The goats Dad got us when we were kids. Come on, you must remember. You weren't so young, then — you were in fourth grade. Come on: that little pen he built out behind the garage?" Though she sometimes believed her sister made faces because she liked to be looked at, Maxine saw that this time Tillie's expression of puzzlement was for real. "I can't believe you don't remember."

"My whole childhood is pretty much one big blank," said Tillie. After a pause she added, "Except of course for the stuff I told you about Dad."

"Yeah, well." Maxine returned to the sofa, where she sat down hard and looked Tillie straight in the eyes. "*That*" — she pointed at her sister — "is total horseshit."

"Ha!" Tillie snorted, which made the baby laugh. "*Now* who has a mouth like a sewer."

"And I'm not born-again." Maxine reached over and took a gulp of her sister's drink, to prove it. "Just because I go to church."

The church she went to was one of those with a long name that didn't say exactly what it believed in, only that it embraced all faiths, and that every genuine seeker was welcome to its pews. Maxine had been drawn in one Sunday in January, a year and a half earlier, when she happened to walk by the door as she struggled to carry the Sunday paper while blowing onto her freezing hands. She caught sight of a sign taped to the door — "It is warm inside" — and, intending only to regain her balance and shift the load in her arms, she opened the door against a blast of wind and felt herself being whooshed through.

From the hall she heard the singing of children and peeked around the corner into the sanctuary. An usher saw her and held out an order of service, and not wanting to disrupt or be rude, Maxine accepted it and sat down. The children were singing a song, the chorus each time in a different language she didn't understand, but she could tell from the inflection and their faces that it was some kind of hymn. When the children finished, the congregation applauded. Maxine had never heard clapping in a church, except at weddings when the couple kissed, and the sound, on a regular Sunday morning, made her start. At the benediction she tried to sneak out, but the people on either side of her reached to take her hand. She stood there stupidly as everyone else, joined by similar squeezes throughout the room, murmured words Maxine did not hear so much as feel. She followed everyone to the coffee hour, where she made five new friends — three of whom she'd told, by the time she left, about her brain tumor. In March she became a member, and last October she'd been one of four lay speakers to give sermons about the relationship of spirituality to their individual lives. A service of testimony, it was called. The woman who signed her up said Maxine could talk about anything she wanted, but she was sure that everyone would be interested in hearing how her faith had been tested by a critical illness. What she had learned by confronting her own death. Maxine could not tell her, of course, that there had never been a time when she believed that her cyst would kill her. It was more of a nuisance than a threat. Maxine often wished — though she hardly dared to acknowledge it, even to herself— that it *had* been more serious; she wished that she could honestly consider it a mortal struggle she had survived.

She went to the library and took out books by people who did have real cancer, and after she delivered her remarks from the lectern at the plain wooden altar, she had to remind herself that what she'd said was a lie. But then she told herself, *No. Not a lie; just someone else's story*. Did it matter who it had happened to, as long as it was the truth? In this way she allowed herself not to feel guilty, and to accept what she saw in people's eyes when they came up to her at coffee hour and expressed their appreciation and concern. "We're so glad you came through all that, that you're here with us," one of them told her. "You're so courageous, so strong."

"Not really," Maxine demurred. But all along she knew that they would take it for modesty.

On Saturday, Max and Tillie packed up for the drive north to their parents' house — their childhood home — where Max had left her car before taking the train down to Pennsylvania the previous week. Their parents hadn't met their granddaughter yet. Tillie's husband couldn't come up with them because he had to work weekends. Besides, he and Maxine had never gotten along very well — he thought she looked down on him because he had never gone to college, and while she knew it was petty of her, this was true. She'd thought she was better at hiding it, though, than she apparently was.

"I bet Mom got Isabelle a christening gown," Maxine said, trying to sound casual as they walked back to the car after stopping for lunch on the Thruway. "She probably thinks it'll change your mind." As she spoke, she held a hand over the baby's forehead to shield it from the June sun.

"That's her problem." Tillie fastened the car seat with a vicious click. "Max, what's the matter with you? Don't you listen, or is there something inside there that just erases everything you hear?" Accelerating, Tillie tapped a finger on her own head. Her small thigh jiggled on the seat.

"I didn't erase it. I just think you're wrong. I mean, I *know* you are. Dad wasn't like that. Isn't."

"Well, maybe not in the daytime." Tillie floored it to pass a truck.

"Not *ever*. I'm not saying I don't believe you. I mean, I know you believe it. I'm not saying you're lying or anything."

"Gee, thanks."

"Don't be like that, Til. Okay? I think you're confused. And I'm not saying that therapist planted it, either. But what you're remembering isn't real." Maxine let out her breath. She hadn't realized she'd been holding it in so long. "Besides, even if it *was* true — like, say, in another family or something — it would be the father's fault. Why punish the mother? You know how much Mom wanted to throw a christening party."

"She can still have a party. She can show off Isabelle all she wants. But I'm not standing up in a church with some guy who raped me and letting him say a prayer on my baby's head." Tillie's voice rang on in the car long after she'd finished speaking. A police car went by flashing its lights but no siren, which made Maxine nervous. Silent emergencies were the most dangerous kind.

"That's a terrible word," she said finally. "*Rape*."

Tillie made a scoffing noise. "No shit."

"I mean, the word itself. It's horrible. It hurts just to hear it."

"Then how do you think *I* feel?" Though the air-conditioning was on, Tillie rolled down the window to suck in some air. She drove like that, with her head halfway out of the car, until Maxine said,

"Hey, what's the matter with you?" and from this weird distance her sister answered, "You think I don't take care of *my* daughter? You wait and see."

From the Thruway they exited onto Route 20, and rising with the altitude as the traffic thinned, they went home. Their parents lived on Sully Hill Road; the turnoff landmark was a silo with a robin's egg blue roof. On Sully Hill, the houses were set far back from the road, and each house was hidden from the others by wild grass and trees. Tillie parked next to their father's Chrysler and carried the baby in while Maxine managed to follow with all the bags.

The house they grew up in smelled, as it always had, like sausage cooking. Her mother never cooked sausage that Maxine could remember, but there it was, anyway — the warm, vaguely broiled scent that stuck to the walls and ceilings, the paint and upholstery, the air they all breathed, in and out of each other's lungs. When she lived there, of course, she hadn't noticed. But when she went away and came back, there it was. It was that family smell of high spirits and misery, celebration and bitterness, comfort and dread. Maxine drank deep with her eyes closed, then thought she might vomit. Leaning forward to kiss her father, letting him hold her close in a hug, Maxine tried to imagine this same weight above her in a bed: an adult man lying on top of her as a child, and what this would feel like — suffocating, titanic, in its very proportions absurd. She knew it had never happened. Yet Tillie was sure that it had. *And if he did it to me, Max, then why wouldn't he do it to you*?

They'd been sitting in the therapist's office when her sister asked her this. The therapist was one of the reasons Tillie had wanted Maxine to come to Pennsylvania. She was a slight, dark woman who sat with her pantsuited ankles arranged in an elegant X. Across from the two of them, Maxine felt like the odd one out. Anyone would have taken the therapist for Tillie's sister, the blood relation. Maxine could have been an in-law or even a stranger. Of all the confidences in the room, she saw that whatever the therapist and Tillie held between them would support the most weight.

"You're wrong, Til," she'd said, knowing that the therapist and Tillie would exchange glances. She could hear the echo of their thoughts bubbling above her: *Deny, deny.* "I know this is what people are into, now. Repressed memory and all that. But haven't you read about the mistakes? Whole families get ruined. Somebody thinks a thing is true, then they find out later it isn't. It's a phenomenon. A vision or something, but you think it's real." The more she talked, the more the two other women receded from her view, until she and Tillie were in the car again on their way back to Tillie's house. "I think it's really sad that you could believe those things," she remembers saying, as she separates now from her father to give her mother a hug. She saw them eight days ago, but in this family they always greet each other as if it has been a long time.

Her mother takes the baby from Tillie, and Maxine watches her sister accept their father's hello, the kiss and tobacco embrace. He's a medium-sized man with shadows under his eyes, where he winces and smiles. When they were little, he used to make his girls laugh by shifting these eyes back and forth to look like a crazy man. They would giggle until Tillie peed.

Now, after letting Tillie go — and is Maxine mistaken, or does he hold her sister longer than he did her? Is she nuts to feel jealous? — he reaches over to stroke the baby under her chin. Only Max perceives the tension in Tillie when he does this, and the way Tillie directs her mother's attention to something outside the window, so that the baby will have to be moved. She hears her mother say the word "church" and sees Tillie shaking her head, and her mother says, "Well, okay. Let's have a *nice* visit," and they all go into the kitchen and sit down. Max braces herself for Tillie to make a scene — a confrontation, like those she has seen on TV, in which grown children accuse their parents of abuse and betrayals a long time ago. The parents always bite their lips, shake their heads and protest, but the audience knows what's true.

Tillie has promised Maxine she won't do this, though. "I'm not interested in having it out with him," she said, on the way home from the therapist. "I don't see him that much. He'll be dead someday, and until then I can put up with him on holidays and whatever. I don't want to do that to Mom. It would kill her, and besides, she wouldn't believe me." At the time, Maxine decided not to point out to her sister that this didn't make sense; if her mother didn't believe what Tillie said, how could it upset her? She decided to feel only her relief, which is what comes back to her as she spoons up the fake-crabmeat salad and takes more crackers than her share from the common plate.

After lunch, Tillie wants to lie down for a nap with the baby, but their mother asks if it can be put off for an hour. There's a sale on at Twice Around, the store that sells "gently worn" children's clothing, and if they go now they might find some nice bargains. Tillie consents but insists on driving, and they pull out with a rush of wheels that Maxine knows, hearing it, will cause her mother to brace herself against the dash.

Still at the table, nursing his Sanka, her father tells her that he's been meaning for a while to clean out the garage. Does Maxine want to help? Of course she doesn't, but she says she will. There are things she wants to find out about him that only he can tell.

But he asked her only so that he would have company, which Maxine discovers, with relief, when she goes out to the garage and finds the lawn chair he's set up for her at the edge of the yard; that way they can talk while he works, and at the same time she can relax. She fixes her gaze on the meadow across the road. When she was little, she thought of it as what heaven must look like, the way the sun lit the grass in sudden circles, as if angels were touching it with wands. Between her fingers she squeezes an old tennis ball as she watches her father begin to sort through piles of junk, tossing it onto the floor in a resounding flurry of dust.

"How's work?" he says finally, and Maxine knows that he really does not remember having asked the same thing only a little more than a week ago, or what her answer was.

"Okay." The last time, she'd gone on to tell her parents about her job as assistant to the editor of a literary magazine. Someday, if the editor ever left, she might have a chance to move up; for now, she was the assistant, and though it didn't pay well, she loved the work. It felt important. There had been times in her life when the only thing that saved her was a book. Her favorite task in her job was reading through the fiction submissions. If she liked them she passed them on to a second, higher-up reader. If she didn't, she got to send the rejection slips, on which she scribbled encouraging messages like "Sorry this isn't right for us" or "Please try again."

"I've never really understood the point of fiction," her mother said, during that conversation, and Max thought, *How did I come out of her?* "I like books about real life."

"Yeah, we know what you like, Amy," her father said, and the three of them smiled because it was a joke that her mother's favorite genre was true crime, especially cases of family members murdering one another.

Maxine knows her parents worry about where she will land in life. They disapprove when she talks about going to graduate school, giving up her regular paycheck. Once you find something with security, you are supposed to stay. *It would be different if you were married, honey*. She doesn't need to hear that again. Instead she says to her father, "How's *yours*?" meaning his job.

"Me?" He pauses in ripping a box open and looks up, surprised. "It's fine, I guess. What can I tell you?" He shrugs. "Nothing very exciting about the insurance game." He tosses the balled-up tape toward a bucket in the corner. In the end, Maxine knows, her father *cleaning out the garage* means that he will only move things from one place to another; he's never been able to throw anything away.

"Do you do everything there? I mean, all kinds? Like property and fire and stuff? Or do you just handle life?" Maxine's heart speeds up as she practices asking her father questions. The felt of the tennis ball frays in her hands.

He laughs. "I can't believe you really want to know a thing like that," he tells her, wiping grime into the side of his pants, "after all these years. But okay. Well, we all have our little specialties. Remember Ned Houghtaling, with the nose? He's strictly auto. Anything involving a car, it goes straight to him. I used to do a little of everything else, but now they mostly give me the real-estate policies. Homeowners and such. Honey, you can't possibly care." Maxine realizes he's caught her staring, way out across the valley to the long bruise-stitch of peak and sky.

"Yes. I do," she said. "Wait a minute. Ned Houghtaling?" She sees her father stiffen, but she doesn't comprehend why until it's too late. "Isn't he the one you were going to start your own agency with?" Only then does she realize she should not have brought it up. Her father lets out the *cch* sound she associates with those moments, over the years, in which he has recognized that another of his ambitions is destined to fail.

"That never worked out," he answers her, muttering down at his shirt. To change the subject, he rummages deep in the box before him. When she sees what he has extracted and holds up to the sunlight, she hears herself gasp.

"You want to hang onto this?" he asks. It is the final X-ray from after her brain surgery, bare ghosts of skull photo-gleaming in gray. "As a souvenir?"

To answer she reaches up and takes it from him, punches the heavy plastic into a clumsy fold, and tucks it under the lawn chair's metal leg. She pauses in letting her memory touch something that scratches, familiar, at the back of her mind. "It reminds me of this novel where this guy falls in love with a woman in a TB clinic, they're both patients, and when she gets better and leaves, she gives her X-ray to him as a present. So that's all he has left of her — this, like, *negative* of her insides — but he carries it around with him and keeps taking it out to look at, after she's gone."

Her father smiles. "I know that book," he says. "Don't think you're the only one in this family who reads," he adds, and along with the teasing there is a serious note in his voice.

"Oh, Dad, I don't." Maxine flushes and leans forward. "I just never thought — I mean, we never talked about it or anything. I never see you read."

"Well, I do it mostly in bed. At night." Her father has stopped working to take a rest. He looks out at the place, miles away, where a few years ago the town assessor was killed by his son in a hunting accident. When the police arrived, the son shot off his own big toe, out of guilt. "*The Magic Mountain*. Right? I thought of that book when Mom and I first saw this house. I always loved the feel of the hospital he describes — how they were all way above the rest of the world, wrapped up in their blankets and beds. Remember how the guy went just for a few days, at the beginning, to visit his cousin? Then the longer he stayed there, the more he didn't want to leave."

Maxine watches her father and bites her lip. "I know. I loved it, too," she says. She wants to cry out, "Dad, did you ever touch Tillie?" (the word *rape* is impossible), but she cannot.

Her father burrows farther into the box. With his face half-hidden, as if it embarrasses him, he says, "Yeah, you're like me. Me and you, we're the types, if we were up in that clinic we'd only come down to the real world kicking and screaming. Mom and Tillie, I think, are the other way. They'd never let themselves get sucked into that kind of fear." He straightens with empty hands as Maxine looks down at her bare wide thighs, wanting to scratch them until they bleed. Her father gestures at the X-ray she is anchoring with her weight. "I'm a little surprised you don't want to get rid of that. Once and for all. Good riddance, that kind of thing."

"Well, it wasn't really such a big deal." Maxine feels breathless, though she isn't sure why. She tosses the tennis ball down the driveway, waiting for her father to contradict her as it bounces.

"What do you mean, not a big deal?" He comes out from the shadow of the garage and stands over her, and she tries to think of it as sinister, a menace, but it won't work — again comes the image of her father kneeling in the grass on that long-ago spring morning, wishing he'd been able to save the last dead goat. "You get cancer, honey, that's a big deal, I don't care *what* book you're reading." He tries to make light of it, a joke, but she sees that his lip trembles around the words.

"But Dad. I didn't *have* cancer." A seize curls inside her. He often has to be reminded about little things, but how could he have forgotten something as important as this?

Her father has flipped his sunglasses back down over his eyes, but she can still sense what lies behind them. He is looking at her with a blend of hesitation and regret. "Actually, honey — Jeez, your mother would kill me for telling you like this." He sucks in air as if it were courage. "But listen: It *was* malignant, that tumor. I was all for telling you then, but Mom thought it would be better if you didn't know." He waits, watching her. She can see through the dark plastic that he doesn't blink.

"What are you *talking* about," Maxine says, astonished to feel laughter rising.

He sighs and comes closer. "I always told her it was a mistake not to tell you, and the doctors did, too. But I went along with it. She convinced me it would be better for you not to get scared. *We* were scared. It was scary. I mean, you want your kids to be okay." He coughs, as if to expel this memory from where it has lodged. "Then when they got it all, and said things looked good, I thought, well, what the hell? Maybe Amy was right.

"Actually, I thought it would have come up before now," he goes on, as Maxine continues laughing. He doesn't show surprise yet at her reaction — he seems distracted by what he has to say. "It's part of your medical records, of course. I assumed a doctor or a nurse by now would have said something, and you'd find out that way." He pauses to allow Maxine a chance to answer, but she thinks it best not to tell him that she hasn't been to a doctor in years, because her job doesn't carry health insurance. When she remains silent, he picks up where he left off. "Your mother and I always planned to sit down with you and have this talk, but we just never did. I kept expecting a phone call from you someday, or an out of the blue visit, with you yelling at us for not telling you the truth. Every time we'd see a scene like that on TV, I'd say, *See? That's going to be us and Maxie, when she finds out what we did.*" He reaches up to brush part of a cobweb from his face. "I'm relieved, actually. Now that it's out in the open. What's so funny?" Finally he lifts his sunglasses to look at her. Maxine is doubled over in the lawn chair. She'd tried to stop laughing for a while, and to get up, but succeeded at neither.

"Oh, God," she says finally, exhaling the last blasts in little sighs. "It's *not* funny. I can't help it. It's just that I was thinking of something else. Another question I wanted to ask you, but I get this instead. Oh, God." A few leftover giggles find their way out.

Her father wipes his hands again and takes another step toward her. This time Maxine stands up, letting the chair topple as she stumbles, crunching the X-ray beneath her. "What?" he says, putting a hand out to steady her. "What did you want to ask me?" but she knows it would only upset him, she knows Tillie has to be wrong, so she shakes her head, kisses him, and tells him to never mind.

At dinner — tuna casserole, peas, tomato slices, iced tea — Maxine's father says to Tillie and her mother, "What did you two buy in town today, anyway? I didn't see any bags."

Tillie and her mother look at each other. "Well, we have a little news," her mother says.

"We didn't go to the store." Tillie takes over, her tone defiant, as if she doesn't trust her mother to tell it right. "We went to the church and got Isabelle baptized instead."

"Baptized?" Her father says the word like someone who's never heard it. He looks at Maxine, confused, and she raises her eyebrows to show him that this is the first she's known of it, too. "But why? I mean, why not do it tomorrow, at the regular service? The way we originally planned?"

Maxine bends intently over her plate. In the corner, her niece lies asleep in her carrier, no doubt worn out from being blessed.

"Dad, could we not get into it?" It is Tillie as a teenager, flush-templed and aggrieved. "It was just spur of the moment. I didn't want a big deal — all that stimulation and people passing her around. She's a fussy baby."

"Well, *you* were a fussy baby. That didn't keep us from having you baptized in front of your own congregation. And what about Max and me?"

"It's okay with me, Dad," Maxine says. She wants to add, *Who cares?* Her parents don't go to church much — mostly at Christmas and Easter. But this baby's baptism has been on their minds since before it was born. She suspects it has something to do with Tillie's husband, who was "brought up as nothing," in her mother's words.

"The church I go to," Max goes on, hoping to divert her father, "doesn't even do baptisms. I mean, they have a service for babies, but it's the same thing as when adults join. They call it a welcoming ritual. There's no water or anything — every new member just goes up to the front and stands there, and somebody gives them a rose." She takes a sip of tea and winces as the ice touches her teeth. "Anyway, about Isabelle — I don't mind. Not having been there, I mean."

"Well, I do." Her father puts his napkin down, stands and paces to the window, looking away from them all as he speaks. "It's not something you take lightly, being baptized in the church. She's a Christian now. She'll go to heaven. And when she sins, she'll be forgiven."

Tillie coughs on something that's gone down the wrong way. "Forgiven for *what*?" Now her whole face is red. "Listen, don't think I actually believe any of that crap. I just did it for Mom. This baby has nothing to be forgiven for. Anyway, *you* should fucking talk."

"Oh, Doug." Her mother waves the tomato fork — with impatience or sympathy, or perhaps disapproval of Tillie's language, it isn't clear. "I'm sorry. But if we hadn't done it this way, it wouldn't have been done. And isn't the important thing, really, that it was?"

Her father looks at Tillie, who stares back at him and refuses to break the gaze. "I just don't get it," he tells her.

Tillie snorts. "Yeah, no shit," she says.

"What's that supposed to mean?" He comes back to the table, but he doesn't sit down. When she was little, Maxine used to play a game with herself. She'd look at someone around her — a kid in her class, or a stranger at the grocery store — and she'd try to imagine what that person was feeling. If the kid was raising his hand, Maxine thought about what it felt like to hold her own arm up in the air. If an old lady was picking through apples, she focused on the sensation of her own fingertips rubbing the smooth red skins. For just an instant, and this was the point of the game, she *knew* she was feeling exactly what they were. She would not have been able to name the satisfaction this gave her, or the relief. She knew only that it made her less afraid to be in the world.

But it has never worked with members of her own family, and it doesn't work now, as she watches her father standing next to her and tries to imagine what it is like to stand on his legs, or rub the edge of the table with his knuckles, or look down at Tillie from his height. "What don't I get?" he says.

Maxine thinks Tillie is going to answer, and her stomach folds over in fear. But at the moment her sister would have opened her mouth, their mother begins brushing crumbs from the table and the baby wakes up. Tillie goes over to get her, and their father sits back down and makes his crazy eyes at his granddaughter, who gapes back. He calls the baby Cutie, which had been his pet name for Tillie when she was young. He reaches out toward Isabelle's cheek. Tillie picks up the baby and turns her away. "Don't call her Cutie," she tells him. Her voice shoots blades.

Maxine watches her father's hand drop. "Listen," she says, urgency swelling at the back of her throat. "I was reminding Tillie this week about those goats you got us, but she doesn't remember. What year was it? Weren't we both about ten?" She addresses the question to her father because he'd been the one who bought the goats and brought them home.

"Goats?" He flashes a look at her and frowns. "No."

"Oh, come on. *Dad.* You bought us two to begin with, but they broke out and got hit by cars. Then we had another one, and it died, too, but not because it escaped or anything; that one was sick."

Her mother says, "That does ring a vague bell with me, Doug. Are you sure?"

"I'm *positive.*" He puts his fork down with a clink. "What kind of an idiot would try to keep animals in that small a space? Besides, who do I look like, Old MacDonald?"

His wife gurgles laughter and he looks pleased.

"See?" Tillie says to Maxine. "I told you."

"Dad?" Max wants to hit him in the chest — not hard, just

enough to startle him into remembering. "I *know* we had them. You built a pen behind the garage. Then, after they all died, you buried them back there."

He shakes his head. "I don't know where you got this," he tells her. "There weren't any goats."

"Maybe you're thinking about the Bardwells, honey," her mother suggests. "They might have raised some for 4-H."

"I'm not thinking about the *Bardwells*." Max tastes saliva souring in her mouth. She feels far away, and she speaks more loudly to bring herself back. "Come on, you guys. This isn't funny. Come on."

The three of them look at each other. Her father clears his throat and shrugs. "Well, okay. So we had goats once. Whatever you say, Maxie." He is trying to sound amused.

"Why are you doing this to me?" She throws her napkin onto her plate, having lost all sense of how much it weighs. She had thought things might shatter.

"Honey, what do you expect us to say?" Her mother stands up to clear the table. "I think Daddy would remember something like that. Besides, does it really matter? Why is it such a big deal?"

Maxine looks across the table at her sister, who smooths her baby's invisible hair. Her father chews a tomato and her mother arranges cookies on a glass plate for dessert. "I'll prove it to you," Max tells them, not even recognizing her own voice. "After supper I'll go out and dig their bones up behind the garage."

Her mother sighs, carrying in the cookies. "It's so muddy back there," she says.

Tillie adds, "You won't find anything."

Her father shrugs again. "Go ahead. If it makes you feel better." He pushes a whole cookie into his mouth.

But when it comes time, Max knows, she won't do it. She isn't brave enough to take that chance. Can't even the hardest things — bones, teeth — disintegrate in the dirt? Instead she lingers at the table with the rest of them, stirring sugar into her tea. On the morning she found Clover's body, she was the first in the family to wake up. It was already hot, and she approached the pen with a dish of carrot shavings, calling Clover's name. Before she ran into the house to get her father, she saw the goat lying there, and she stopped, blind, her head rushing away from her and the sound stuck in her throat, because in that moment she knew what it felt like to be dead.

Please Come Back To Me

> Before us lies eternity; our souls
> Are love, and a continual farewell.
> — W. B. YEATS, "Ephemera"

THE DAY AFTER CHRISTMAS, Dorrie was finishing the last carton of eggnog with her mother and Jeanne Marie Ettlinger, who had been her best friend when they were children and who now went to medical school.

"I want to show you a picture," Dorrie said to Jeanne Marie. "Tell me what you think." Out of an envelope in her purse she pulled a snapshot of her husband, Chris, sitting on the beach. She directed Jeanne Marie's attention to Chris's left arm, which was bare from the shoulder down (he wore a sleeveless tee that said "Endangered Species"), and which rested on a cooler containing Michelobs and Diet Cokes.

"The mole," Dorrie added, pointing further when Jeanne Marie seemed not to see. "That brown thing."

Jeanne Marie drew the photograph closer and peered. "You expect me to diagnose that little dot?" she asked. "It looks like a poppy seed."

Dorrie's mother sat across from them, folding salvaged sheets of wrapping paper to use next year. "Silly," she said to her daughter. "He's twenty-six years old. Nothing's wrong with him. Where do you get these ideas?" She paused in packing the paper, and lit a cigarette with the lighter her boss had given her for a Christmas present. It was silver, classy looking, and when she'd gotten home that day, she threw away all her Bics.

"But could it be something?" Dorrie persisted. She took the photo back and rubbed her finger over the spot she was looking at, as if she could feel it—the round brown bump in the top half of Chris's arm, at the place where a short sleeve hem would meet the skin. "We just noticed it this summer. It wasn't there before."

"It couldn't hurt to have it checked," Jeanne Marie said. "Where is Chris, anyway?"

"At home. I mean, his parents'." Dorrie put the photograph back in her purse, which she set on the floor beside the pile of presents she and Chris had received from her mother. The gifts from his family were already packed in the trunk. Chris's parents gave them a wine rack; an espresso machine, though Dorrie herself had never drunk any; a set of towels from Lord & Taylor; two sweaters apiece; a microwave oven; and another subscription to *Smithsonian*, which she told herself she would read this year. When her mother asked her what Chris's family had given them, Dorrie said, "Oh, sweaters," and had to remind herself that she was telling the truth.

Dorrie's mother crocheted them a rug that didn't match anything, though they would lay it down beneath the bedroom window, where the cats tended to sleep. She also sewed them hand towels with their initials embroidered. Chris's were CRM (Christopher Richard Manning) but Dorrie's spelled DUM (she had been Doreen Udell) and the sight of the letters made her wince. She knew she would not hang the towels in her home except when her mother was visiting.

"They're just an hour from here, over in Esperance," she said to Jeanne Marie, referring to Chris's family. "We were there for Christmas Eve and half of yesterday, and then we came here. He went back this morning to say good-bye."

"Oh, right." Jeanne Marie had never really learned any details of Chris's origin or his history, but it was easier to pretend that she had. She had met him only once, at the wedding, a year and a half ago. "Are you guys going to have kids?" she asked Dorrie, and in the next moment it occurred to her that maybe she shouldn't have brought this up in front of Dorrie's mother.

"Good question," Dorrie's mother said to Jeanne Marie. "I've been wondering the same thing myself."

"A boy and a girl, we hope," Dorrie answered, ignoring her mother's tone. "Luke and Olivia. They're waiting up on the moon somewhere, for us to call them down." She looked up at the ceiling because even though she knew better, in her most private heart she really was tempted to believe it, and she wanted the children to know that she thought about them even now, when they were still the distant, lunar fantasies she and Chris had invented during the first meal she cooked after their honeymoon, over a bottle of cheap champagne. "But not for another three years or so. We wouldn't be ready before then."

"Nobody's ever ready," her mother said.

They sat in the living room, across from the tree. The lights clipped to the branches were turned on, but the corner where the tree stood looked darker than in the days before Christmas, when the wrapped packages underneath gave it a bright, winking height. Outside they could hear the wind skimming down Cobb's Hill, where as kids they used to sled all day until patches of dead grass showed through the snow.

It was time for Jeanne Marie to leave, but she didn't seem to be picking up on this. *Maybe if I start talking about something personal,*

Dorrie thought. She said to her mother, "Do you ever miss Dad?" Next to her, Jeanne Marie poured rum straight into her glass.

"Of course I do."

"Especially around this time?"

"Well, I wish he hadn't died so close to Christmas, if that's what you mean." Her mother smoked slowly and took a long sip. "Do you remember him, honey?"

"I think so."

"He was a good man."

"I know he was."

"Sometimes I'm sure he's here with me again." Her mother put out the cigarette before it was finished, and she settled back in the armchair holding her drink in hands folded across her stomach. She closed her eyes. "Sometimes I'll hear the wind outside, like tonight, and I think he's trying to get in."

The remark did not require an answer, but Dorrie felt she should give one. "You do?" she said, because it was all she could come up with.

"I know it sounds crazy. Maybe not to you. But I'm sure Jeanne Marie thinks so."

In her chair, Jeanne Marie slurped the dregs from her glass. "No offense, Mrs. Udell, but you're right." Ordinarily she was not bold in any way, but she had, by this time, consumed a lot of rum. "I'm a scientist; I can't be believing in souls blowing in the wind." When neither Dorrie nor her mother objected, she gathered steam and forged ahead. "What happens after a person dies is their body starts decomposing, and that includes the brain. The brain is what makes us think and feel. If a person's brain is dead, he can't exactly be in a relationship with anyone. Right?" Without waiting for them to acknowledge the truth of her argument, she went on. "So how could it really be Mr. Udell out there? He wouldn't know where to go because he couldn't think, and he wouldn't feel anything for anybody, no offense." About halfway through her speech she'd realized it would have been better left undelivered, but it was too late. She plunked her glass down and said, "Well, I better go." She stood with a little trouble and twirled one way and then the other, not sure which direction her coat was in. Dorrie got it down from the hook in the kitchen and held it open for her. "Say hello to Chris," Jeanne Marie said, shrugging the sleeves on, "if he even remembers me."

"Of course he does." Dorrie gave her a hug and recalled, when Jeanne Marie pulled away from the embrace, how her friend used to take the mandatory shower after fifth-grade gym class with a towel wrapped around her body, holding it closed and sopping under the water in a tight fist at her breasts. Dorrie and her mother watched until Jeanne Marie vanished behind the white banks piled at the side of the street.

"She used to be so cute," her mother said. "It's too bad."

"I think she still is." Dorrie stacked up the eggnog glasses. "It's just not as obvious."

Now her mother smiled, because she wondered again how (it was not in the bloodline) her daughter had grown up to be so consistently kind. "Don't you ever say anything nasty about anybody?" she asked.

"I'll say something nasty about Chris, if he doesn't get here soon." Dorrie pressed back into the sofa and cradled a pillow to her chest.

They both sat with their eyes closed for a few minutes. Then her mother opened hers and turned to look at Dorrie. "You know, you don't have to protect me, honey. I know what you must think."

"What are you *talking* about?" Dorrie shot forward in her seat.

"I know I'm not the mother you would ask for. I believe in things that don't make sense to you. I know my presents are embarrassing. But I do the best I can, and I do love you."

"Mom, I know that." Dorrie's voice came out angry, because

she hated her mother for talking this way. "Stop it, will you? I love you too."

"I know." In the eaves the wind paused for a moment, then started up again. "See? There's your father now," her mother told her, pointing toward the sound.

On the drive home to New Jersey, Dorrie held the cats by turn — there were two of them, Bonnie and Clyde, though both were girls — while the one not being petted paced the back seat, waiting and making petulant noises, nestling among the gifts. Rain or snow fell on the windshield, depending on how hilly the road was at any given point.

Dorrie felt safer than she could remember ever feeling before in her life; even the idea of dying was, strangely, not so bad. She was not afraid of anything that might happen, as long as Chris knew about it, as long as he was there. Even dying together, in a warm car with the four familiar heartbeats moving forward through the night, felt right — people always say we are born and we die alone, but Dorrie believed that these people did not know love the way she knew it, the way it was possible to inhabit another person as if you breathed with the same lungs.

She shivered without knowing she was going to and said, "My friend Jeanne Marie says you should do something about that mole."

"How does she know?"

"I showed her the pictures. Of you on the beach." They both realized how silly this sounded and laughed, Chris's sharp hoot sending Bonnie's ears into the air.

"She say anything about the rest of my body? What a fine specimen I am?"

"No." Dorrie turned and giggled at the window. "She didn't."

"Well, how good a doctor can she be?" The look on his face (he really appeared to be serious) made Dorrie laugh again, but when the car skidded on a slick patch, sliding sideways on the road, the sound in her throat backed into a gasp.

"Will you make an appointment?" she said.

"It's just a mole."

"Well, I'll make one for you." They were passing through a slick stretch of the Thruway, freezing rain glazing the glass. Crystals pelted the roof and hood. Dorrie took both of the cats into her lap, and turned the radio down so Chris could concentrate. "This is scary," she said.

"You could go to sleep." He did not look at her when he spoke, because his focus was aimed straight ahead, but she knew she would always have his first attention when she needed it. "When you wake up, it'll be over."

"I wouldn't leave you alone in this," she said.

She tried a few different dermatologists before she scheduled Chris with one who could see him as early as three weeks later. At supper that night, she told him about the appointment and he made a small sound she couldn't interpret, but she let it pass without asking him what he meant.

For dessert they ate chocolate-covered graham crackers, passing the bag between them while they lay on the couch together and watched *Jeopardy!* Chris usually knew a lot of the science and history questions, and Dorrie answered the ones about popular culture and quotes. The only categories they overlapped on were Music and, sometimes, Potpourri. The cats always perched on top of the couch during the game, like sentinels or referees. "What is carbon dioxide," Chris might say, crunching around a cookie, and when he turned out to be right — especially if it was a Daily Double — he made a noise with his mouth meant to sound like a crowd reverberating in awe. Whenever Dorrie got one — hers were more like "Who was the Sundance Kid?" — Chris high-fived her, and sometimes the clap between their hands was loud enough to scare Clyde away.

On New Year's Eve they went over to Steve and Linda's. Steve and Chris worked for the same company in Newark, and when they discovered they lived in the same apartment complex, they'd introduced their wives and began doing things together on weekends. At first Dorrie had felt anxious, because they were all professionals while she was not, but Chris told her not to be ridiculous, that none of them could hold a candle to her. She wasn't sure what he meant by this, but didn't want to put him on the spot by asking. Gradually she grew used to Steve and Linda's company, and even convinced herself that she enjoyed it, despite the fact that Linda was always trying to lend Dorrie books about the supernatural — ESP, reincarnation, bending spoons with your mind. Dorrie accepted the books, but didn't plan to read them. Chris applauded her for this, because he thought it was all hocus-pocus, so she didn't tell him that the real reason she returned the books unopened was that she was afraid she might come to believe some of it, and he would think less of her.

Steve and Linda's apartment was laid out exactly like Chris and Dorrie's, but on the other side of the complex. Visiting them Dorrie felt disoriented at times, because it felt like being home and *not* being home at the same time.

Still, Steve and Linda decorated differently, so there was the pale excitement of being surrounded by objects and colors not their own. Linda set the hot pan on the table, which was set with Mexican dinnerware and woven place mats. Candles threw a festive light to all four corners, and they sat down without recognizing, yet, how much they had to be grateful for.

After they'd filled their plates and clinked glasses of sangria, Linda said, "Are you guys making resolutions? I have one. Starting tomorrow" — the force of her words made the flame closest to her waver in front of her face — "or the day after, I'm going to exercise three times a week if it kills me. I swear to God. It cost me a lot of money to join that club, and I'm just letting it sit there." When nobody responded (because it was obvious that they all knew how this resolution was going to work out), she plowed through her embarrassment and turned to Chris. "Your turn."

"I don't have any," he said. Across the table he noticed Dorrie pointedly dabbing her own mouth with her napkin as she looked at him, and he reached to blot a dot of sauce above his lip.

"Why not?"

He shrugged. "My life is perfect. I don't want anything to change."

Steve raised his eyebrows. Then he jerked his thumb toward Chris and said to Linda, "Do you believe this guy?"

"What? I think it's nice." She ripped off her third hunk of bread from the loaf they were all sharing.

"*My life is perfect*? Nobody says that and means it. It's impossible." He shook his head and turned to Dorrie, and it did not escape any of them that although he pretended to think his friend was either lying or joking, he felt jealous of what Chris had said. "Your husband needs serious help."

"I don't think so," she said, smiling. She did not even have to look at Chris to know he was smiling, too. To take the pressure off him, she put her fork down and announced, "Okay, I'll make one. My resolution is to smile at my boss at least once a day, even when I feel like killing her."

"What good will *that* do you?" Linda asked.

"I don't know. But I heard somebody on Oprah say that when you forgive somebody, you don't really do it for them. You do it for yourself." A pause followed during which she felt chagrined and guilty, because she had wandered into territory far steeper than they had all contracted for, and pulled them in with her. Luckily, Steve got them out of it with his resolution not to fart in his cubicle at work anymore, to which Chris replied, "I give that ten minutes, tops."

Later, as they watched the ball drop over Times Square on TV, Dorrie squeezed Chris's hand and said, "I love you." She whispered it so Steve and Linda wouldn't hear, as if it were something they needed to hide.

But Chris wouldn't let her get away with this. In a normal voice he said, "You too," because the word *love* came harder to him. Even though their friends had already finished their short kiss, he held Dorrie close, assuming that she would grow embarrassed and push him away. But instead she held on until he started laughing, and even after that she told him, "I'm not letting you go."

January started slowly, and cold. They couldn't do much outside in the way of fun, except sometimes on a couple of Sundays when Steve and Linda got together a few couples from the complex for touch football, and invited everyone over afterward for chili and beer.

At work Dorrie continued to hate her boss, but Evelyn was working on a big case and spent a lot of time in the law library, so Dorrie didn't have to see her that often. She passed most of her days transcribing tapes Evelyn had dictated the night before. The morning Dorrie found a pencil in Evelyn's OUT box and put it back on the desk, assuming it had fallen out of a file, and Evelyn called her on the intercom to explain that she'd put it in the box because she wanted it sharpened, Dorrie barely managed to hold back the tears as she called Chris at work and whispered into the phone after stabbing the pencil into a sharpener. There were sharpeners all over the building, including on Evelyn's desk.

She could hear his outrage on the other end of the line. "What does she think you are?" he said. "A *monkey* can sharpen a pencil."

When this caused a fresh, louder gust of tears, he realized he'd said exactly the wrong thing, and rushed to explain himself. "Dorrie,

I'm sorry. But you know what I'm saying. She treats you like crap. You have to get out of there."

"It's not so bad," she said, because hearing him say this had made her feel better. "I wouldn't make the same money anywhere else. As long as *you* know I'm smarter than a monkey, that's all I need."

It made Chris angry to hear her talk this way. He liked his job, and he often felt guilty that Dorrie didn't like hers. He tried to keep in mind that it was her choice, but when they came home at the end of the day and he saw how she looked — it took her a couple of *Three's Company* reruns, stroking both cats, to unwind — he wanted to tell her to quit, it wasn't worth it, he couldn't stand to see her so tense.

On other days he felt less sorry for her, and on those days they fought. "If you hate it so much, then do something else," he would tell her, taking his tie off so he could dangle it in front of Bonnie and Clyde. "You went to college. You don't have to be a secretary."

"I know," Dorrie would say, though she did not, in fact, know this. Her own mother had been a secretary, and her grandmother, too. Dorrie hadn't finished her degree, which would have been in English, anyway, and what could you do with that? She could spell and write a good sentence, which was part of the reason Evelyn had hired her. "I'll go back to school someday. Chris, don't tease them that way." She was talking about the cats, who leapt in frustration for the tie.

When he wouldn't stop, she went on, "Besides, it's easy for you to talk. You've been to graduate school. You have your pick of jobs."

"That's because I work hard."

"And I don't?"

"I didn't say that."

Chris worked for a company that designed computer programs using geographical data. Someday soon, he told Dorrie, we'll all be driving cars with computers built into the dash. When we get lost, all we'll have to do is punch in our destination, and the cursor will lead us there.

Dorrie loved to hear Chris talk about his job, especially to other people, because he always found a way to make sure they understood how what he did could potentially affect their lives. This was what was missing in her own job, besides the respect she wanted from her boss — she could never see, no matter how hard she tried, how anything she did might influence anything, in even the most distant or peripheral ways. All Dorrie did was type, file, and set up meetings between Evelyn and her clients. Her initials (at work she dropped the Udell, so she was just *dm*) came at the end of every document she produced, so she *did* get to make a mark, but of course she was always in lowercase, after the slash preceded by Evelyn's assertive capitals.

When spring arrived early, at the beginning of March, she cleaned one Saturday the miniature grill they kept on the miniature deck by their back door, and they invited Steve and Linda over for steaks and beer, which they ate and drank sitting in a circle on the deck's floor, each person's knees touching two others. Everyone wore short sleeves to the supper picnic. Linda, who was sitting next to Chris on the left side, squirted steak juice on him by accident when she cut in, and she went to wipe his arm off with her napkin. "Ooh," she said, noticing the mole, "what's that?"

"It's a mole," Chris said.

"Well I know *that*," Linda told him. She leaned closer and peered. "It just doesn't look good, I mean."

"He was supposed to go to the doctor about it last month." Dorrie passed another napkin to Linda. "But did he keep the appointment I made for him? No."

"I had to go to Atlanta," Chris said, "for a sales thing."

"It's all dark," Linda said, lifting a finger to the raised spot, "and it — yuck — squishes."

"I'm trying to eat here," Steve said. "Do you mind?"

"You'd better go in and have it looked at, Chris." Linda wiped her finger on the clean napkin and picked up her knife again. "We had a woman in HR who had a mole on her back, but she lived alone, so she never even knew about it until it was too late."

"What happened to her?" Chris asked.

"Well," Linda said. She shrugged and smiled a little, to imply that he didn't really want to know. Then they decided that it was too cold to sit outside, after all, and went back in to where everything felt familiar.

The doctor was a man the age of Chris's father, and he even looked like him — small stature, thin shoulders, recessed eyes. It threw Chris off when he stood to shake hands, and he found himself smiling as he sat down on the examining table and rolled up his sleeve.

"Something amuses you?" the doctor said. His name was Elliott Gruberman, and he looked apprehensive about what it might be that Chris found funny.

"No," Chris said. "It's just that you look a lot like my father. Except he's blind."

The doctor narrowed his gaze, as if he weren't sure how to take this. "You mean really blind, or he just doesn't see things the way you think he should?"

"He's really blind. Since he was a kid."

"What happened? Some kind of fever?"

"No, more bizarre than that. He just came in the house one day — he'd been playing ball with a bunch of kids — and screamed that a big light split the sky open, and now he couldn't see. The doctors told his mother it was just temporary, something called flash blindness. But it never went away. And they never figured out where the light came from. It wasn't lightning or an eclipse, or anything. And the *really* weird thing is, none of the other kids saw it."

He didn't quite know why he went on at such length to the doctor. But later he realized it was because he was trying to delay talking about the mole on his arm.

"I know what you're thinking," Chris continued. "He's crazy, right? It's psychological.

"But the doctors didn't think so. They thought it was just one of those things that happens — he was in the wrong place at the wrong time, it hit him at an angle nobody else saw, and bam! The next thing he knows, he can't see."

"Wow." The doctor whistled, though his face was serious. "Your dad religious at all?"

"No. Why?" Even as he answered, Chris realized he'd been wanting to ask the same question all his life.

The doctor shrugged. "It sounds kind of biblical. 'And now men see not the light which is bright in the skies.' Book of Job."

Chris wasn't sure whether to be alarmed or comforted, so he decided to feel both. Luckily, the doctor had taken his arm up by then, and turned it toward him to look at the mole. "So this is the guest that won't go home, I gather?" Under the swivel light, Chris forced himself to look at the brown spot, which he had routinely avoided — in the shower and when he dressed or took his clothes off — since Dorrie started pestering him about it.

"My wife made me come," he told the doctor, who was pressing the mole and looking at it from all angles.

"And you're complaining?"

Something in the doctor's voice gave Chris a lift of surprise that made him want to laugh, and it rose to his face in the form of a blush. "I mean come *here*," he said, and Dr. Gruberman slapped himself on the back of his hand.

"Forgive me," he said. "I've been on vacation. I'm not back in doctorly mode."

"That's okay," Chris told him.

"You have to say that. I've got your life in my hands." The doctor took his finger off the mole and, seeing the look on Chris's face, he said, "That was a joke. We'll take it off to be on the safe side, but most often these guys turn out to be benign."

"Take it off?" Instinctively, Chris's right hand went up to cover the mole, as if to protect it from what the doctor was saying.

"Excise it surgically. Give it the boot." Dr. Gruberman swabbed the arm yellow, then prepared a needle of anesthetic.

"I didn't think anything would happen today." Chris got to his feet, but there was no place to go. His shirt was on the other side of the room, and the doctor stood blocking the door. His arm fell numb and heavy by his side, and when he saw what the doctor was preparing, he felt faint at the stomach and thought he might fall.

"Well, there's no point in waiting. We need to get rid of it, just in case, so we can run some tests." Dr. Gruberman raised a metal instrument — it looked like something Dorrie might cook with — above Chris's arm and said, "If I were you, I'd look the other way. Imagine Kathleen Turner sitting on the sink. Or Debra Winger — I'm a Debra Winger man, myself."

"Okay." Chris turned and closed his eyes, but at this moment when he floated in fear it was Dorrie he thought of, and their first date, a minor-league baseball game, the Albany-Colonie A's. Chris and Dorrie got to the park late, and they were on their way up the short rise of bleachers when the field and stands stilled for the singing of the anthem. At the end of the song, before she started following Chris up the steps, Dorrie felt a wet splash against her sandaled heels, and turned to see that someone — a teenage boy, ugly with acne — had vomited over a railing from the row above them, and she'd been hit with spray. The boy looked guilty, and hung his head over his knees. When Chris saw what had happened, he came back down to where Dorrie was standing, and he yelled into the aisle at the boy, "Geez, what are you, drunk?" because he could not believe the evening was starting this way, someone throwing up on his date.

The boy didn't say anything, and the friend sitting next to him was also silent, looking out to the field as if he might have come by himself. Dorrie told Chris, "Wait a minute," and she said to the boy, "Are you okay?" and he shook his head and started crying.

"Dorrie, the kid's drunk," Chris said. "Come on."

"I am not." The boy was shaky, and he sounded scared. "I'm sick. I'm hot, but I keep shivering. I just want to go home."

"How did you get here?" Dorrie said.

"His father." The boy pointed a weak finger at his companion, who gave a shy nod to Dorrie as if he were being introduced. "But we're supposed to take the bus back."

"Well, we could drive you," Dorrie told him. "Right, Chris?"

"Are you kidding?" Chris said.

"Chris." She moved closer to him as if to confide something, and he smelled the lemon of shampoo in her hair and knew she had washed it for him. She was using a napkin someone handed her to wipe the vomit from her heels, and her voice near his cheek felt like an embrace of his entire body. She held the soiled napkin by the corner — he would have let it fall between the seats — and added, "He's sick. Think how you would feel."

Chris looked at the boy again and remembered the misery of nausea, worse in a public place among strangers, and because he did not want to lose Dorrie or let her know that he was not a good person, he said, "Yeah, okay. Let's go," to the boy, and the two teenagers followed Chris and Dorrie out to the parking lot, silently, until the boy who had been sick on Dorrie paused before getting into the backseat of Chris's Impala and said to her, "I'm, you know, sorry."

"It's okay," Dorrie said, and Chris, getting in on the other side, was jealous of the look she gave the boy, of the sympathy her face showed and the tenderness in her smile. He would have pushed the car across town to know what it felt like to receive these things from her, and in that moment, as he started the car and watched her eyes approving and thanking him from the next seat, he vowed that he would let himself learn from this woman (for although she had barely just started college, he could see that this was what she was), no matter how much he had to give up of what he believed he already knew.

A hot star exploded in his arm, followed by a deep pull. Chris bowed his head over his lap and tried not to pass out. When it was over, and Dr. Gruberman had finished stitching, the arm felt stiff and tight under the bandage. "How are you going to get home?" the doctor said. "You really shouldn't drive."

"My wife came with me," Chris told him, and then he smiled in spite of the pain and warned the doctor, "Don't say it."

"Ah, good boy. You're going to be fine." Dr. Gruberman wrote a prescription and held it out to the hand at the end of Chris's good arm. "I'll call you when we get the results in," he said. "Five days, maybe a week."

"What are the tests for?" Chris asked. He couldn't button his shirt, so the doctor did it for him, and he felt like a child being bundled up by his mother to go out in the snow.

"Well, cancer," Dr. Gruberman said, "but that's a long shot." He snapped the tail of Chris's shirt down and pulled the collar out at the neck. "Don't worry about it. Looks like we got it early."

Chris said, "Do I just leave now?" He did not want the doctor to let him go.

When she saw him in the corridor, Dorrie got up from the seat where she was taking a quiz in a magazine. "What did they do?" she said, seeing the bandage, and Chris could tell from her face that he didn't look good.

"Took it off."

"What does that mean?"

He shrugged, and the motion felt wild, as if he might not be able to ever stop. "He said it could be cancer."

"No," Dorrie said, although Chris's last word was what finally scratched the itch that had been picking at her heart. She blasted out a laugh that did not sound like one, and rolled the magazine into a tube. "I mean, they probably have to say that. But it's not."

"I know." He winced.

"It hurts?" She recognized the thinnest reflection of tears in his eyes, and it frightened her more than if he had spilled sobs on the sterile floor.

"Not too bad," Chris said.

"Then why — " But she realized she didn't want him to tell her why he was crying, and she took his hand as they walked out together, each of them blinking as if it were too bright, though the sun was on its way down.

In the car she was still talking but his mind was not with hers. They drove the streets he had come to know because he lived here, but this time he saw them as part of a foreign place, a city far from home, which was the kitchen his mother stood in and the touch of her tired hand.

All the moments we think we will tell someday: they were fighting for the front of the line at his lips, then in his throat, where they waited to be whispered into the world's ear. It began with the warmth of sunlight on the crib sheet, and the vibration of stroller wheels struggling across snow. The memory of his grandmother jumping over a puddle. The taste of blood and ice cream when a tooth comes out in a cone. The moment he realized he could not look at one thing without his eye also taking in everything around it, even the ocean, which included the sky. What it felt like to be himself, waking up on a Saturday morning; how the smell of rain in the summer could make him angry or want to cry. Every secret between him and God that would someday be only God's — each came forward with all the others now because it was time to be counted, and Chris knew this in a way that came not from logic but intuition, the same way we understand love.

When they got home, a message blinked on the answering machine, but it was not for them. The male voice carried a burry, thick-tongued accent Dorrie felt sure came from some country she would not be able to identify on a map. "Hello? I call about the opportunity you are offering. I think I am your right man. Please come back to me as soon as possibly." He left a name, which they could not make out, and a phone number, which they could.

"Oh, I love that," Dorrie said, letting herself feel momentarily amused. "*Come back to me.*" She was standing by the phone table with her coat on, and Chris stood next to her, looking at the wall, where a frame containing vignettes of their wedding day — the kiss at the altar, the kiss through bites of cake — hung at the level of his eyes. He had teased Dorrie when she put the montage together, calling it corny, but sometimes she caught him studying it as he did now, when he didn't realize he was being watched. "The mistakes people make are so cute sometimes. Remember when Li Ching at the Christmas party said it was half of one, six dozen of the other?"

"Yeah," Chris said, but he wasn't smiling. He lifted his right hand to run a finger across the surface of the photo frame. "Dusty," he added.

"So clean it." Dorrie took her coat off and snapped it back against the couch. "They shouldn't have told you it might be cancer. That was a stupid thing to say."

"I wonder what opportunity that guy was calling about." Chris nodded toward the phone.

"A job, probably. What difference does it make?"

"We should call him back and tell him he got the wrong number."

Dorrie was shaking cat food into the two bowls. The sound called Bonnie and Clyde to hover around her hands. "See?" she said to Chris, putting her arms around him from behind. "You're a better man than you think you are."

They lay on the bed for a few minutes without speaking, Dorrie being careful not to jostle his bad arm. Then Chris said, "You're glad you married me, right?" He knew he did not have to elaborate; she would understand why he asked.

Dorrie made room for the cats among the covers, and he felt rather than saw her smiling in the dark. "I'll think about it," she told him. "Let me come back to you on that."

The news, when they got it, wasn't good. It took longer than the doctor had expected, and after eight days Dorrie made Chris call to find out why they hadn't heard anything; it turned out that the mole — or at least part of it — had been sent to a hospital in Minnesota and then one in California, and nobody could tell anything from the tests, until they flew it back to the East Coast and Boston, where it was finally found to be malignant.

Before they received that last piece of information, on the eleventh day, they traced in their imaginations the mole's route across the country. It started when Dorrie said to Chris, "I can't believe this, and you won't believe it either, but I'm actually jealous of your mole. I've never been to California."

"Neither have I," Chris said. They entertained each other with visions of the mole traveling in first class, all expenses paid, living it up. It felt safe to laugh at something so silly, spending their energy on the absurd.

But on the eleventh day — it was a Monday — Dorrie was sitting at her desk when the phone rang, twice which meant it was an outside line, and at her personal extension, which meant it was Chris.

She picked up the receiver and instead of *Hello*, she said, "Listen, I have to work Friday." Sunday would be Easter, and his office was giving people Friday off. They planned to drive to upstate New York to visit both of their families for the long weekend. "I thought I'd be able to get out early, but Evelyn has this deadline. So we won't be able to leave till that night, which'll be bad traffic-wise, but — "

"Dorrie," Chris said, and the sound of his voice made her stomach feel as if it were being sliced open. "The doctor just called. It was cancer." Then there was nothing at all on the other end, as if the line between them had been pulled.

"Are you there?" she cried, and Anita, who worked in the next cubicle, stood up and looked over the top to see what was happening.

"Of course," Chris said. Then he laughed without happiness and added, "At least, for now."

"Shut up," Dorrie told him. She had pulled a thumbtack from the bulletin board over her desk, letting fall to the floor a memo about comp time, and she began stabbing the sharp end into the paper on the pad that said *From the Desk of Doreen Manning*. "Don't say things like that. What are you telling me? Wait a minute. *Was* cancer? What do they mean by *was*?" Suddenly hope opened her lungs wide and let her breathe again.

"I can't really talk too much right now," Chris said, and she could tell he was afraid of being overheard. "But he thinks there's a good chance they got it all. I have to go back and let them take out some more tissue, to make sure, but he says I'm probably okay."

"That's not good enough," Dorrie said. "*Probably*."

"Dorrie, I have to go."

"Wait a minute." Anita's face was still hanging over the top of the cubicle, and Dorrie tilted her face up to gesture — though politely — that she should sit back down. "How are we supposed to work all day?" she whispered. "Chris, I can't. I want to see you. Take the rest of the day off, and meet me back home."

"I can't just leave," he said, and now she heard that it was not discretion but terror that tinted his tone.

"Tell them you have a family emergency."

"They'll think it's you."

"Then tell them you're sick," she said. "Oh, my God — that's the truth."

But when they got to the apartment, they didn't know what to do or how to feel. It was late morning, and the cats were lying in the tunnel of sunlight coming in through the bedroom window. Usually when Chris and Dorrie arrived at the end of the day, Bonnie and Clyde ran to the door at the sound of the key, but at this hour they were too comfortable to move, and not hungry, and they only opened their eyes when their nap was interrupted by the early voices and shadows of their owners coming home.

Dorrie wanted to hold Chris, attach herself to him physically, but he didn't feel like touching in the middle of the day; when he let her know this, with a movement of his shoulders and his head, she felt as if she were being shaken off, like dandruff or a pest. He saw this in her face and tried to hug her then, but it was too late.

"What should we do?" he said. He sat on the bed's edge while Dorrie took her jewelry off. "I feel guilty, being home instead of working."

She took her skirt and blouse off, hung them up in the closet, and stepped into her jeans. "I don't know," she said. "Why do we have to do anything? I mean, you have cancer. God. I can't believe this." She was holding a sweatshirt and she had been about to put it on, but as her arms went up they lost their momentum and fell, and she stood with her hands tangled in the fabric, the flesh of her breasts looking blanched in the noon's sharp light.

"I have an idea," Chris said, getting up from the bed to nuzzle her neck.

"Chris," she said. "I'm too scared. Shouldn't we think about everything?"

"What's to think about?"

"What could happen."

"This could happen," he told her, and he leaned her back on the bed.

She whispered, "Then we'll *really* feel guilty," but she lifted her lips to his. When they woke up a few hours later, it took them both longer than it should have to remember that something was wrong.

Chris voted for waiting to tell anybody else in the family, even his parents, until the operation was over and he had been cleared. But Dorrie convinced him that it would be too hard to hide all weekend. "I'll do it," she said, during the ride to Esperance. "I'll just say it when we get there, and it'll be over with."

Chris told her, "No, let me," but it took him a while, at his parents' house, to bring it up. They arrived late on Good Friday, and only had time for tea and beer in the kitchen before everyone went to bed. As it was, they had to speak softly because Chris's niece, who was a year and a half old, was asleep in the next room. Chris's sister Charlotte, the baby's mother, had come home to live without her husband, who had not wanted a baby, and who had not forgiven Charlotte — even after Tess was born — for getting pregnant on purpose without talking to him about it first. When Tess was two months old, the husband had moved out, taking another apartment in the same town. Chris's sister, after a period of not believing that this was her life, took the love she had once felt for her husband and gave it to Tess, along with all the mother love Tess would have received, anyway, and the baby was bright with the power and danger of it; if love were radioactive, she would have glowed.

On Saturday morning they were all up early — Tess sang them awake — and when they had finished eating the waffles Chris's father had made, Chris rubbed the fold of his napkin between his fingers and said, in the moment before Dorrie and his mother would have begun clearing the table, "Listen, we have some news."

There was a short silence, during which even the baby paused to look at him; then Charlotte, who sat next to Dorrie, exclaimed, "You're pregnant!" and moved to put her arms around her sister-in-law. When Dorrie held her hands up to fend her off (not because she disliked Charlotte, but because she couldn't encourage the mistake), Charlotte looked hurt, and Chris hurried to tell her, "Charl, it isn't that."

"Then what?" His mother, who wore earrings with her robe to the breakfast table, reached across to tilt Chris's face toward her, as she might have when he was three.

"I had a little mole here, remember?" he said, pushing up the sleeve of his rugby shirt to show them the small gauze square.

"What happened to you there?" his father said, turning his head as if he could see with the rest of them. He took the arm in much the same way Dr. Gruberman had, and ran his fingers slowly up the skin until they found the bandage.

"They took it off. The mole," Dorrie said. "So they could send it for tests."

"And they found something," Chris added, before she could tell it all.

"When did this happen?" his mother said, and they all recognized that it was her way of delaying the real question.

"The week before last."

"And you didn't tell us?"

"Frances, stop." Her husband gave Chris's arm back, folding it gently at the elbow. He sold insurance for a living, and he was comfortable asking people for personal information. And people — maybe because his voice contained more comprehension than the average set of eyes — were comfortable giving it to him. "They found what?"

"Malignant melanoma," Dorrie said.

"But they think they got it all." Chris held the plastic syrup bottle between his fingers and squeezed the contents to the top. "So it's really like a thing that already happened — bad news in the past."

"You mean cancer?" His mother's voice went so high and loud that Tess, sitting on her lap, flinched from her grandmother.

"Well, I guess so," Chris said, as if the force of her dismay made him doubt what he knew to be true.

"But they think they got it," Dorrie repeated.

"But they're not sure?" Mrs. Manning untied the sash of her robe without looking down at it, then pulled the lapels closer together across her breasts and retied the sash in a knot they could all tell was too tight.

"I have to go back this week so they can take out more tissue."

"When?" his mother asked.

"Wednesday."

"Then why are you telling us this now?" She said it in such a reasonable tone that it took them all a few seconds to realize their surprise. "Why didn't you wait until it was all over, when you knew everything was fine?" She had taken the syrup from Chris, made him stop squeezing the bottle to look at her.

"Frances," her husband said. He knew exactly where her hand would be, and reached out to touch it. "Come on."

"I was going to wait." Chris turned to Dorrie, and his expression said *See*? "I wanted to, but Dorrie said we should tell you."

"I thought you would want to know," Dorrie said, and it was all she could do to keep from adding, "for Christ's sake."

"She does. We do. Of course," Chris's father said. "Don't mind Mom, she just went off the beam for a minute. It's just such a shock, because he's so young." He nodded in Chris's direction with an expression of deference to what his son now knew about mortality, which he himself did not.

"But you hear about skin cancer a lot," he went on. "Like the president's nose, remember? They take the bad part off, you're home free."

Charlotte told Chris, "Listen, you're going to be fine." She stood up, lifting Tess to her hip, and Dorrie sensed in the motion an impulse to put distance between the baby and her brother, as if cancer were contagious. "You're strong. They got it in time. You have Dorrie. But make sure you call us, the minute they find out."

"Okay," Chris said, and Dorrie could tell that neither he nor Charlotte quite knew how to handle it when the attention tilted from her toward him. "Hey, stinky," he said to his niece, who was trying to escape, "where do you think you're going?"

"See the bunny," Tess said.

"The Easter egg hunt at the firehouse," Charlotte translated. "Mom, are you going to come?"

Chris's mother looked as if she were making a choice as to what to think about, and then Dorrie saw her decide. "If we go, we have to hard-boil some eggs," she said, collecting the breakfast dishes. "That's how they work it — everybody chips in." She put the plates down in the sink, went over to stand behind her son, and put her fingers around his neck gently in a collar of support.

"Someday you'll have someone to bring to the egg hunt, too," she told him.

"Why can't I bring Dorrie?"

"Too tall," his father answered, and they all laughed as if he had said something funny. Only everyone's laughter — including her own — sounded different to Dorrie from the laughter she had known until now.

Because of the experience with Chris's family, they didn't tell Dorrie's mother that weekend. They left Esperance Saturday afternoon, after the egg hunt, and arrived at Mrs. Udell's house in time for supper. Easter morning, Chris and Dorrie got up to find miniature baskets, filled with paper grass and chocolate marshmallow chicks, in their places at the table.

"I couldn't help it," her mother said, serving them bacon and scrambled eggs. Instead of eating, she had a cigarette going in an ashtray on her placemat. Outside, the day was dark but warm, and they could see people jogging and walking their dogs along Krumkill Avenue. "I used to love being the Easter Bunny for you when you were little," she told Dorrie, who had, of course, heard this before. "That, and Santa Claus. And the tooth fairy. I dreaded the day you would ask me if they were real. I kept you going until you were ten."

"Guess what, Mom," Dorrie said. She grinned across the table. She would have been embarrassed about the baskets, if Chris had not so immediately shown how happy his made him — if he had hidden his pleasure instead of kissing her mother's cheek and unwrapping one of the chicks to eat before the scrambled eggs were ready.

"You mean there's no Santa Claus?" he said.

After breakfast, Dorrie kissed her mother too, and asked what time they needed to leave for church.

"You're going to church?" her mother asked.

"I thought we all were," Dorrie said. She looked at Chris, surprised. His suit and her spring dress were hanging from the hook above the backseat window. "I just assumed."

"Well, I wasn't planning to. I haven't been there in over a year." Her mother took a sip of coffee, wincing at how cold it had gotten.

"What?" Dorrie said. "What are you talking about?"

Her mother shrugged as she pushed her mug away. "It wasn't doing anything for me. I got bored. And with my new schedule, Sunday's the only day I can sleep in."

Dorrie got up to refill the coffee cups. She didn't really want more coffee, but she had to do something. When she came back to the table, she said, "Are you kidding, Mom? It wasn't *doing anything* for you? You made me go to church every Sunday of my life until I got married, and now you're not even going on *Easter*?"

Her mother shrugged. "So sue me. Come on, Dorrie. It's not that big a deal."

"How can you say that?" If someone had asked Dorrie at that moment what exactly was upsetting her, she would not have been able to identify it. All she knew was that she didn't need this right now — her mother giving up what she'd always had faith in — on top of everything else.

Under the table, Chris reached for Dorrie's hand and squeezed it. "It's okay," he told her, and though she wasn't even sure what he referred to, she chose to believe he knew what he was talking about.

That night in bed, Dorrie said, "What if— " and then tried to turn the words into a cough she hoped Chris hadn't heard, but it was too late.

"What if what?" he said.

She shook her head. "I was just thinking. Not about us, really, and this cancer thing" (she was lying, which they both knew), "but what if two people who were married found out that one of them might, you know, *die*, and they had to decide whether to have a kid or not?" She pressed in close to him, which normally made him feel too crowded, but this time he let her stay. "It would be awful to think of the kid growing up without his father — or mother — but I can also see, say, the woman wanting to have the baby. To have something of the man left. To remind her of him."

"Would she need something to remind her?" Chris felt his breath go sour.

"No, of course not. Silly." Dorrie reached up to touch his chin, where tomorrow's whiskers were already taking shape. "But if she had a baby, it would be like part of her husband was still alive."

When he spoke again, the words came quietly, into her hair. "I think it would be awful for the husband to know a baby was coming that he was never going to know."

Dorrie kicked aside the comforter to rearrange the sheets Chris had twisted by his feet. "Look, it's crazy to talk this way. I'm sorry I brought it up."

"Me, too," he said, but he wasn't angry. He lay awake marveling at how young and foolish they had been once (was it only two years ago?), conjuring up their someday children waving from the moon.

The next time Steve and Linda came over was the night of the day Chris had his surgery. He was lying on his back in bed, and they pulled chairs in from the kitchen and ate pizza, using Dorrie's hope chest (which contained spare bedsheets and the Christmas presents they'd never used) as a table.

"When I woke up, all I could think about was Dorrie in the other room," Chris said, making faces of pain as he told them what the experience had been like. He was not hungry, and he lay with his arm in a sling, resting on a hill of pillows Dorrie arranged for him. The arm had an incision eight inches long, the flesh at either end tucked into itself and pinched together, like darts in a homemade dress. With every motion he felt a hot, sharp flash as he had on the day the mole itself was removed from the surface.

"All I wanted was to be clear enough so they would let her take me home," he continued. "That's the first thing I thought of, when I came to. I hated thinking of her sitting all day, waiting around, while I was just lying there." He was aware that this might make him sound suspiciously noble, but it was the truth; a vision of Dorrie was what kept him struggling to stay conscious and alert, what brought him back to his feet and, hesitant, leaning against his small wife, out from the hospital to the bright air of the spring afternoon.

Dorrie said, "When I saw *him* trying not to cry, and holding his arm that funny way — " She lifted her own arm to imitate the angle of his elbow — "all I could think was, *I'm twenty-three, he's twenty-six, we shouldn't have to be going through this.*"

The talk was making Steve and Linda nervous; Dorrie could see it in the look they exchanged before Linda scraped the pepperoni off her pieces and slipped it onto Steve's. "Well, it's over now," Linda said. She was a year older than her husband and Chris, but she had not yet realized that she was going to die. "Listen, we were thinking of renting that place at the shore again this year. You want to go in with us?"

"When?" Dorrie said.

"End of July."

"Maybe," Dorrie told her.

"I can't think about it right now." Chris gave a little kick to his covers and made another face. He knew he was being a drag, but he couldn't help it — they wanted to talk about vacations, while he was feeling the bite and gouge of something that had wanted to kill him, and might still. He saw, suddenly, how small the room was, compared to the world; how easily the walls could fold in around them, and how little noise they would all make, collapsing underneath.

"I'm sorry," Linda told him, but they could see that she wasn't really. She wadded up her napkin and lofted it like a basketball toward the wastebasket in the corner. But it missed and hit Bonnie on the nose, and the cat made a noise and began batting it around on the floor with her paw. They all laughed, even Chris, and then Linda reached down into her bag to pull out a stack of paperbacks.

"You're going to love this one, Dorrie," she said, holding up one with stars on the cover, scattered in a galaxy of floating eyes. "The guy who wrote it is a shrink who couldn't figure out why this patient of his was so screwed up — she didn't have any big traumas in her life — so he hypnotized her and found out that she was remembering stuff that happened in her *past* lives, and not only that, she remembered all her *deaths*." Linda opened the book and flipped through the pages to remind herself of the fascination she had found there.

"Right, Lin," Steve said. He reached for the last piece of pizza. "And then she strapped her wings on and flew back to the moon."

Linda hit his shoulder with the book. "I know it sounds weird," she said. "I'm not the type who usually believes this kind of stuff. But neither was the guy who wrote it, the shrink. He taped all their sessions, and he found out that the woman knew things, when she was hypnotized, that she never would have known in real life. Like what it was like to be a slave girl in Egypt, or a prisoner in a gulag. Sometimes she even remembered what it was like to be a *guy*." She turned the book over. "I wish there was a picture of her in here. The patient, I mean."

Her husband asked, "She say whether they had jock itch in the Middle Ages?"

"The coolest part," Linda went on, ignoring him, "is about the Masters, they're called — I don't know if they're male or female — who speak through the woman. Like, their voices come out of her mouth. The Masters say there are all these different planes we live on, and after we die, we just go on to another plane."

Steve spiraled his index finger next to his head. "After a layover in Cuckooville, you mean?"

"And this is my favorite part: they say that our souls keep finding each other, from plane to plane. It's called soul migration. After we die from one life, we can kind of hang out for a while and choose how we'll come back. But you always end up being around the same people, from one life to the next."

"You mean we all knew each other before?" Dorrie popped open a new can of Coke, put a straw in it and held it up to Chris's mouth. "Like I could have been a queen somewhere, and you were all my subjects?"

"Or your children," Linda said. "Or maybe you were a *king*."

"So we'll all end up together, even after we die?" Steve tried to hold back a belch, but failed. "That seems like it should be a good thing, but it depresses me. I think I like the idea of there being an end to all of this. Not having to try anymore. Like taking a long, perfect nap and never having to wake up."

"Maybe we could talk about something else," Chris suggested. He felt swept by a flush through his center, and his arm throbbed to a beat faster than the one coming from his heart.

"Oh, sweetie. We should let you rest." Dorrie began to pack up the pizza crusts and plastic cups. "Come on, you guys. Let's move out to the living room."

After they'd had left, the words *living room* lingered in Chris's ears, because he'd heard them in a way he never had, before. It was right that they should go there without him; it was a place he didn't belong.

In a few days he was up and moving around again, the arm out of its sling, the last pills of the prescription stored in the medicine cabinet where Dorrie would find the bottle a year later, cleaning; she let it fall into the trash bag, but reached in right afterward to save it from the tissues and the used dental floss, and she shook the pills in the bottle like the beans of a baby's rattle, a comforting tumble between the round plastic walls.

It was the middle of April, and kids were already out playing baseball down the hill from the junior high. They gathered by the backstop at three twenty, as soon as school let out. In the week after his surgery, when Dorrie went back to work and Chris spent his days going crazy in the apartment — flipping TV channels, eating more than he should in combinations that disgusted him, exercising his arm, and tossing toy mice for the cats to chase — he looked forward each afternoon to the arrival of voices at the field, and to the entertainment of watching the choosing of teams, the warm-up pitches, then the game itself. By Wednesday he recognized most of the kids by their throwing motions and their postures at the plate. They were eighth or ninth graders, Chris guessed; it was the age at which two of them could share a birthday and still stand a foot apart in height.

On Thursday, he went outside to watch, covering his wound carefully with a new bandage and with his windbreaker from the high school swim team, which had his name sewn across the chest. He had spent so much time lying on the couch or in bed that it felt strange to be standing under the sun, with the spring breeze soft on his face. The air was so fresh it made him dizzy, rushing to his brain, and he walked slowly over to the field, stepping in mud on purpose so he would have something to do — clean his shoes off — when he got home.

They chose teams quickly, and before they scattered across the sloppy diamond, some of the kids looked at Chris standing on the sidelines and he saw a few of them whispering. He tried to look bored and harmless at the same time, as if he had just happened upon the game while he was out for a stroll. He thought he might be able to sit down on the playground, but both benches were broken, and a sign said "Swings Are for Children Only." He closed his eyes, smelled mud and grass, saw the shadow of a cloud moving darkly over his lids. Then he fell.

It was as simple as that; without tripping or even moving his feet, he fell forward and slightly sideways, and did not even know it was happening in time to put his hands out to blunt the blow. When he opened his eyes, he was looking at third base — which was somebody's bunched-up jacket — from the level of the ground, his cheek pressed against damp earth. Half the kids stood in a cautious circle around him, while the other half stayed back and watched. He realized that it would have taken time for them to move into these positions from the field, so he calculated he'd been out for a minute or more.

He tried to sit up, but the world in front of his face went gray, then black, with details of the day still clear around the edges, like the borders of a photograph destroyed at its center by a flame. He felt himself fall toward the ground again, but before he made impact a pressure supported him from behind, and when his eyes focused he found that two of the children were together holding him up.

"Geez," Chris said. He felt embarrassed.

"Maybe he's drunk," one of the kids warned from the back of the circle.

"I'm not," Chris said, but his voice sounded distorted even to him, and when he put a hand to his lip, he saw blood on his finger where it had touched his face.

"Can you stand up?" one of the girls asked. She told him her name was Beth. "You're okay, Chris," she said, and he was startled until he realized she was reading his name from the embroidered breast of his jacket. She patted his shoulder like a mother or an aunt. "You live around here?" she asked.

"Over there." He was steadier now, and he gestured toward the apartment with a nod. The other kids were shifting in their sneakers, and the sky was going orange. He felt like an idiot. "You should get back to your game," he told them, trying to smile so they would leave him alone. "It's no big deal, I'm going home now."

"I'll go with you," Beth said.

"Don't be silly," Chris told her. "It's right there." But when he began walking he realized that something was terribly, terrifyingly wrong. He could not make his legs work, and he felt as if he were revolving in the air, feet first, the way he always did in the dentist's chair after the mask of nitrous oxide went over his nose. He allowed Beth to guide him home, and by the time they made it to the door the kids had begun a new inning.

She stayed with him until Dorrie got home. He lay on the couch and she slipped his jacket off, and then because he said he was hot, she unbuttoned and rolled up his sleeves. She didn't ask about the bandage on his arm; she brought him Coke in a Yankees mug with ice, and a stack of Saltines.

"You don't have to eat these," she said. "It's just what my mother gives me, whenever I'm sick." She wetted a washcloth in the bathroom and held it against his head. He felt better — the walls had stopped moving — but he was still scared, with the kind of fear there is no solution for, even sleep; this he knew the way he knew the sounds and scents of Dorrie as she dressed in the morning, or the rhythm of his own breath.

Beth read to him, the Milestones column at the back of *Sports Illustrated*. She had gotten through all but the last when Chris heard Dorrie's car outside, the engine's familiar cough before it agreed to die.

"That's my wife," Chris said, and Beth got up from the floor where she had been leaning back against the couch as she read to him. Dorrie did not seem surprised to see the teenager there, as she stepped inside and over one of the cats; it was almost as if the two women already knew each other, in the way they both ignored the formality of a greeting and bent together over Chris.

"You don't feel hot or anything," Dorrie murmured, feeling his cheek with the backs of her fingers.

"He fainted watching our game."

"I'm calling the doctor." Dorrie's face held a calm that made Chris feel better, even though he knew it to be false. Dorrie spoke to a nurse and when she hung up, he wanted to warn her not to say anything, but he couldn't get the words out in time.

"We have to go in," she said.

The cancer had spread. It was not what the doctor had expected, and it was the first and only time in his practice — he told them this as if they had won a contest — that the metastasis of a melanoma showed up so soon after the original diagnosis. "Usually it takes years," Dr. Gruberman said. "Or months, at least." As he spoke, he looked not at them, Dorrie noticed, but at the diplomas hanging on his wall, behind Chris's head. He had attended important, impressive schools. Dorrie thought she sensed a desire on the doctor's part to hide the certificates, because in this case they had done no good.

Chris started treatment the following week. He went on leave from his job, but Dorrie couldn't, so she worked out a schedule: on the days of his appointments, she took personal time to bring him to the hospital and back home again, and for the afternoons she hired Beth, the teenager, to stay with him. Beth got out of school at noon — she was a senior, she had more than enough credits to graduate — and she'd put in an application at the A & P before Dorrie called her, the night after Chris's trip to the emergency room, to offer her the job.

"A lot of the time they said he'll just be sleeping," Dorrie had told her, "so you can watch TV or read. I just want to make sure somebody's here in case he needs anything. They said they'll be giving him pills for pain and everything, but he might be throwing up and stuff. I mean, can you handle that? It might be kind of gross."

Beth said she thought so and Dorrie told her, "It would be great if you could do it. I'd feel safe. You don't seem like a kid to me. I mean that as a compliment." She blushed at how she thought she must sound to Beth. Dorrie was a married woman — a wife! She still couldn't get over it sometimes. But she was only seven years older than the girl, and she remembered her senior year, and those long talks with Jeanne Marie Ettlinger on the way to and from school, more vividly than her wedding day or the night Chris had proposed.

Beth asked, "When do you want me to start?"

They arranged a time. But the whole week of that first treatment, Chris's mother and sister Charlotte and the baby came to visit and to help, so it was crowded and awkward in the afternoons, before Dorrie returned home from work. Her mother-in-law had asked why she didn't just cancel Beth for the week, but Dorrie said she'd already hired her, and besides, this way Chris's mother and Charlotte could go out, if they wanted to — they wouldn't be trapped in the house, because Beth would also take care of Tess.

As it turned out, Chris responded better than anyone expected, and although he spent the hours directly afterward in bed, he often felt well enough by midafternoon to want to get out in the fresh air, so his mother and Charlotte took him places — the movies, the mall — while Beth babysat Tess in the apartment. The baby was obsessed with basketball. She had her own plastic backboard, and a ball she could put through the low hoop seven times out of ten. "I figure I don't even have to save for college," Charlotte said, one night after supper as they watched Tess tire herself out with foul shots from the edge of the living-room rug. "Her layup will put her through."

"I always thought any kid of mine would have a baseball scholarship," Chris said.

"What if it was a girl?"

"By that time, they'll let girls play." He clicked to another channel during the inning break, and seemed surprised when his mother got up and left the room, too late to hide that she was crying.

"Oh, shit," Charlotte said, getting up to follow her.

Dorrie was folding laundry at the side of the TV. She asked Chris, "Did you really mean it when you said it would be too sad to think you could ever have a kid now, because you'd never get to know him?" She seemed intent on getting the crease in his pants just right, though he had no reason to wear anything but sweats anymore.

"When did I say *that*?" His tone suggested she might have accused him of cheering secretly for the Mets.

"Well, you didn't, exactly. We were talking about what *if*."

He turned the sound down, which impressed her. Tess made another basket and began clapping for herself. "I must have been crazy," Chris said, reaching to caress the scar on his arm, which Dorrie had been trying not to notice he touched, now, more than he touched her. "I'd give anything to think you were going to have my baby. Our guy. Luke. Or Olivia." He looked up at her, his face washed flat by hope. "Why?"

She began to smile, but then her lips collapsed. "I've been puking," she told him, watching her shoulders shake out of the corners of her eyes. "And I'm late."

"Oh, my God." He wanted to hold her, but she knew he didn't have the strength. "I thought all those chemicals were supposed to make me — " He wasn't sure how to finish. *Sterile? Shoot blanks*?

Dorrie smiled. "I guess your guys can swim through anything."

He wanted to say something that would let her know how he felt, but nothing seemed adequate. Though it wasn't like him, he mimicked his friend Steve in resorting, at this serious moment, to a joke. "I guess the toilet's really getting a workout, between the two of us."

Dorrie groaned and laughed and cried at the same time. "Shut up," she said, hitting him softly with a sad fist. "Stupid."

Their niece's eyes lit up at the word, which she was forbidden to say. "'Tupid, 'tupid," she chanted, and when her mother came back into the room Chris grinned as he whispered to Dorrie, "Now see what you've done?"

She kept thinking they would have a conversation about the future, but they never did, and afterward she realized it was because they were each afraid that by admitting the worst that might happen, they would make it come true. *Come true* — even in her head, she caught herself using the language of childhood. If she were ever going to become a grown-up, shouldn't it be now?

Yet, still, because of what she had learned in Sunday school, or perhaps from TV, she imagined what followed death to be a place in the sky with white vapors, a camera's-eye view of the world. She wanted to ask Chris if, after he died, he would give her some signal, in whatever form might be allowed — a breeze, a tap on the window, a shaft of sunlight — but a certain shyness prevented her. Chris felt shy, too, though for a different reason (he felt guilty about making his young wife a widow, even though he knew it wasn't his fault), so they never had the talk they both longed for, except in their own minds.

Luke Udell Manning was born on February nineteenth, and his father Christopher died ten days later, in the same hospital but on a different floor, having been present for the birth, although he had to sit in a chair at his wife's bedside while he encouraged her, and despite her pain she had to be careful — because of *his* pain, which could make him pass out — about how hard she gripped his hand.

In those first ten days of Luke's life, she took twenty-six rolls of film, and had them all developed at the one-hour kiosk so Chris could see them before he died. Somehow, it seemed crucial to her that he be able to carry these static images into unconsciousness, and she didn't understand *why* she thought this until Luke became old enough to look at the pictures, when she realized that somehow she believed (though she knew it was silly) that Chris would be able to look at the same photos, whenever he wanted, from wherever he was.

Sometimes she caught her breath suddenly, especially in that first year, and felt almost like laughing. It just seemed so absurd. Who was she, this woman alone with a baby and, on the shelf below her wedding album, a book containing mourners' names, an obituary, and a poem Anita, her friend from work, had copied for her out of something called *Sorrow's Embrace*? (She didn't like the poem and it didn't comfort her, but Anita had had it laminated, so she felt obliged to keep it.)

Charlotte, her sister-in-law, said she understood how Dorrie felt. "When your husband leaves, it's like you have to start over," she told her, and it was all Dorrie could do to keep from retorting, "My husband didn't *leave*." But then, she supposed, he had.

She didn't work for more than two years after Chris died, thanks to Dr. Gruberman's commission of insurance fraud. He told them not to tell anyone because he could lose his license: when he found out that they didn't have any life insurance, he offered to change the date of Chris's diagnosis, so that the cancer wouldn't be a preexisting condition. Chris's dad bought them a sizable policy through his own agency, and though he knew of the doctor's criminality, he ignored it for Dorrie's and Luke's sake.

She quit her job, and she thought there would at least be some satisfaction in doing that, but to her surprise and discomfort, her boss seemed genuinely shaken about Chris's death. The day Dorrie left, Evelyn gave her a sizable savings bond for Luke, and told Dorrie that if she ever needed a job or a reference, not to hesitate to call.

She bought a house in a development called Great Meadows, which had three separate pools for its residents, along with a golf course, two playgrounds, and a clubhouse where her mother, when she came to live with Dorrie and Luke, became a regular in the rotating bridge game every Tuesday night.

Mrs. Udell moved in just after Luke's third birthday. She'd been talking about it since even before Chris died — though of course she treaded extremely delicately on the subject at that point, to the degree that Dorrie didn't even realize what her mother was talking about until she lay in bed at night, with Chris wheezing at her side, and ran the day's phone conversation through her head. Then it made her angry, and she told her mother not to bring it up again.

But now it had been three years, the new house had four bedrooms, and she knew it would be good for Luke to have his grandmother around, so Dorrie said the necessary words and it was all arranged. The weekend her mother settled in, Dorrie invited Steve and Linda and their new baby over for a welcoming dinner. She also invited Beth, who was now a junior at Rutgers but who spent a lot of her time with Dorrie and Luke. She and Dorrie had remained friends after Chris died, and the baby and Beth adored each other like nephew and aunt.

Within fifteen minutes of everyone's having gathered and greeted each other in the wide and echoing foyer, it became clear that there would be trouble in the form of jealousy, on Mrs. Udell's part, over her grandson's affection. Luke gravitated toward Beth all evening, when he wasn't trying to get at Steve and Linda's daughter, Caitlin, so he could pinch her arm. At first Mrs. Udell tried to make a joke of it: she said, "What am I, chopped liver?" with a mock indignation that disguised nothing, but when dessert time rolled around and Luke still hadn't shown her any interest, she insisted on being the one to give him his bath, even though he screamed when she picked him up and carried him off up the stairs. Luckily, the house was big enough that with the bathroom door shut and the water running, they could hardly hear him as they finished their meal.

"Maybe I shouldn't have come," Beth said, though — despite her effort to hide it — the others could see she was partly pleased by Luke's preference for her.

"Don't be silly," Dorrie said. "He just hasn't seen my mother that much in his lifetime. He'll get used to her."

Linda said, "I wonder if it bothers her that he looks exactly like Chris?" She had opened her shirt and was breastfeeding Caitlin, and the rest of them shifted their eyes.

"You really think so?" Dorrie seemed surprised. "I thought that when he was first born, but now I don't see it. He just looks like himself."

"Oh, my God. It's unbelievable." Linda shook her head. "I don't know how it doesn't freak *you* out. To be reminded all the time."

"But I don't see it," Dorrie said. It was true, and yet she knew there had to be a reason she couldn't look at her son, except with her eyes squinted, when she went to wake him from a nap, or in the early mornings when he came into bed with her for a final hour of sleep, during which she turned her cheek to feel his breath across the pillow. She had thought it would be a comfort to have a piece of Chris after he died, but as it turned out, she hesitated to recognize his face in the baby's, because of what she might feel.

But, oh, that face! Nobody had told Dorrie about the fear: how afraid you always were for your child, and how the fear came when you looked at his face and tried to imagine what he would be like as an adult, when he had felt so much more of what it was possible to feel, and learned how to mask it with his eyes and mouth. Part of you wanted to keep it from happening, this education; but if it *didn't* happen, he would be killed by life. So sometimes she held Luke's cheeks between her hands and said, in her head to Chris, *Take care of him.* This was a consolation she derived from his being dead — she could ask more of him than if he were still with her, though she never let herself think too long about whether she actually believed he received her messages.

But on a day that started like any other when Luke was almost four, she found out, or thought she did.

Dorrie had gone back to finish her degree after Chris died, then taken a job in the publications office for the school district, where her favorite task was to write profiles of children in different grades for the Student Spotlight section of the monthly newsletter that went out to all parents. She dropped Luke off at preschool every morning, and Beth picked him up in the afternoons, though she didn't linger with him at home because Mrs. Udell was usually there, and things were still a bit touchy between the two of them.

On this day, Beth saw him inside and took off his raincoat, and set on the kitchen table the macaroni map of New Jersey that Luke had made at school. She was in something of a hurry because she had a study date with a junior and the emphasis was on "date." The door to the downstairs bathroom was closed, and later Beth would swear that when she called "Hello" to Mrs. Udell through the door, Mrs. Udell answered her back, so Beth set Luke up with his Legos in the living room and took off.

But Mrs. Udell wasn't, in fact, at home; it must have been one of the kittens, Bert or Ernie, that Beth heard when she called out. Instead of being in the bathroom, Dorrie's mother was stuck in traffic on her way home from the Livingston Mall. She still thought she would make it in time to meet Beth, which was why she hadn't left a note or found a pay phone to call and leave a message, and by the time she realized that she *wouldn't* make it, there she was stuck in the middle of all those cars, and though she realized that this was the exact situation for which Beth had suggested she get one of those cell phones, she had demurred because it seemed so complicated. Anyway, there was nothing she could do about it *now*.

So Luke was home alone after Beth left, though he didn't realize it at first. He played with the Legos for a while, but then he got hungry, and in the kitchen, after he called for Gammer to give him a snack but she didn't come, he got out some crackers and chocolate chips by pulling a chair over to the counter. Then he went out the back door and then to the front yard and down to the street, then stepped into the street because he saw a pebble he wanted. He was leaning down to pick it up when Linda, who had moved with Steve and Caitlin to the same development as Dorrie, was driving down the street on her way to drop off at Dorrie's a book about children who remembered their past lives. The GPS in her dashboard was acting up, sending out annoying staccato beeps, and Linda fiddled with the controls. As she smacked the panel, she took her eyes away from the road, and at that moment Luke stumbled farther away from the curb, having kicked the pebble accidentally ahead of himself. He would have fallen under the wheels of Linda's van if not for what Linda referred to, later, as a miracle.

"I swear to God, Dorrie, and I'm not proud of it, but I wasn't paying attention, and the last thing I expected was for there to be a kid in the road, let alone Luke. But there I was trying to get that damn beeping to stop, and I swear to God I saw Chris's face in front of me, and he put his hand up, and I slammed on the brakes and saw Luke in front of the car, just standing there. I swear to *God*, Dorrie, it *was* Chris. He appeared in front of me because he knew Luke was in trouble. He probably even saved Luke's life. Well, I wasn't going that fast, but at least it kept him from being hit, and hurt. It's the most bizarre thing I've ever had happen to me in my life — you mean you've never seen him before, in all this time? He's never appeared to *you*?"

And even though she thought Linda had always been a little kooky, and even though of course she was upset about Luke's near accident, once she had calmed down Dorrie found herself feeling jealous of Linda, because in fact Chris had *not* appeared, ever, to her. She had to settle for her memories, and photographs. Because of her jealousy she decided that it was just a product of Linda's kookiness, the apparition in the road. Still, even years later, she found herself continuing to look for her husband around the next corner, at the bottom of a stairwell, behind a bush she was trimming in front of the house. "That's normal," her mother told her, when Dorrie confessed it once. "I still listen for your father in the wind."

"That is *such* a load of crap," Luke said, tossing the bag of pretzels back across the couch to Caitlin. "Your mother's a nice woman, Cait, but she's a total nutcase."

"I know," Caitlin said. Did he think this could possibly be news to her? "But forget my mother for a minute, and the whole thing with you and the van. Forget your father, even. Just in general terms, do you think there could actually *be* anything, after we die? Even if it isn't a place — could it be like a state of mind, or something, that keeps going?" She cracked a pretzel open with her teeth, and one of the flying crumbs caught Luke in the eye. "Oh, sorry," she said, when he put a hand up too late to deflect it.

He told her it was okay as he rubbed away pretzel flakes. When after a minute she saw that he still looked flustered she said, "What's the big deal? It's a pretzel."

"Didn't I ever tell you I have a thing about going blind? Like, a phobia?"

"You do?" She looked at him amused, and he could feel the fondness in it.

"My grandfather's blind. You never knew that? When he was a kid, some big light supposedly flashed through the sky. Nobody else saw it, and they never figured out what it could have been. I know, he's probably nuts, right? Hysterical blindness. But still. I get nervous."

"Does your grandpa walk around with his hands out in front of him all the time?"

"Not really. He gets around pretty well. You develop a certain kind of radar, he told me. You make up for what you don't have, with other parts of yourself."

"That's kind of cool."

"I know." They sat in silence for a few minutes. "Wanna go get some slices?" Luke asked her.

"Nah."

"Well, what do you want to do?"

Caitlin stretched out on the couch as Luke sat on the floor, leaning against it and petting Ernie, who was sitting in his lap and who hadn't been the same since they'd had to put his sister Bert down the year before. Luke and Caitlin were fifteen, and had never done anything more, with each other or anyone else, than hold hands. Though they had never discussed it, they both knew that this would come later, and that they would both regret letting it happen too soon. "I think that movie where the kid sees dead people is on," she said, picking up the remote and switching on the TV.

"I hate that movie."

"You do not." She was right, and Luke felt a flush of gratitude for this woman who knew him so well. They watched for a while until they both felt too tired to follow it, fell asleep, then woke up an hour later at exactly the same time.

When the doctor told Rona Udell that she had cancer in her lungs and that it had spread to other parts of her body, she wanted to light up, right there in front of him. It was a natural instinct, she supposed later — a reaction to stress, and what could be more stressful than being told you were going to die? Because that's what he was telling her, though he was using other words (*metastasis*, *morbidity*). The worst part was wondering how she was going to tell Dorrie. She remembered when they had broken the news to her about Chris; Dorrie just came right out and said it: "Mom, Chris has skin cancer, and they tried but they couldn't fix it, and he's, well, he's probably gonna die." Chris was sitting right next to her when she said it. There was that equivocation and quiver in her voice — on *probably* — and that's when Chris took Dorrie's hand and put his head down on top of her jeaned knees. To Rona it seemed an inappropriate gesture, almost sexually obscene, but then she was ashamed of herself, because she realized it was, instead, grief.

So she thought that's how Dorrie would want to hear about it — straight, no sugarcoating — but she was wrong. After dinner that night, after Luke and Caitlin had left to go rent a movie, Rona said, when Dorrie got up to clear the table, "Wait a sec, honey. I have something to tell you." Dorrie sat down again and gave her mother an apprehensive look. After Chris's death, she had never heard the words *I have something to tell you* without expecting it to be bad. And usually, of course, she was right. Rona told her about the doctor and finished up by saying, "He said it might be fast, because it's spread so much. It's all over, he said. He meant the cancer was all over my body, but I heard him as telling me my life was all over, and isn't that funny, how it meant both?"

Dorrie was staring at her, gripping the table with both hands. Rona could tell how strongly she was holding on, because Dorrie's skin turned so white. "How long," she said to her mother, in the voice that Rona had not heard now for so many years.

"Well, see, I asked him that, and he said it would probably be a couple of months. Or it could be shorter or longer, he said. He said we should think about whether we want it to be in a hospital, or here."

"Hospital," Dorrie answered immediately. Then, trying to cover up her quick response, she added, "I mean, they can do more for you there. Like manage the pain and everything. Plus — " But she stopped herself. She didn't want her mother to know that she would not put Luke through watching his grandmother die every day.

She was not allowing in, yet, the full significance of what her mother had told her. She could not. From her experience with Chris, she knew that this would come later, in moments she didn't expect, as when she leaned over the water fountain at work, or tried to fasten a bracelet around her wrist. Her mind had a beautiful trick of being able to tuck whatever it couldn't manage, at the moment, into a mental folder like the manila ones she used in the office: tasks she didn't want to deal with now, but would have to face eventually. "Let's clean up," she said to her mother. "*Jeopardy!*'s almost on."

"Wait a minute," Rona said, without moving. "Honey. Who's going to tell Luke? Do you want me to?"

"I'll do it," Dorrie said. She knew Luke would not be surprised, and that he would hide whatever tender feelings he might have when he heard the news. "How can she keep smoking, with that hack of hers?" he often asked Dorrie, when they heard Rona in the bathroom as they were eating their breakfast. In fifth grade somebody's father, a doctor, had brought in a diseased lung for health class, and though Luke never told his mother, he had ever since imagined, even after he understood that he was wrong, that his father's arm had been some black, rotted, speckled thing that must have fallen off just before he died.

Dorrie was stabbing slits in the margarine with her knife. "Mom," she said, "I don't want to be having this conversation. I don't want to hear what you're telling me. Maybe the doctor doesn't know what he's talking about. You should at least get another opinion." Just saying this seemed to erase the feelings her mother's news had brought on, and she surged forward, cheered. "Go to Dr. Gruberman," she said. "Remember, the one who helped Chris?"

"But honey." Rona put the napkin down and smoothed it out with her fingers. "Chris died," she reminded her daughter as gently as she could.

What she knew she could not tell her daughter — probably, she could not tell anyone — was that she didn't really mind the idea of dying. In fact, she almost welcomed it. She'd been to a funeral once where one of the readings was a poem by Walt Whitman, and she wrote down the last line on the program because it struck her as so right: "To die is different from what any one supposed, and luckier." She understood that there was no way Whitman could know any better than anyone else what dying was like, but maybe, being a poet, he had some kind of inside scoop — maybe God had sent him to the world with that gift of intuition, so he could spread the word.

Or maybe she was just a negative person. Maybe she was lazy, all too ready to stop putting in the work. Whatever the case, ever since the doctor had made his pronouncement, she'd gone over the tally in her head, and the pluses kept adding up. She didn't do all that much with her days now, anyway; she was bored with Dorrie's house and the routine they had settled into, and the near-constant ache in her ribs made her feel like screaming. On top of all this was the fact that she believed — well, okay, she *hoped* — that she really would be reunited with her husband, who had died so many years before. She had not allowed herself to imagine the nature of this reunion — A hug? Was heaven's version of a hug anything like what we did here on earth? Did you recognize the person right away, or did God have to reintroduce you? — because she was afraid that if she thought about it too much, she might realize how foolish she was and, beyond that, that nothing awaited her besides a big blank.

She felt she should be wiser about life at this point in it, and that she should mourn what she was losing. Yes, she'd miss her daughter and grandson; she supposed she might have lived long enough, if it weren't for the cancer, to see Luke marry (though she hoped it wouldn't be to that Caitlin, who like her mother Linda had *no* delicacy whatsoever) and have his own babies.

But to be honest, she'd never really gotten all that much out of it — life — except for maybe the few years when she was married and it was just plain fun, to think about Ross coming home from work, and their evenings and weekends together. Even then, though, there were so many chores — with Dorrie, of course, and the housework; every time she found herself folding another batch of clothes, she thought *That's it, that's the last one, I can't do this anymore.* And that was when she was *healthy.* When Dorrie had married Chris, and Rona met Peter Manning for the first time, he took her hand and held it, while his eyes looked somewhere to the right of her, and she thought, *I couldn't stand being blind*, and she may have even thought, *Why don't people like that kill themselves?* because she had heard the story about the flash of light that took his eyes out, and knew he had never seen his wife or children or his baby granddaughter, and she didn't know how he could bear all that.

But people did. Bear things. Her secret was this: she knew that they were made of stronger stuff than she. So when the doctor said she was dying, she basically gave up. Another secret: she thought, *I don't regret even one of those cigarettes. That's how I made it through.* She was ashamed of these thoughts. But they were secrets and they would die with her, so what did it matter?

Dorrie said, "I'm not saying he could save you, necessarily. Gruberman. Just that he knows our family, and maybe there's something he could think of that your doctor doesn't know."

But of course this wasn't the case. The cancer was too far advanced, and Dr. Gruberman couldn't help. (Hadn't he done enough for them already?) Rona Nichols Udell died seven weeks after her diagnosis, and Dorrie comforted herself by thinking of her parents being together again, finally, although of course she never mentioned this to anyone. She missed her mother. She could tell that Luke missed her, too, though he was not a big talker, particularly about emotions.

Except for the day on which he asked his mother what it felt like to be in love. Dorrie could tell that he was embarrassed, but also that he had decided to suffer it in service of an answer. Dorrie thought for a moment about what to say, and in the way that had become a habit for her, she asked Chris for help. Immediately came the memory of the drive through the snow with the cats, from her mother's house that Christmas, before they discovered Chris's cancer, before Luke was born. She told her son about not being afraid to die if her husband was with her. He thought about *that* for a moment and said, "Then I think I love Caitlin."

"You think?"

"No. I know."

The day of the wedding dawned clear but cool, and the forecast was for rain in the afternoon. It was May, and Luke and Caitlin had both just graduated from college. Steve and Linda thought they were too young, but Dorrie was all for it — she knew how fast things could change, and she wanted Luke to grab love when he found it, and hang on for dear life.

Beth had been invited, of course, and she sat with the families up front. She wore a sheer dress, which became completely translucent when a downpour soaked everyone between the ceremony and the reception. She was thirty-nine, but Dorrie still thought of her as a kid.

Beth had become a nurse, and she worked now in a hospice center just outside of town. She had dated doctors and a few male nurses over the years, but not much seemed to come of any of it. She was downwind of pretty, but she had much love to give, and it caused

Dorrie heartache to see her alone. It reminded her of the feeling she used to have about Jeanne Marie Ettlinger, her friend from grammar school, who had planned to be a doctor for the children she wouldn't have. Dorrie had lost touch with her, but somehow she thought that if Jeanne Marie had ended up marrying or becoming a mother, she would have heard about it somehow.

But, she thought, *I'm just a romantic. Maybe they don't mind, Beth and Jeanne Marie. Aren't there worse things than being alone?* Then Beth caught the bouquet, and Dorrie saw that she *did* want to find someone. She sent a plea to Chris, whom she thought of as floating somewhere above them all: *Help her*.

After the reception, the families and their close friends gathered at Dorrie's house, to open presents and drink the leftover wine. Linda came over to hug her from behind. "Can you believe our babies got *married*?" Her breath smelled of cabernet as Dorrie pulled away and tried to smile. "Remember the good old days when they were babies? Remember *before* that, when the four of us used to get together, before — " She stopped herself from saying *before Chris died*, and Dorrie knew she didn't want to jinx the wedding day by mentioning death. She nodded to her friend.

"Remember those books you used to give me?" she said, wanting to keep up her end of the conversation. "About all that weird stuff?"

"Oh, I remember that one about reincarnation. I forget the details now, but wasn't it by a psychiatrist or something?" Dorrie made an assenting noise; she didn't want to let on how many times she had read it.

"I can't get over what we used to believe," Linda said. "It's like when you're a kid, with Santa Claus, when you're just on the verge of finding out — you want to believe it so bad, you'll do anything to hang on, even though you know you're only fooling yourself." She paused to take another sip. "You know?"

Dorrie nodded, casting her eyes around the room at the people she loved. Tess, Charlotte's daughter, had turned out to be not a basketball player, as Charlotte had predicted when she was a baby, but an alcoholic. Dr. Gruberman took Dorrie aside and asked about the young woman at the end of the couch, who had quietly drunk one bottle by herself and was halfway through her second. "That's my niece," Dorrie said.

"I think I can help her."

"We've all tried. She doesn't want to stop."

"Well, will you give her my card, anyway?" He fished one out of his pocket and scribbled his home number on the back. Dorrie took it, but she said, "Forgive me, but what makes you think you — ?"

She didn't have to finish, because he interrupted to say, "I'm seventeen years sober." He gave her a few moments to register what he had said, watching her calculate.

"That means when you were treating Chris — "

He interrupted again. "Yes. I was still drinking. But never on the job, Dorrie. Although I did have a hangover the first time I saw him. I remember because I was saying things I ordinarily wouldn't have, and I kept telling myself to shut up, but it didn't work. I think I might even have talked about God. I was looking for help myself back then. It didn't come till years later." He lowered his voice. "I think that's why I did what I did, fixing the insurance. I felt guilty, somehow."

She was looking at the floor as she asked him, "He wouldn't still be alive, would he?"

"Oh, my God, Dorrie." She looked up and saw that she had stung him close to the core. As gently as he could manage in the face of such feelings, he told her, "No."

"I'm sorry," she said, drawing him close in a hug. "Sometimes I would just give anything to have him back. That was thoughtless of me."

"You had a right to ask it."

"I'm happy for you. Your — sobriety, is that what they call it?"

"Yes. I'm happy, too." He motioned to the card he had handed her. "So if there's anything I can do for your niece, let me know."

She thanked him, and turned again when someone else touched her arm. It took her a moment to recognize that it was one of the caterers from the reception, because the woman had taken off her apron before ferrying the remaining food to the house. "Now that everything's over, I just wanted to say hello in person," she said to Dorrie, who had to lean forward to hear her, because the woman's voice was as pale as her skin. "You wouldn't know me. But you wrote about my son in the newsletter, when he was in seventh grade. The Spotlight column we all got sent? His name is Scott Wozniak. I don't expect you to remember, there were so many kids." Still, her face looked hopeful that Dorrie *might* remember, and though at first Dorrie cast about wildly and found nothing triggered by the name, in the next moment her vision did settle on the image of a slim blond boy with a face full of blemishes who had been referred to her by his guidance counselor, when Dorrie asked for the names of students who might make good profile subjects.

"But I do remember," she told the woman, who looked so delighted it made Dorrie want to cry. "The macaroni sculpture of Richard Nixon, right?"

"That's it!" When the woman looked as if she wanted to reach forward to hug her, Dorrie took a step back. The woman realized this, without seeming insulted, and lowered her tone again. "They were studying Watergate in history, and for some reason Scott became obsessed with Tricky Dick. In art class they were supposed to make sculptures of famous people, and the other kids did people like Madonna and Michael Jordan. They laughed at Scott for picking Nixon. He felt bad, like a screwup, until you wrote that story.

Do you know that he kept it taped up above his bed until he started high school?" She laughed at herself. "Of course you didn't know. Anyway, I wanted to thank you. He had a few rocky years there, but he's a teacher himself now. History, not art. I'm not saying it's all because of that one article, but you never know."

"Thank you for telling me," Dorrie said. Blushing, she turned her attention back to the presents. The others were playing a game during which they set each wrapped gift before Chris's father, who guessed what it was from the size and shape. He was eerily accurate at sensing what was inside all the packages. His wife sat beside him, and Dorrie caught her looking at her husband for much longer than she would have gotten away with, if he had not been blind. She wondered what her mother-in-law was thinking — if she still ever wished her husband could see, or if she had exchanged this for being grateful. *Probably not*, Dorrie thought. *Don't we all want what we can't have? Look at me, still wishing I could have Chris.*

"Excuse me," she said, though no one could hear her, and still smiling at the roomful of people, she drifted with backward steps toward the kitchen. It had stopped raining, but the air remained moist. She stepped onto the back deck, sliding the door against the crowd and the noise behind her. She looked up at the moon, hoping it would be clear now, but it was still covered by clouds. "Give me a sign," she whispered to Chris. "Anything, I don't care what. Please." When a minute went by and she felt nothing, she moved on in her request. "Mom?" Another minute and still nothing. All she heard was the low murmur behind her of the celebrating guests. All she saw was the gray sky above her and the backyard, with its wet grass and the swing set Luke had not allowed her to get rid of, even after he had far outgrown it, even after it began to rust.

What had she expected? That the clouds would part suddenly, and that she would see, in their mist, the faces of the people she had lost? What made her think that she might be the one person on Earth graced with the knowledge everyone wanted, but no one could have? She understood now that she had been receiving signs all along—they just hadn't come from the source she had sought them from. And they were the same signs everyone else got, whether they recognized them or not. "You're an idiot, Dorrie," she said out loud, though she smiled to herself as she did so, reaching to press her finger to a raindrop on the railing. She went back inside and stepped over crumpled wrapping paper, strewn across the floor where all the presents lay revealed. As she reentered the living room, everyone stopped talking and turned to look, as if her arrival had just been announced.

The Flannery O'Connor Award for Short Fiction

David Walton, *Evening Out*
Leigh Allison Wilson, *From the Bottom Up*
Sandra Thompson, *Close-Ups*
Susan Neville, *The Invention of Flight*
Mary Hood, *How Far She Went*
François Camoin, *Why Men Are Afraid of Women*
Molly Giles, *Rough Translations*
Daniel Curley, *Living with Snakes*
Peter Meinke, *The Piano Tuner*
Tony Ardizzone, *The Evening News*
Salvatore La Puma, *The Boys of Bensonhurst*
Melissa Pritchard, *Spirit Seizures*
Philip F. Deaver, *Silent Retreats*
Gail Galloway Adams, *The Purchase of Order*
Carole L. Glickfeld, *Useful Gifts*
Antonya Nelson, *The Expendables*
Nancy Zafris, *The People I Know*
Debra Monroe, *The Source of Trouble*
Robert H. Abel, *Ghost Traps*
T. M. McNally, *Low Flying Aircraft*
Alfred DePew, *The Melancholy of Departure*
Dennis Hathaway, *The Consequences of Desire*
Rita Ciresi, *Mother Rocket*
Dianne Nelson, *A Brief History of Male Nudes in America*
Christopher McIlroy, *All My Relations*
Alyce Miller, *The Nature of Longing*
Carol Lee Lorenzo, *Nervous Dancer*
C. M. Mayo, *Sky over El Nido*

Wendy Brenner, *Large Animals in Everyday Life*
Paul Rawlins, *No Lie Like Love*
Harvey Grossinger, *The Quarry*
Ha Jin, *Under the Red Flag*
Andy Plattner, *Winter Money*
Frank Soos, *Unified Field Theory*
Mary Clyde, *Survival Rates*
Hester Kaplan, *The Edge of Marriage*
Darrell Spencer, *CAUTION Men in Trees*
Robert Anderson, *Ice Age*
Bill Roorbach, *Big Bend*
Dana Johnson, *Break Any Woman Down*
Gina Ochsner, *The Necessary Grace to Fall*
Kellie Wells, *Compression Scars*
Eric Shade, *Eyesores*
Catherine Brady, *Curled in the Bed of Love*
Ed Allen, *Ate It Anyway*
Gary Fincke, *Sorry I Worried You*
Barbara Sutton, *The Send-Away Girl*
David Crouse, *Copy Cats*
Randy F. Nelson, *The Imaginary Lives of Mechanical Men*
Greg Downs, *Spit Baths*
Peter LaSalle, *Tell Borges If You See Him: Tales of Contemporary Somnambulism*
Anne Panning, *Super America*
Margot Singer, *The Pale of Settlement*
Andrew Porter, *The Theory of Light and Matter*
Peter Selgin, *Drowning Lessons*
Geoffrey Becker, *Black Elvis*
Lori Ostlund, *The Bigness of the World*
Linda L. Grover, *The Dance Boots*
Jessica Treadway, *Please Come Back To Me*